THE AMAZING CASE OF THE ANZAC KARMA

THEY SHOT HIS MUM AND DAD: THEY SHOULDN'T HAVE

KENN LORD

LUMINOSITY
PUBLISHING

LUMINOSITY PUBLISHING LLP

THE AMAZING CASE OF THE ANZAC KARMA
They Shot His Mum and Dad: They Shouldn't Have
Copyright © JUNE 2021 KENN LORD

ISBN: 978-1-8383183-2-1

Cover Art by Kenn Lord

DEDICATION

THIS BOOK IS DEDICATED TO the many free-thinking people of my country who believe that our governments are elected and paid to govern responsibility and to act for the common good of everyone. In such a perfect world there can be no room for corruption, or for any kind of interference that demeans the lives and wishes of the people.

A perfect world being governed by perfect politicians is the eternal hope for any country. When that hope runs off the rails, stories like the one I've written are not the way good things are meant to happen.

QUOTES:

There are more things in Heaven and Earth, Horatio, than are dreamt of in your philosophy.

—Hamlet, William Shakespeare

Karma and Payback are soulmates.

—*Cynthia Del Largo*

BOOK ONE

ANZAC DAY: THE BROKEN WORLD

AT 3:50 A.M. ON THE MORNING of Anzac Day, Mary Cameron stood on the wide front veranda of her big house overlooking the Manly Boat Harbour on the shores of Waterloo Bay in south-east Queensland.

Hundreds of boats lay at anchor in light rain. There was no wind—the bay was eerie and still in the pre-dawn light. As the sun rose, it cast a misty glow over the rain-washed boats; masts etched against a pale sky.

Mary's husband Jack walked through the open shutters of the living room, joined her on the veranda, looked up at the sky and said, "What's the verdict?"

Mary smiled. "It's only light rain, and you've never missed a Dawn Service. We can take umbrellas."

Jack put a hand on hers. "If that's okay with you."

"It's Anzac Day, Jack."

A special day for the Camerons.

Jack's grandfather fought on Gallipoli; his uncle was one of the Rats of Tobruk, his father flew a Kitty Hawk in the Battle of the Coral Sea; his cousin fought in Korea, his nephew was killed in Vietnam.

Mary said, "I'll get the umbrellas."

The Dawn Service was to be held, as always, at the Manly War Memorial in Russell Park, a small grassy triangle at the junction of two streets on a gentle slope of the suburban landscape.

Mary and Jack drove the short distance in light rain that stopped before they arrived. The tiny park was packed. Two of the Boy Scouts in a troop near the monument shuffled around to make room for the Camerons, who joined them.

The thirty-minute service began—and continued with hymns sung by the students of the Manly State School, a reading of the service, and wreaths laid against the monument.

Then the bugler took his place to play the "Last Post."

Few people took any notice of the car that had driven slowly down the street on the eastern side of the park. It stopped with a clear view of the monument.

One of a group of uniformed servicemen in the crowd, glanced at the car to see its three young occupants climb on to the vehicle's bonnet.

Assuming it was to get a better view of the bugler, the serviceman turned away, expecting to hear the first notes of the "Last Post."

They were never played.

Out of nowhere, Russell Park was shattered by the sounds of gunfire.

A bullet smashed into the shining brass bugle and blasted it from the bugler's lips. Two more bullets hit the statue of the soldier on the monument.

More bullets sprayed the startled crowd.

When the shooters on the car lost their balance on the slippery wet bonnet—the soldiers charged, grabbed the legs of two of them and brought them down.

Before the third man could be caught, he jumped to the car's bonnet and fired three more shots. The crowd, dazed and confused, was in total shock.

Screaming sirens heralded the arrival of police and ambulances.

The shooters, restrained by the soldiers, were anything but subdued.

"Anzac Day is for infidels," yelled the man who fired the last shots.

The police took them into custody while Ambulance crews cruised the crowd.

Casualties were relatively light—the servicemen and the rain had stalled a major tragedy. One of the last three shots hit Jack Cameron. The other two hit Mary.

She died in the bloodied arms of the Boy Scout holding her. Jack, seriously wounded, was taken to the Wesley Hospital in Brisbane.

It was the opening of a door that would never close.

NOTTING HILL, LONDON: THE BROKEN HEART

TIM CAMERON, HIS FLAT MATE Brett, and Patti, Brett's current squeeze were in a bubbly mood. They had spent a casual evening with their buds in Bobby Fitzpatrick, a trendy West Hampstead pizza hangout. Brett and Patti were making coffee in the kitchen when the doorbell rang. Patti left the kitchen to open the door.

She returned to speak to Tim with a concerned look on her face.

"There's someone from the Australian Embassy to see you."

Tim went to the door. Minutes later, he walked back into the room.

His face was ashen, and he stood, shaking, supporting himself against the kitchen bench with has hand.

Brett started at him, "What? What is it, mate? What?"

Tim spoke three words, "Mum and Dad."

Patti was beside him. "What's happened?"

Still ashen-face and shaking, Tim stood staring at the wall.

3

THE TIMES THAT HAD TO END

AT THE AUSTRALIAN EMBASSY, TIM Cameron heard the details of the Dawn Service attack on his parents and had trouble taking it in. His one thought was to get home. He was urgently ticketed on an early morning flight to Singapore, with a connecting flight to Brisbane.

Brett and Patti helped him pack, sat with him through the night, and drove him to Heathrow. He took on the twenty-five-hour flight in a daze; hardly eating, hardly drinking; hardly able to think. His world had been wiped out.

He was met at the Brisbane airport by Charlie Cameron, recent widow of John Cameron, his father's older brother. Charlie, a down-to-earth country lady of sixty-two, took him under her wing and didn't waste words when Tim asked about his father.

"He took a bullet that tore into his heart muscle. It's lodged, and they can't operate until the swelling goes down. It's touch and go. He knows you're coming, but don't expect sunshine and roses."

At the Wesley Hospital, Jack Cameron was fading fast. There were massive complications. Tim sat by his Dad's bed in a daze. The man he'd grown up with could barely move. He looked weak and shattered, but his eyes shone when he reached for his son's hand.

"They got Mary, Tim, she died beside me, and the bastards got me, too. I won't be getting out of here, you're all that's left of us, son. Be brave."

Long hours later, Jack lost consciousness. He died with his son holding his hand.

CHARLIE WAS A ROCK. SHE drove Tim to the Manly house—and she was with him when he mounted the front steps, and when he turned the key on the front door.

She took his arm. "Nothing's been touched," she said. "It's not going to be easy for either of us, but you've got to do what you've got to do. I've closed my place in town, and I'm staying as long as you need me."

When he walked down the hallway of the beautiful big house, Tim steeled himself. The breakfast nook was set with crockery and cutlery. A frying pan sat on the stove top. A bowl with four eggs and rashers of bacon sat on a bench beside it; slices of bread sat on a cutting board; beside it, a bowl of fruit—the Anzac Day breakfast Mary would never make. The nook windows were open to the breezes from the bay, and the perfume of the mock orange blossoms on the trees in the garden drifted in.

Other rooms were filled with arrested life—an open newspaper, pens and pencils on Jack's desk, his coats, and a hat hanging on a rack, a partially opened drawer, and Mary's shopping list, held by a decorative magnet on the refrigerator door.

Tim stood anchored in the doorway of the main bedroom. The big bed had been made on that fatal morning. Mary had turned down the sheets as she always did, and she'd fluffed up the pillows. Tim couldn't speak.

With Charlie at his side, he sorted through possessions, making decisions on what to keep, what to discard—his mother's cosmetics and perfumes, his father's collection of medals, letters and books.

They went through wardrobes; sorting, packing and discarding.

Charlie ordered meals from a local restaurant, insisted on his eating, listened while he talked about his young life in the big house, made his bed, washed his clothes, fixed his nightcaps, and kept him focused. Three days later, with nothing more to do, Tim was broken.

"Cry it away, boy," said Charlie, "it will eat you if you don't."

She took him in her arms and held him, sensing his pain, holding him tighter, feeling his heartbreak, soothing him, urging him to cry his sad rivers and to sob away his hurt. She held him until he was still and calm in her arms.

But the worst wasn't over. Charlie was ready.

The funerals she arranged at the crematorium were testing. Too many friends; too many relatives; too many curious people; too much anguish; too many questions; too many affectionately spoken words; none that made any difference:

Tim didn't need to be told who his mother and father were by a minster holding a book, or by one of his father's grieving friends making speeches. He didn't need the words offered to him in well-meant sympathy. He nodded and tried to be grateful.

As the coffins slid away, a curtain closed on his consciousness.

Charlie kept him steady and drove him home. He resisted other offers of help and shut himself off. She stayed though the following week, then sat with him on the wide front veranda overlooking the bay. He was spent, he looked drawn and haunted, his energy reserves were busted.

"You need to make decisions," said Charlie, "make them now, and decide what you're going to do."

"I don't want to go back to London. I want to be near them, Charlie."

"Then don't stay in this house. It will haunt you. You're barely twenty-nine, you've got a life to live. You have a career. Make the break."

"I won't be the same, not ever."

"Make the break, boy."

He took her advice, sold everything with the exception of a collection of photographs and things he knew his mother and father loved. The furniture he grew up with was the last to go. He watched as it was carried down the high front steps and loaded into the removal van.

"It's all gone," said Charlie, "now you can start again."

He put the big bay-side house on the market, and it sold for a small fortune. He was not short of money, but he had to get out of Manly and as far away from Richard Russell Park as possible. Charlie took him to her place in Brisbane and encouraged him to make decisions. He told her about his plans.

"Before I look for a job, I want to spend some time on the Sunshine Coast. We went there a lot when I was a kid, and I've always loved it."

"Beautiful memories won't hurt," she said, "they never do."

He bought a car and made his move. On the day he left, Charlie sat with him over morning coffee. "It will take time, but you'll be fine. Stay strong."

"You've done so much, Charlie. How can I tell you what I need to say?"

"Say nothing. Stay in touch. You're Jack's boy, and I'll want to know everything."

It was a bitter-sweet goodbye.

4

THE DARKNESS BEFORE THE DAWN

TIM LEASED A UNIT IN an exclusive apartment complex on the beachfront at Peregian Beach on the Queensland Sunshine Coast, and sat on the balcony every day, gazing at the sea. His life was a jigsaw puzzle, but he was slowly putting it back together.

It wasn't easy.

The Anzac Day tragedy had developed into a hot topic that was gobbled up by the cold machinery of the press and television. He knew there would have to be an inquest and assumed that the three shooters would be kept in custody; charged, convicted, and sent to jail, an open and shut case.

That would be the end of it, and he could get on with his life. It didn't happen; the case was complicated by one word.

The word was *'ethnic.'*

The three young men who fired the bullets were immigrants. Excuses were made. They came from a country where violence was a way of life; they were not responsible; their 'ethnic background' was used as a shield by the Human Rights advocates who protected them. They received bureaucratic legal aid worth tens of thousands of dollars—their actions were excused on 'ethnic' grounds.

One of the men sustained a broken leg and head injuries when he was attacked by the servicemen at the Dawn Service. His legal aid representatives were suing the Army. He appeared in court on crutches, with his leg in plaster and bandages around his head. He claimed he'd been unfairly treated by the

Australian soldiers who had roughed him up for standing on the bonnet of his car.

He denied he'd been armed. The magistrate was sympathetic, and the case was progressing. It got worse. The shooter who fired the bullets that killed Jack and Mary had been previously arrested after an attack on two teenage girls who resisted his advances. He said he was 'insulted' when they called him a 'grub.'

He went wild; punched them out, and they finished up in hospital.

His claim that the girls deserved what they got was backed by his legal representatives, who cast aspersions on the morals of the girls who'd worn tight T-shirts and short denim skirts.

The police gave sworn evidence against him, but the magistrate let him off on 'ethnic' grounds and admonished the two girls by suggesting that calling him a grub, was not appropriate. He was allowed to go home to continue living on welfare.

Tim's legal rep was slack-jawed that the magistrate had chosen to ignore evidence that the shooter had been under surveillance when he masterminded and carried out the Anzac Day attack. The word 'ethnic 'had become his shield.

Tim and his solicitor were caught in a tangle of bureaucratic red tape. The Human Rights activates ranted and raved, and the media, riding a juicy scandal that was selling newspapers and titillating the eyes and ears of television viewers, was keeping everything on the boil. The Anzac Day incident crashed into the news as a 'Terror Attack' that involved a group of armed servicemen, who heavied three over-zealous youths at an Anzac Day Dawn Service.

There was scant mention of the servicemen's actions in preventing a major tragedy. The lone shooter could not be blamed for the fatal 'accident' and his two friends were innocent participants whose violent upbringing in a foreign country failed to give them a clear understanding of what they were doing. Local and federal Members of Parliament were deeply sympathetic but didn't want to know.

"It's a matter for the courts, and we can't be involved."

Weeks of wrangling resulted in nothing: The over-zealous trio were being held in custody at tax-payers' expense until a decision could be made on their futures.

They were receiving counselling and were reported to be receptive.

As a last gasp, Tim reluctantly agreed to a television interview to plead for justice.

Big mistake:

He was thrown into the pit with a sexually ambiguous female reporter who had earned a reputation as 'gotcha' interviewer. Smarmy as hell, she trapped him by casting doubt on the validly of Anzac Day—calling it a *"glorification of war"* that came with obvious risks in *"a modern multicultural society."* She implied that Jack and Mary had put themselves in harm's way by attending the Dawn Service, and in so doing *"took the consequences."* Tim's attempts to explain his family's deep associations with Anzac Day were discarded as *"over-emotional and naïve."*

That enflamed him and he erupted. Too late: it was exactly what his interviewer wanted. She had made him look like a petulant loser.

End of story.

The interview caused a tidal wave of reaction to the interviewer's attitude, but it was a storm in a teacup that lasted no more than a few days, then quietly went away.

When the *"Terror Attack"* had been milked for all it was worth, it faded from public view and disappeared from the mainstream into the limbo of yesterday's news.

Tim was left with nowhere to go.

His pain deepened. He couldn't come to terms with the injustice and the way he'd been treated. His thinking turned dark. He felt himself being pulled toward thoughts of revenge. He told himself there had to be some kind of payback, and he began to harbour destructive feelings toward the three men who were walking free after having committed such a wilful act. His mother and father were gone, and he was losing out to anger and grief. As the days churned on, he knew he was getting worse. He was living in one of the most beautiful seaside resorts in the country, and he was unable to feel anything but hate and despair.

And then, unexpectedly, something wonderful happened.

5

THE GLOW OF THE ELEVENTH HOUR

APRIL DAWN KNOCKED ON TIM'S unit door. He opened it, she introduced herself, and said, "Your Aunt Charlie sent me to check you out. She wants to make sure you're all right. Are you all right?"

"All right?"

"You're not, are you? You're a mess. You look like a mess."

"A mess?"

"You're not on the planet."

April kept staring at him and shaking her head, then she said, "Charlie told me about the bad time you've had. I knew about it anyway; everyone knows about it. Can I tell you something? Don't bother to answer, I'll tell you anyway. It won't do any good to stay sad and angry. It will only make things worse. I'm here because I understand how you feel, and I want to be your friend. I want to make you feel better."

She kept staring at him; waiting for him to respond.

He didn't, not right away.

She smiled and said, "Well?"

Tim took a long look at her, and without realising it, he relaxed.

The word "*alive*" leapt into his head. April Dawn was alive. She was pretty too, as fresh as a summer breeze; bright as a hundred fields of poppies in a short pink dress with ribbons in her hair and pink bangles around her wrists.

She was still smiling at him when she asked, "Are you going to invite me in?"

Without a second's hesitation, Tim said, "Yes."

She walked into his unit and looked around. "Fancy unit, let's hit the balcony, I love looking at the sea.'

She was behaving as if she'd known him all her life. His acceptance of her was instant. He relaxed even more.

With the vast sweep of the South Pacific Ocean in the background, April opened up. "I'm a freelance journalist, I live up the road in Noosa, and I write for feature magazines. I saw your interview with that bitch on television. She's a sad case, a latent dike with two kids, and a dud husband. She hates the world and everything in it. She sure gave you the works."

"How do you know she's a latent dike."

"She used to live up here, people talk, what do you care? You came out on top. Everyone felt sorry for you. Me too."

"I don't want people to feel sorry for me."

"Too late. You're a steamy looking guy. Do you do sex with chicks?"

"Yes."

"How long since your last screw?"

"Some time."

"That's ridiculous. How long will it take you to get your gear off?"

Tim's jaw dropped an inch. "Are you kidding?"

"Of course I'm not. Where's the bedroom?"

While he was undressing, he realised it had been ages since he'd thought about sex, and his mind was suddenly back on track. Excitement hit, and by the time he'd lost his clothes, he was up and ready.

April, who'd outstripped him by ten seconds, gave him an admiring look. "That's nice," she said, "do you like mouth-works?"

"What guy doesn't?"

"That wasn't the question, honey."

"Yes, I do."

"Put your hands behind your head, and don't move."

She dropped to her knees and went to work. She put a grip on his buttocks and held him tight. When she had him shuddering and shaking, she rose, took his mouth with hers and said, "You poor baby, you've had a rotten time. Stretch out on the bed and relax. You know how to do that, don't you? Just lie there and let me chase all the bad times away. It won't hurt a bit."

With prefect precision, she took him over, twisting and writhing, moaning and sighing. Her fingers teased his nipples, and her eyes continued to drink in his ongoing expressions of rapture. When it was time for phase two, she rolled over and waited for the move she'd primed him to make. One second later, he made it, sending them both into the breathless world of primal pleasures.

For the first time since his arrival from London, Tim felt like a man again, and he knew straight away that things would be easier.

His mind spoke. *Thanks, Charlie, you're never far away.*

April made the coffee and said, "I'm taking you to dinner in the best restaurant on the Sunshine Coast. It's called *The Spirit House*, it's the middle of a bamboo forest in the hinterland, about half an hour's drive up the highway. I'm going to feed you fantastic food. No fancy dress. Any objections?"

He smiled, shook his head, and said nothing.

The Spirit House was a revelation. Softly illuminated by concealed spots and twinkling fairy lights, its dining tables skirted a man-made lake. In it, lived tame water dragons that didn't mind bonding with customers. The edgy tucker took the place to the next level—sheer indulgence. In this idyllic atmosphere, April launched candidly into the problems of the human race and its inhabitants.

"You know it wasn't bullets that killed your mum and dad, it was The System."

Tim was caught out. "I don't know what you're talking about."

"I'll go into detail, then."

She did, with gusto. As April told it, The System was the ultimate *Bad Guy* that made it easy for the young hoods who staged the Anzac Day attack to exist; the same System that fed them; housed them; helped them and protected them.

"That's why there was no justice, and there will be none. The System makes the rules and makes sure everyone toes the line."

Tim was all ears, and all confused.

April wound up. "The System is a no-win situation for amateurs. It's been known to test the mettle of spirited fighters. It's a Big Money Game, and it's played by a united army of superrich power brokers, charlatan judges, weak magistrates, wanky public servants, and two-faced politicians. Its preachers are the media's loud-mouthed clowns, who con everyone by making up fake news and serving it as the truth."

"So, what's the real truth?"

"The Big Money Game is The Force, kid. It can buy a charmed life, it can buy a way out of trouble, misery, and boredom. It can buy respect, admiration and awe. Sometimes, money can even buy love. Money makes people look up to the people obsessed by the game they're playing. They can be bastards and crooks, and it doesn't matter. They can do anything. They can rob, cheat and lie, and get away with it. Their System can buy and manipulate the law and get rid of troublemakers who get in the way."

April paused. "Am I boring you?"

"Fuck, no!"

She patted his hand and continued her sermon. "Big Game players are a protected species, and they're always safe. If you're on the rich list, you're a Somebody, you've got it made!"

Tim frowned. "Are you telling me that everyone who has money is like that?"

"Of course not. It's only the ego-driven deviates who use it to shape the world; to make everything work for them. They buy powerful friends in the bureaucracy. They fix it so they pay no taxes, they out-smart everyone; they're the masters of the game, and little people like you are their victims."

Tim listened in awe. April was only a girl, obviously younger than he was. He asked how she came to form such opinions at her young age.

"You don't have to be old to have opinions, baby, I've been working and observing since I was fifteen, and I've always been independent. I don't work for people, I work for the satisfaction writing gives me, and I don't take crap from anybody. I live to look and look to live. When you do that, no one can control how you feel or what you do."

Tim, lost for words, resorted to one. "Amazing!"

"It's only amazing because it's common sense. Look at you, you're a victim of The System. You've been bashed around by bullies, and you've got to make a stand. If you don't, you'll lose yourself, and your self-respect."

That hit home with a wallop. Then she floored him. "What are you going to do about what they did to you?"

It was as if she'd read his secret thoughts.

When he didn't answer right away, she said, "If you feel unfairly used and degraded, you've got to do something. You can't just go on feeling messed-up."

"What the hell can I do, April?"

"Take their System on. Target the thugs who got your mum and dad, the politicians who wouldn't do anything, the magistrates who let them off, and the journos who put you down. Play the Karma Game. You've earned your chance."

Something stirred inside, and Tim gave her an interested look. "The Karma Game?"

"That's it, kiddo. That's the pushback!"

April could see him thinking, she knew she was getting to him, so she fired another shot. "Karma is the great leveller, baby. It makes the world go around—it's Nature's Law. It's out there, but you've got to look for it and check it out. You have to believe in it; you have to believe there's a chance to get even, and if you truly believe, Karma will put you on the right road."

Tim held her with his eyes. He said nothing, but he was smiling inside.

April's final word. "Think about a pushback plan, baby. Put it out there; let it take root and settle, believe in it, give it life in your mind. Tell yourself it can happen. Trust it and never deny it. Be ready for it when it knocks on your door. Am I connecting with you?"

"All the way." He meant it.

"Okay. I'm off the subject. Did you have a nice time tonight?"

"Wonderful."

"Don't you just love this wild restaurant?"

"I do."

"Are we gonna screw again?"

"When?"

"As soon as we get back to your fancy pad."

Tim locked her eyes. "I'd rather not wait that long. What's wrong with my car?"

April smiled a cheeky smile. "Okay, we'll skip the cheese and biscuits."

"Let's ask for a doggie bag," said Tim, "I love blue cheese."

"Your Aunt Charlie was right about you, kiddo. She said you were worth looking after, and she's right, you are. I'm glad we met, now let's get out of here."

APRIL STAYED WITH HIM FOR three more days, revealing a talent for cooking and housekeeping. She bought little things for the unit, added pots of greenery, flowers, and herbs, and made sure Tim knew how to look after them. Her lovemaking broadened his technique in the bedroom, and her lectures were pure gold.

"Forget the *Kama Sutra*," she said, "take no notice of all that fancy stuff. You can break your back trying to screw like a contortionist. The object of sex is majoring in the art of perfected pleasure, so relax and do what comes naturally. Adam and Eve didn't need a manual, and they did okay. They didn't need snakes and apples either, that stuff is only for people who take the Bible literally."

"And you don't?"

"Of course not. It's Disneyland."

They were seated on the balcony. The lazy surf was bubbling away in the background while the setting sun was spraying the breakers with a golden glow. April was sipping on a frosted glass of guava juice, smiling at him with her sparkling eyes.

She had successfully baited the statement that hooked him.

"The Bible is Disneyland?"

"Here's a prime example. Moses was Mickey Mouse in *The Sorcerer's Apprentice*. Didn't you see *Fantasia?*"

"I did, but it never occurred to me that Mickey Mouse was Moses."

"The chosen people are the broom that Moses bewitches, and the Promised Land is the cauldron they have to fill, so Mickey calls on the broom for help to do the job. Things get out of hand when the lazy broom turns into more brooms and they all run amok, so the Sorcerer has to step in to keep them in line."

Tim, as usual, was intrigued. "So, who's the Sorcerer?'

"He's the God figure. He fixes the brooms, then to make sure they stay fixed, he waves his arms around like mad and conjures up the Ten Commandments."

"That's pretty off-the-wall, April."

"So were the Ten Commandments."

"What do you mean?"

"They weren't worth the tablet they were forged on, and they're still not. Try this. '*Thou shalt not covet.*' Everyone covets. Shopping Centres would go broke if there was no coveting. It's the backbone of Big-Money business. Supply and demand. Coveting. Got it?"

Tim nodded.

April continued, "*Thou shalt not commit adultery.* God had to be kidding. The suburbs are rife with it. Again, supply and demand. Shall I go on?"

"I think, I've got the message."

"Great, then I don't have to explain the other eight commandments. I don't want to talk anymore anyway, how about you get your gear off—I'm into looking at you in the buff—your equipment is one-hundred-per-cent eye candy."

"I could say the same for yours."

"Then let's forget the Ten Commandments and make a few of our own."

"Okay."

April closed in. "Right here on the balcony. Are you up for that?"

"Sure."

She wiggled her body. "We can sell tickets."

"Or binoculars."

April put her frosted glass down. Her face ignited. "I'm really into you Tim. You do wonderful things to me, and it's not just the sex. I could easily get interested big time in you, but you're not ready."

"Why do you say that?"

She took his face in her hands. "You're too full of hurt, baby. It doesn't show, but it's there, and you've got to get rid of it. If not, you'll have to carry it around and you'll never be free. You're too beautiful to be a prisoner. You don't belong behind bars."

"That's it?"

"The talking, yes. Are you into screwing standing up?

"I can be."

He registered her sweet little giggle as she breathed against his cheek. He held her close when she twisted in his arms, then pulled his hands up to cup her breasts.

Their skimpy clothes fell away, and he melted into her. Her sighs matched the rhythm of the golden breakers rolling up the beach in the fading sunlight.

One or two walkers on the sand gazed up, a couple stopped for a minute or two to watch what was happening. But on the terrace, two people were too busy to notice, and they were having too much fun to care.

APRIL EXPERTLY COOKED THE FRESH green prawns she'd bought from the man with the trawler, spiced them with green ginger root, thickened the pan juices with fish stock and cream, served them on clear glass plates, and watched Tim's face when he took his first bite.

"Wonderful," he said.

"The object of the exercise," she replied.

He gazed at her. "I've never met anyone like you."

"There isn't anyone like me."

"You didn't have to tell me."

She filled two glasses with chilled green wine, looked at him in the candlelight, sipped on the wine, and said, "I can only stay for another day. I have assignments."

"Can't you do them here?"

"I wouldn't be concentrating, and there's research."

"How about afterwards?"

"There's always afterwards, Tim."

"I'll miss you."

"Your Aunt Charlie asked me to make sure you're okay. You are, for now, but there's more to be done."

"I suppose there is."

She got serious. "You do know what I mean, don't you?"

He got serious, too. "You've helped me more than you know."

April waited a moment or two, then abruptly changed the subject. "There's someone I want you to meet, someone special; someone who can help you take the next pushback step. She'll put you on the right track and keep you there."

He was curious. "Who is she? Some kind of magician?"

"You can make up your mind about that after you've seen her. Do you know anything about astrology? Not magazine mumbo-jumbo. The real thing."

"Is there a real thing?"

"Do you want to find out?"

"If you think I should."

"I'll give you something to read. There are things you should know about this person. It's best not to meet her cold."

April rose from the table, went into the bedroom, and came back holding a magazine. She sat down again, flipped a few pages searching for the ones she wanted. Then she handed him the magazine, indicated the article, and said, "Read this, read it all, and concentrate, I mean, concentrate. Can you do that?"

He took the magazine. "I think so."

April's *'something to read'* was a well-written, in-depth article in a prestigious circulation magazine that focused on people with colourful occupations.

While she cleared the dishes, Tim settled down to read. After two minutes, he was captivated.

The mystic astrologer had the unlikely name of Cynthia Del Largo.

In the eyes of her fans, she had the amazing ability to connect with messages sent though space from the sun, moon, and planets in Earth's solar system. She believed in extra-terrestrial influences on human life and existed to share her knowledge with those who believed in her. Her residence was a two-storey house in the Montville rainforest high up in the Sunshine Coast hinterland.

Her previous home had been in New York, where she hosted a weekly astrology segment for a popular lifestyle television show. As such, she had been sent to Australia as a consultant on a movie about astrology.

Montville had been one of the film's locations. A week later she'd fallen in love with it and interpreted that as a positive message from the planets. She returned to New York, cut all her ties, migrated to Montville, shopped around with a real estate agent, paid cash for the rainforest house that took her fancy and moved in to be surrounded by creative people who understood and admired her.

At the age of eighty, she was ageless.

She wore wispy pastel-coloured dresses, floaty scarves of mushroom pink and turquoise blue and dangly beaten silver earrings that went with her silver hair and fine delicate skin. Her emerald-green eyes were shiny bright and deep, her laser gaze scared the hell out of people with things to hide. She was never taken lightly.

Her seventy-year-old companion, Enid Avery, answered Cynthia's advertisement for a live-in housekeeper. Cancer had stolen Enid's husband; it had also taken Cynthia's. They bonded at once.

Tim, totally rapt, read on:

There were no television sets or radios, no newspapers or magazines in Cynthia's house. She was modern enough to appreciate the Internet, which supplied the information she needed. The only opinions that grabbed her, were her own, and the only visitors to her home and workplace were people who consulted her for astrological readings.

Enid took enquiring phone calls between eight a.m. and noon every day. Callers were required to leave specific personal details: name, year and place of birth; time of birth preferable. A date and time for a consultancy would be arranged if Cynthia was interested or challenged.

No fee was charged.

Tim raised his eyebrows when he read that, but it was true.

Clients were simply requested to leave a donation. They were frequently large. Return consultations for satisfied visitors were not unusual. Her clients were received in an intimate and beautiful room on the ground floor. The walls were painted deep blue; the carpet was blue, and she sat at a carved cedar desk in front of a wide bay window that looked out on a spectacular garden overgrown with crepe myrtle and magnolia trees, flowering geraniums, periwinkles and daisies, two avocado trees, two pink grapefruit trees, and one macadamia nut tree.

Cynthia delivered her readings in a softly modulated voice with perfect diction; rarely repeating herself. In every way possible, she was as perfect as a human being could be—so perfect that fanciful people were convinced that she had come from another planet.

Tim finished reading.

He put the magazine down and looked at April.

She could tell he was blown away. "Don't ask questions," she said. "Trust me."

"You've been right about everything else."

April nodded. "I hate being wrong."

"Do you know this astrologer?"

"I listen to what she says."

"She's influenced you."

"You said you'd be willing to think about a plan to put things right."

He answered positively, "And I meant it."

"Have you come to any conclusions?"

Tim got the drift. "Do you think this astrologer can fine-tune me?"

"Will you lose anything by seeing her?"

"No."

"Then do it."

The subject was closed.

April left early the following morning.

"I'm not saying goodbye," she said. "It's not the finish of anything. I'm giving you time to sort yourself out, and you can't do that if we're screwing all the time."

"Will you stay in touch?"

"Don't ask silly questions. Just take the next step."

6

THE ALL-SEEING EYES OF CYNTHIA DEL LARGO

TIM CALLED CYNTHIA'S NUMBER. As requested, he left details of his birth and waited for a reply. Two days later, Enid Avery called him. His appointment was confirmed for the Wednesday of the following week at ten a.m. As the day drew closer, he found himself getting excited about the meeting, but he had taken precautions.

He realised that newspapers, magazines and television sets were not regular features in the Montville house, but he was still sensitive. His pictures had been splashed over front pages, he'd been on television as the centre of racial controversy, and he didn't want awkward questions.

He arrived at Montville driving a rented car and wearing perfectly boring everyday clothes that looked nothing like him. He had removed his expensive designer watch, and the gold Cameron family ring he wore on the third finger of his right hand.

He hadn't used his real name and believed he was incognito—but he did not know Cynthia De Largo and had no way of knowing how much his astrological chart had intrigued her, or how eager she'd been to meet him.

Two kindred souls were about to discover each other.

Cynthia watched him closely as he moved to take the seat opposite her on the far side of the cedar desk. She noted his keen almost furtive but positive interest in her beautiful room as he took the chair, adjusted its position, calmly looked into her eyes, and waited.

She looked calmly back, her silence encouraging him to speak.

The sound of his voice pleased her. She found it deep and even; well-controlled, with no traces of awkwardness or nerves. "I understand that you don't read newspapers or magazines and that you don't have a television set."

"Do you find that strange?"

"A little, yes."

"Newspapers and magazines are no longer selective about what they print. What was once real news is now tailored to the demands of advertising and fanciful opinions. Honest opinions in print are rare. Information is dressed up to appear real when that's often not the case."

Tim was all ears. "I have very few positive thoughts about newspapers."

"Television is worse. It hasn't progressed at all since the fifties. It is bland and uninspiring. Its messages come with pictures, but its words are delivered with such bland earnestness that they go in one ear and straight out the other."

Tim smiled. "I've never thought about television like that."

"Hardly anyone does; that's the trick."

"I suppose it is."

He started to tell her why he'd come to see her.

She cut him off. "I know why you're here. I've studied your chart. Your Sun sign is Scorpio, and you have Scorpio in the ascendant. You are true to your sign: purposeful and emotional, subtle, persistent, and determined, you are the masculine personification of the typical Scorpio man but the Moon in Aquarius in your chart softens you. It makes you intuitive."

She was watching him as she spoke and went on, "You are a wonderful friend, and a robust enemy. If you like someone, it's adoration; if you don't, they may as well not be there." She paused before she said, "Intimate pleasures comes naturally to you."

A smile curled his lips. "That's the same with most people, isn't it?

She shook her head. "Intimate pleasures can cause problems."

His smile broadened. "And often do."

She smiled and continued, "As of now, Pluto, the planet of secrets and creative destruction, is in negative aspect to your birth sign, and you are secretive about your dark feelings."

He needed clarification and asked for it.

"You are a man with two faces. You are not who you pretend to be, and because you are unusually secretive and furtive under the current aspect of Pluto, I suspect that you may have used a false name when you made your appointment to see me."

"Amazing."

"There's something else that betrays you. The clothes you're wearing don't match who you are, and they're too new. You bought them to fool me."

His smiled in spite of himself. "That's true."

She smiled back, letting him know he'd met his match. "Shall I go on?"

"Please do."

"The Pluto effect is strong. You've been taken over by dark thinking; it's obsessing you and I can help you understand it." She paused for a moment. "Do you want me to tell you who you are?"

He shifted in his chair. "I know who I am."

"I'm talking about how you came to be who you are. There's a difference."

Cynthia launched into her spiel: She told him about his childhood; his formative years; his love affairs; his deep closeness to his parents, and important episodes of his life so far. Her detailing floored him. She knew it all. She had read him perfectly and laid his life out in front of him. Looking squarely at him with her all-knowing eyes, she continued.

"You've been touched by a deep tragedy. I won't go on about that because you're still coming to terms with it and it's making you angry and resentful."

He was bowled over. "You've read all that in an astrology chart?"

"It's what I do."

He moved forward to lean on the desk. "You said you could help me."

"I want to help you understand your dark thinking and what you feel you should do about it."

He took that in. "You don't believe my dark thinking is wrong?"

"I believe it's your right, but you need guidance. If you agree, you should come to see me again."

He read that as a sign that the consultation was over. "When?"

"Whenever you need to talk."

"You mean when I'm more together about things."

"Are you happy with that?

"I am."

Cynthia's smile was bright and friendly. "Use your real name when you come here next time, and please wear your real wardrobe—I don't want to advise the person you pretend to be."

He sat back. "Did I make mistake?"

"I understand the disguise."

He looked a bit sheepish. "I'm sorry."

"Don't be. Is there anything else?"

"No."

"You're satisfied?"

"I'm grateful for your interest."

"Grateful goes without saying. Are you satisfied?"

"I'm over the moon."

"It's nice over there."

"I agree."

Cynthia handed him a card. "My private telephone number."

"You don't mind if I call you?"

"That's what the card's for."

He smiled and nodded. "It's already on my mind."

"And it's already in the stars."

He rose from the chair. "You don't charge a fee."

"I don't believe in fees."

"I feel I should pay you."

"That's up to you. Money is only money."

He gave her a long appreciative look. "I'm glad I came."

She looked back. "So am I."

Her laser eyes beamed at him, and they were shining. It hit him then, that he'd found a friend. In twenty minutes, he'd found a friend. He stood for a long moment looking at her and saw that she'd found a friend too.

He turned, left the room, and closed the door.

A few minutes later, Enid opened it and approached Cynthia's desk.

"He left a lot of money," she said.

"He'll be back. He'll need to stay in contact."

"Who is he? There's something strange about his name."

"Forget it, Enid, it's not his name."

"It's familiar, somehow."

"Is it?"

Enid frowned. "Is he in trouble?"

"He may be capable of causing trouble."

Enid was silent for a few moments: "Should we tell someone?"

"Tell them what?"

"That he may be capable of causing trouble."

"If it's in the stars, there's nothing we can do about it. What will be, will be."

Enid smiled a knowing smile. "You like him."

"I think he's worthwhile. Worthwhile people need worthwhile advice."

TIM DROVE HIS RENTED CAR along the lane that curved away from Cynthia's magic cottage and turned it into the street that connected with the road that ran down the mountain to the Sunshine Coast. He was reeling with a sense of elation. Cynthia Del Largo was his new best friend and she'd come right out of a story in the astrology magazine April Dawn had given him—*a miracle.*

The miracle word had dropped into his mind from out of nowhere.

Astrology—what did he know about it? Aries, Taurus, Gemini, Cancer and stuff. Whatever, it was important enough for newspapers, magazines and web sites to give it space— valuable space sometimes. There it was—mostly frivolous and fatuous but read with enormous fascination by hordes of groupies every day—messages that the stars were beaming out from the twelve houses of the Zodiac.

Familiar messages covered the spectrum—a great time to buy a lottery ticket; your mother-in-law has a surprise for you; a long-lost friend will contact you; good luck is waiting in the wings; a perfect day to think about a holiday; look forward to a fun weekend, and best of all—you'll meet someone who'll be more than interested in you. Don't rule out excitement.

The groupies lapped it up. It hardly mattered that it was not really a perfect time to think about a holiday, or that the interesting someone didn't come along. Tomorrow, there would be a whole new set of predictions, gleefully accepted as a possibility, even though the wording was so ambiguous that only wishful thinking could make it seem real.

The smart-money astrologers who pushed the predictions barrel were making small fortunes. It was big business— coveting by the Stars!

The exception was Cynthia Del Largo—the wonder woman who had followed her own star; selling up to live in a far-away rainforest, all because that's where she believed she should be.

Tim couldn't estimate how much money the move would have cost, or how much money she might have had, but he reasoned that she was obviously comfortable, and certainly committed to her profession.

She accepted donations of cash. No doubt there would be quite a bundle of enlightened clients leaving fat tips on Enid Avery's desk.

The point was that Tim was convinced he'd found another someone who understood him, and beyond that, someone who understood his reasons for wanting what he wanted. He was so elated he could barely see the road. He was driving by numbers, and his head was spinning.

He stopped the car.

He admitted to himself then, that he'd had doubts. His plans were not together.

April had advised him to play the Karma game. Cynthia picked up on it. She pushed a button that had given his wild thoughts a green light. Without knowing exactly what he had in mind, she not only announced her approval she had offered her cooperation.

How much more could he have hoped for?

He sat there in his rented car on the side of the road and stared out at the lush countryside. A kind of wacky little smile lingered on his lips and a thought flashed in his mind.

I'm going to even the score Dad, for you and for Mum; when you see her, tell her how much I love you both.

He sat for a while longer then started the rented car's engine, wheeled out onto the road, and headed for his rented apartment at the beach.

He wasn't sure how long the drive took. Still elated when he unlocked the door, he walked in, picked up the telephone and dialled April's number.

When she answered, he said, "I've been with Cynthia Del Largo."

"Congratulations."

"It was like talking to you."

"You noticed."

"You speak the same language."

"We believe the same things."

Tim warmed his voice. "Am I going to see you?"

"Tell me what happened."

He told her everything. The line was silent for a long moment.

Finally, April spoke. "How do you feel?

"Kinda whacked out."

He caught her little giggle when she said, "Goes with the territory."

"I feel I've been given a green light to screw the planet."

"In your case, it deserves to be screwed."

"Cynthia De Largo is . . . I can't say what she is."

"She's exactly what you think she is. Stay close to her, Tim. Trust her."

"I already do. I never thought anything like this could happen."

"Listen to what she tells you. She'll help you get it right."

He paused a moment. "For weeks I've been raging inside about how unfair everything has been. All I wanted was an understanding of how I felt, that's all. I wanted those guys to be punished for what they did, and I was made to feel like a criminal. I don't feel like that anymore. I feel like it's all going to be okay."

"Stay with the feeling . . . you're on the right track."

"When will I see you?"

"Be patient."

April ended the brief conversation and called Charlie.

"Your boy is okay, Charlie. He'll be fine, just fine."

"You're an angel."

"I've done what you asked me to do."

"I knew you would."

"Everything's cool with him, he just needs time."

AT SIX P.M. TIM SETTLED down in front of the TV set to watch the news. He hit the remote and waited to see if there was anything to interest him. Now that 'clarity' was his second name, he could see everything with new eyes.

He thought of what Cynthia Del Largo said.

Television hasn't progressed at all since the fifties. It is bland and uninspiring . . . its words are delivered with such bland earnestness that they go in one ear and straight out the other.

The evidence was on the screen in front of him. He watched in amused wonder. Same-old newsreaders; same-old earnest expressions; same-old deadpan reads of the auto cue; a bloke with sculptured hair in a neat suit and tie; a chick in trendy threads with trendy hair and glossy lips. The same-old format he'd grown up with. A lead story designed to grab attention followed by a *'stay tuned'* pitch for more after the hard-sell commercial break. Then more ads and more stories escalating down in importance.

Finally, breathless pointers for the Sports News; a must-watch presented by an ex-sports star whose crusty face and macho presentation were his passport to the minds of the groupies.

After sport, the weather report delivered by an *'expert'* with a talent for making hot news out of cold fronts, hurricanes, heatwaves, highs, lows, isobars, depressions, and mercury readings.

Then the Big Wrap. The weather journo's ad-lib time with the newsreaders; casual jokes and jolly talk to prove that television newsreaders are human after all.

Tim was having a ball.

He hadn't realised that the art of earnest news-reading had been set in concrete from the very birth of television; and there it stayed; anchored in the glory days of the box when television news had been a must-see living-room adventure—the gospel according to the wonderworld of commercialism— *World News with pictures all drummed up to sell things with more pictures—brilliant!*

All that had given rise to the Current Affairs and Opinion yap-fests—showcases for brittle-edged commentators to mouth-off about political moves and the dos and don'ts of elected Members of Parliament who pretend to be serving the public but who exist like VIPs in a world of freebies and A-List invitations.

Three days of April Dawn and one meeting with Cynthia Del Largo had sharpened him. How times had changed. Once upon a time, everyone talked television: The country's pulse pumped for prime-time soap operas, homemade cop shows and dramas, homespun series, games shows with bubbly hosts, cuddly kid's stuff, variety shows with real stars, and heaps of fabulous folksy afternoon fluff.

All gone like the dinosaurs!

Now this—Who cooks the best pasta? Who does the best home renovations? Who sings the best songs? Which judge judges fair, and which judge doesn't—Gossipy show hosts in laugh-fests with glittery celebs driven by a genuine aim to look as natural as possible while making fools of themselves.

Then out of nowhere, it happened.

In the midst of his nostalgic reverie and despite his critical awakening, one story on the small screen trapped his attention and it was interesting enough to stay with him. When he switched the television set off, he began to think about it; not for any specific reason; it had just grabbed him. The story was about a man called Mackenzie Forbes. His very name rang a bell.

He sat up, suddenly. Another story coming his way, just like the Cynthia story had done—This one had hooked him, and he had to know more.

7

THE WONDERLAND OF A WONDER MAN

MACKENZIE FORBES WAS AN EXTRAORDINARY man in anyone's language. His way-out ideas on all fronts had labelled him a wild risk-taker. He didn't give a damn what anyone thought. He was well-heeled enough to bankroll his way-out ideas; some of which failed to ring bells at the bank but so what?

Easy come, easy go.

Although he was a second-generation Aussie, Mackenzie's fortune had come from South African diamonds via the wise investments of his father and grandfather.

Diamonds were Mackenzie's best friend.

Among the obvious benefits of this sparkling friendship, was Mackenzie's freedom to be fiercely independent. He could easily have been a solid player in the Big Money Game, but he gave that game—and those who played it to people's detriment—the middle finger whenever he got the chance.

He preferred to be a man of the people.

He trumpeted himself as the 'Ultimate True-Blue Aussie' and took pot-shots at politicians, corporations and the CEOs who didn't throw bouquets at his patriotic 'Australia-First' philosophy: When he aimed, he usually hit a bullseye.

"You blokes don't come within coo-ee of dinkum Aussie behaviour. You all take and no give, and you don't give a rats for the lives of decent Aussies. You're lower than a truckload of witchetty grubs and just as gutless!"

He was critical of government doors that opened to support shonky tax-funded schemes that helped rich con men get richer. Bureaucrats howled him down as a 'nut-case' but if anyone took him on, his standard answer was:

"You can get stuffed; if you don't like my mouth, take it to court!"

Mackenzie was very much his own man. His marriage had so far been in vogue for thirty years, mainly due to the fact that he was hardly ever home with his wife and son, both of whom had learned to understand that nothing comes for free. Nevertheless, it was a happy home. He was fit, good-looking and virile. You would have expected his son Josh, who had just turned twenty-one, to be Cock of the Walk. He wasn't.

He was definitely a Dad's lad who thought his Dad was '*awesome*" and that everything he did was '*awesome.'* Seriously.

Mackenzie's latest project was a theme park that was the very antithesis of Disney glitz. It was based on much-loved and lately neglected fictional Aussie characters called *Dad and Dave,* who lived and loved in the make-believe but familiar bush town of *Snake Gully.* These two *'dinkum blokes'* were married respectively to Mum and Mabel, and their *ups-and-downs-and-ins-and-outs* had enlivened the lives of the population in the thirties and forties.

They had been brought to life by a gifted Aussie storyteller, who wrote under the pen name of *Steele Rudd,* and Mackenzie thought it was time to bring them back to life in a dinkum Southern Cross theme park.

The television story that caught Tim's attention was a vocal shoot-out that '*Moneybags Forbes'* was allegedly having with the local council over the development of his theme park, set to happen in the woody hinterland o Wide Bay, close to the city of Maryborough in south-east Queensland. It was denigrated in the television report as a *"duelling banjo concept for hillbillies."*

Mackenzie's reply was typical:

"Aussie families and kids should not be fed exclusively on Yankee stuff like Dreamworld and Movie World. They should know what 'dinkum Aussie' used to mean, and still means to

me. *I'm on good terms with the council, and if you don't believe me, ask 'em!'"*

True to his new-found form, Tim decided to find out more about the Forbes theme park. He dug around for a couple of days and turned up a detailed Internet report on the project that had been written by a senior member of the Wide Bay Independent Investment Council.

Tim settled down to read it. It was long and detailed, but he stayed with it.

The Forbes theme park—simply touted *as Dave and World,* was well planned to take place close to Lake Lenthall to the near north-west of Maryborough.

The Wide Bay Council that administered the land had not been in the mood to be dictated to by any '*nutty diamond billionaire.*' The councillors were cautious about the setting up of a theme park on beautiful virgin land that had been virgin or near-virgin since Captain Cook.

Mackenzie was not to be swayed. After a week of perseverance, he managed to arrange a crucial meeting with the Wide Bay Council. Facing a roomful of reluctant council members, he tabled his plans in words and promises that were deliberately colourful and extravagant.

'*Dad and Dave World'* would not be honky-tonk. It would not be thrown open to bogans and yobbos. It would not be a cash cow to be milked indiscriminately. It would respect the environment and protect it. It would not interfere with Lake Lenthall's prized camping sites, nor would it upset the lake's natural colonies of freshwater fish, water dragons and native birds.

The room was quiet.

Taking note, Mackenzie moved on:

The park would have its own power plant; its own water; its own sewerage treatment plant; its own garbage collection, and its own First Aid facilities under the charge of competent medical personnel. It would have its own dairy farms; three of them, its own butter factory; with pasteurised milk and cheese making facilities.

The Wide Bay Councillors, wide-eyed with fascination, could scarcely believe what they were hearing. Mackenzie rode on:

Snake Gully staffers and park attendants would include specially tutored actors as Dave, Dave, Mum, Mabel, and other members of the permanent Snake Gully population—policemen, a mayor, farmers, shopkeepers, and their families.

There would be a Snake Gully Band and Snake Gully Dances; picnics with all kinds of country-picnic funning: three-legged races, egg and spoon races, tugs of war and talent quests. There would be an old-fashioned merry-go-round, a tilt-a-whirl, an octopus ride and an old-time steam train with a barrel funnel engine and open carriages that would *choof* around on rails circling the township on sight-seeing tours.

One of the starriest attractions scored the next rave.

A gushing waterslide with a heating plant for the cold weather would cascade into its own filtered pond built to look like a natural water hole surrounded by weeping willows, heliconias, lillipillies and morning glory vines. The waterslide's take-off platform would be higher than the natural gum trees in the vicinity accessed by a water-proofed escalator. Slide riders would be supplied with an inflated foam mat and take off like a rocket into a gushing fountain of water triggered by the opening of a giant valve—fantastic family fun, and as clean as a whistle.

Chuffed by the positive response, Mackenzie became lyrical:

"With as few modern touches as possible, Dad and Dave World will celebrate what life was like under the Southern Cross in the good old days of our grandfathers."

He kept drawing amazing mind pictures:

The main street would have a vintage Bakery Bar and Café that served proper country tucker—freshly baked meat pies, corned beef sandwiches, fish and chips, malted milks and milkshakes, freshly brewed ginger beer, cream buns, apple pies, proper billy tea, and true-blue Snake Gully Craft Beer.

There would be an upmarket Dining Room where visitors could sit at linen-covered tables and order fresh prawn cocktails, Burnett River scallops, Mum's vegetable soup; fish in breadcrumbs with tartare sauce, roasted chook lamb or beef, Gladstone mud crabs (in season), Mum's bread and butter custard, hot fruit pudding with cream, and buckets of homemade ice cream.

Taking further note of the rapt silence in the Council Boardroom, Mackenzie kept on giving out while his audience kept on giving in.

"*All my on-site staff, including cooks and kitchen hands will be recruited from the ranks of Maryborough townspeople. I'm talking jobs for skilled applicants across the board. In the main street, I'm building a licensed hotel, with a lounge bar and a classy private bar with vintage Aussie décor and leather chairs in respectful homage to the appointments and furniture in the original Hotel Australia in Sydney. There will be a theatre with a stage for live shows, a dance hall, a bank with ATM facilities, a diary food shop that sells Snake Gully milk, butter, cream, ice cream and cheese. I'm building a picture theatre that will screen the thirties movies of Dad and Dave, with George Wallace, and Roy Rene, and I am investing in re-mastered copies of Aussie film classics like Forty Thousand Horsemen, The Sons of Matthew, Smithy, A Bush Christmas, The Overlanders, and Dad Rudd MP. This is all as fair dinkum as you'll get and it's True-Blue Aussie to a T!*"

Positive euphoria held the room in its grip, then one of the councillors rallied to ask this all-important question:

"*Exactly how do visitors get to your theme park, Mr Forbes? After all, it will be a little out of the way, and they won't all be driving cars.*"

Every pair of ears in the room tuned in to Mackenzie's answer.

Arrangements had been made with Queensland Rail to lay a branch line from Maryborough Train Station to a Train Station at Snake Gully. Construction was set to begin as soon as possible. Two of the vintage steam engines presently in storage at the Ipswich Rail Museum had been purchased and will take turns pulling the vintage Ipswich Museum train carriages which will be re-conditioned, polished and revarnished—each identified by a logo that will read '*The Snake Gully Express.*'

Mackenzie took a breath for the home run:

"*Dad and Dave flags will flutter from the tops of the carriages. When the Snake Gully Express takes off it will be a one-hundred per cent thrill ride all the way down memory lane. It will run between Maryborough and Snake Gully and the ride will take thirty-five minutes. At Maryborough, the train will link to high-speed electric trains from Brisbane, Rockhampton, Bundaberg, Gladstone, and all points north to Cairns. Overnight accommodation, if needed, can be supplied by hotels and motels in Maryborough, and I'm expecting business to be brisk. If it's as brisk as I think, I will look at investing in new hotels in Maryborough to take up the slack.*"

The Wide Bay councillors, swept away by the Forbes tsunami, were open-mouthed with glee. Pretty Maryborough's future was suddenly brighter than it had been for years. It had once been the vibrant centre of cotton mills, shipbuilding, and sugar cane, but times had changed. Mackenzie had just announced his intention to change the times back. At the end of the meeting, '*Dad and Dave World*' was unanimously '*Go.*'

THE GREAT MAN WASTED NO time. He was on the case the very next day, and a few days later his theme park leapt off the drawing board to take its first steps as a true-life happening, due to open in a matter of months.

The next day, he briefed his work force:

"*Put an urgent stamp on everything; any problems must be ironed out pronto. This is a blockbuster. Let's make it big enough to set the world on fire! Let's rock and roll!*"

TIM FINISHED READING THE REPORT in wonder and amazement.

He could tell that Mackenzie was an Aussie mover who played it straight—the kind of man he wanted to be around, fearless, and individual, someone who could move mountains and put them on a plate. Tim was convinced that they had to meet.

Dad and Dave World could well be part of the plan that April Dawn wanted for him, the plan that Cynthia Del Largo had told him to think about. If that was it, he had to find a way to get to Mackenzie Forbes.

So, what does a nobody have to do to get close enough to a somebody who takes pot-shots at everybody? After an assault on his think tank, Tim nailed one chance:

One of the big man's few supporters was Wide Bay Senator Kaye Mallory. Her support wasn't effusive, it was mid-field. But the Forbes theme park was in her electorate and it would certainly be on her mind. Because part of her job was to keep her voters happy, Tim felt she may be able to help him make a contact. It was well worth a try.

8

WIDE BAY'S GUARDIAN ANGEL

ALTHOUGH MACKENZIE FORBES AND HIS *'White Elephant Theme Park'* were not the flavour of the month on the political and bureaucratic fronts. In Wide Bay, people could barely think or talk about anything else. Everyone had caught *'Snake Gully Fever'* and the sun was shining brightly.

Queensland's Federal Senator, Kate Mallory, who lived and worked in Maryborough, was smart enough to realise that if she supported the Forbes project from the kick-start, she'd be able to reap all kinds of rewards for the people who voted for her.

Still, she was walking softly.

She was more than a pretty face; she was a pretty face with a fine form that didn't escape the notice of the randy masculine Members of Parliament she mixed with. At forty-two, she was a divorced mother with two girls—both in a secondary boarding school and doing well. But because she was a charming eyeful who knew how to dress, how to walk, and how to talk with authority on a variety of subjects, the natural assumption was that she had 'hot pants' that needed the services of a fire engine.

But Kate was too switched-on to play fire engines with any of the twitchy gents in the political stratosphere, and she treated them like eunuchs in the sultan's harem.

It was with care and discretion, that Kate cast curious eyes over *Dad and Dave World.* She admired the concept, loved its patriotic approach, and thought it had a lot of merit as a treat for families. The biggest factor in its favour was its potential as a uniquely Australian lure for tourists.

One thing bothered her—the heavy media and bureaucratic criticism of anything and everything Mackenzie Forbes. In the '*Tall Poppy Zone,*' his head was higher than the Milky Way.

Kate had a mate in the public relations business, and he was not one of her heavy breathing firemen. Barney Ericson was fifty-eight, with a tribe of grandkids, four sons and daughters-in-law, a delightful wife, a great big house, a mind that was in good shape, and a mouth that dripped good sense on cue.

Kate trusted him: he gave trust back.

Their friendship was not freely advertised. There was good reason: Whatever Kate was or wasn't; in the eyes of the public, she was a politician on a lavish salary, and she collected her own fair share of critics and envious glances. Due to Barney's position as CEO of a small but prestigious public relations outfit, he was able to keep her (secretly) up to speed with what was happening or not happening, in and around the world that occupied and paid her.

The pair kept in touch via email, but their favourite face-to-face was on the cosy veranda of Kate's gracious private home on the banks of the Mary River in Maryborough. Barney piloted his own plane, a Cessna Citation, that stood by in a hangar at Archerfield in Brisbane. In answer to Kate's urgent phone call regarding the current rowdy antics of Mackenzie Forbes, Barney flew to Maryborough to meet with her, a pleasant hour-long flight.

She met him at the airport, and they drove to her house.

He sat in a comfortable white cane chair at a white cane table on Kate's front veranda, with a view of the river. She poured him a cold beer and broached the reason for his trip—Mackenzie's theme park.

Barney sat quietly, idly tapped the table a few times, then fixed her with wise eyes and said, "Forbes is a cowboy, Kate."

"Everyone knows that Barney."

"He shoots from the lip, but he's no airhead; he's no fool either. He doesn't care what anyone thinks because his enormous wealth makes him independent. As a diamond billionaire, he's cock of the walk."

"The talk is that he inherited all his money."

Barney sat forward. "Empty talk. He's made some very canny investments that very few people know about. He likes to keep quiet about them."

Kate brow crinkled. "Are these investments above board?

"He simply prefers not to blow trumpets."

"What kind of investments Barney?"

"Shopping centres, minerals, a beach resort or two, apartment complexes," Barney paused, "and motion pictures."

Kate was more interested than surprised. "Movies! You're kidding."

"One movie—ever heard of *The Outback Jackaroo?*"

"Who hasn't?"

"Nobody wanted it. They said it was an Aussie movie, and Aussie movies don't make money. The producers were ready to let it slide. Then along comes Mackenzie who says, *'If it's Aussie it's good enough for me.'* He agreed to underwrite the entire production if his name was kept out of it."

"That movie made a fortune,"

"Several fortunes, worldwide. That was twelve years ago, and the royalty cheques are still lobbing. Now tell me why you're asking questions about the genius who got the movie the starting post."

"I want to know what ordinary people are saying about him."

"He's the man on the white horse."

"That's not the media's opinion."

"Because he never stops bashing them. He has no time for politicians, either."

"That's no secret."

"What's your interest?"

Kate took a moment. "What's your take on *Dad and Dave World*?"

"Brilliant."

"Brilliant?"

"If gets a chance to fly."

"There's a chance it won't?"

Barney nodded. "It's no sure thing."

"Wide Bay is all over it."

"Tinkerbell-thinking. Wave a wand, ring a bell, and let fly with the magic fairy dust."

"Why do you say that?"

Barney took a long sip of the chilled beer. "Forbes has enemies in the boardrooms of the faceless bureaucracy. They don't like him because they see him as a threat to their power base. They'll do anything to bring him down, and they're forever searching for chinks in his armour."

"Does he have any?"

"If they're not there, it's easy to put them there. In Mackenzie's case, the best way to put them there is to ridicule his every move."

"I see. If you keep saying something often enough, it's bound to sound like the truth."

"Look at it this way, Kate, *Dad and Dave World* looks like a winner. Wide Bay loves it; it won't be long before the country loves it too. Forbes will be King Kong. He'll have the general public in the palm of his hand, and he'll be in a position to unmask the faceless bureaucrats who dictate the government's policies. They're forever pushing their United Nations barrows, and Forbes is no fan."

Kate got the message. "So, you think I'd be making a mistake to show my support for his theme park?"

"If you don't support a venture that's obviously good for your voters, you may strain their trust. If you do support it, you'll raise the ire of the faceless bureaucrats."

What's your advice?"

"Don't go big. You could be compromised if everything goes belly-up."

Kate frowned. "Is there a chance it will?"

"I'll keep my radar focused on the whispers."

"Whispers?"

"The social underground—always critical, mostly negative enough to cause waves in the mainstream."

"How important are they?"

"I'd prefer not to have you, or anything connected with you as one of the topics."

"Appreciated, Barney."

With that out of the way, Barney changed the subject. "How are the girls?"

"Just fine."

"Not missing a father?"

"Divorce isn't pretty, but I'm on top of it."

"Stay there."

Kate smiled. "Do you have time for lunch?"

"I have time for you, and if that includes lunch, it's a bonus."

9

THE ROAD TO WIDE BAY

LIKE MOST MEN OBSESSED BY a cause, Tim Cameron wavered from time to time but not often, and not for long: When he wavered, he refuelled his obsession by focusing on what had been taken from him.

It was a move that worked every time.

The morning after his visit to Cynthia Del Largo he sat on his Sunshine Coast balcony gazing at the sea, idly recalling the story his father told him when he was no more than a kid of four or five. It was the old one about David and Goliath. Might isn't always right, and big doesn't always mean winning—unless you're as big as someone like Mackenzie Forbes—the kind of big that impressed people.

Tim sat there in the sun, his eyes on the seagulls dipping and diving all over the white-collared waves. Since reading the Wide Bay Business report on Mackenzie Forbes, he had been watching for news on the *Dad and Dave* front.

Despite the critical barbs, the news was hot. Mackenzie Forbes was hot. Tim was impatient to meet him, and he was convinced that Senator Kate Mallory was the key. But who was she and what was she like?

The seagulls were still at it, turning the Sunshine Coast seascape into their private playground and easing his mind at the same time. A bright thought slipped into his consciousness and he grabbed it before it slipped away. Hit by a sudden idea, he left the sunny balcony and called Cynthia Del Largo on her private number.

She picked up immediately.

He identified himself. He was brief. "You said to call if I needed you."

Cynthia was equally brief. "Go ahead."

"I'd like you to read someone's chart."

"Put a name on it."

"Kate Mallory."

"Oh yes, the Wide Bay Senator."

"Is that possible?"

"Her details are public property. Her chart will be easy. I'll need to see you."

"When?"

"Tomorrow morning at nine. I'm free for an hour."

"Perfect."

"Nine, sharp. Don't be late."

"I'll stop at the shop and get takeaway coffee."

"You'll do no such thing. Enid will make peppermint tea."

"I love peppermint tea."

Cynthia gave a little chuckle. "Good boy"

THE FOLLOWING MORNING, TIM, DRESSED in his own wardrobe and driving his own car, arrived in Montville, turned into Cynthia's little street, and marvelled again at the sheer charm of the decorative two-storey cottage she lived in. It appeared to have grown exactly where it was, and all the trees, shrubs and flowers appeared to have grown with it.

He walked along the cobblestone path and rang the front doorbell. Enid opened the door and said, "You're right on time."

"On purpose."

She walked in front of him to the study and opened the door.

Cynthia was seated at her desk and her eyes drank him in. "You've changed your wardrobe. Perfect. You look like you belong to your astrology chart. I approve."

"I made a special effort."

"Peppermint teatime," said Cynthia.

The pot sat on her desk. She poured some into two fine china cups. Tim took a seat, picked up one; inhaled the aroma, and smiled.

Cynthia raised her cup, took a sip, and said, "You're anxious."

"Yes."

"Kate Mallory is puzzling."

"Puzzling?"

"Not your run-of-the-mill politician."

"Tell me more."

"She's a Gemini with Aquarius rising."

"So?"

"I'm speaking astrologically."

"Always a foreign language to me."

"I'll translate." Cynthia smiled and took another sip of the peppermint tea.

Tim listened intently. Cynthia's interpretation had Kate Mallory pegged as a humanitarian with a sharp mind and excellent communication skills, a forward thinker with a bright personality, and a charming disposition.

Tim asked his question. "Why is she not run-of-the-mill?"

"No subterfuge; she's direct; she means what she says and says what she means."

He smiled a big smile. "Sounds like my kind of person."

Cynthia took another couple of sips of the peppermint tea. "She is the near-perfect mother, and a too-perfect wife. She cannot allow a man to take full control. In her eyes, marriage is a partnership and quite definitely a two-way street."

"Is that why hers didn't work?"

"Exactly. You may find her attractive."

"Attractive how?"

"Attraction is attraction."

His comment had a cheeky edge. "She's forty-two, and I'm twenty-nine. So what?"

"Arithmetic has nothing to do with attraction."

"That's true."

Cynthia's eyes twinkled. "The Earl of Essex was twenty-two and Queen Elizabeth was fifty-five."

"And he lost his head."

"Make sure you don't lose yours. Kate Mallory is off your shopping list."

"Officially?"

"Don't even think about it."

"Is that a warning?"

"If you need her for something it's not the way to get her approval."

Tim was adamant. "I still want to meet her."

"Tell me why."

Tim revealed his fascination with the Mackenzie Forbes theme park; why he was so interested in it; and how Kate Mallory was the only important person not to trash it.

"In fact," he added, "she hasn't said anything much at all. I'd like to know how she feels about it, because I'm hoping she'll help me get to Mackenzie Forbes."

"Finish your tea," said Cynthia, "I need to make you aware of a few things."

Tim drank the tea and waited. Cynthia rose from her chair and moved to the centre of the room. For the first time, he saw her full length. She wasn't tall, but her body, swirled in some sort of filmy fabric in shades of turquoise and lime green, was slender and elegant. Her fine grey hair was piled on top of her head in soft waves held in place with silver combs.

She was a handsome feminine woman.

Take away thirty years, thought Tim, and Cynthia would have me hypnotised; clear visible proof that arithmetic has nothing to do with attraction.

She opened up in her beautifully modulated voice. "The Mackenzie Forbes theme park is attracting you; there's no doubt that your stars are drawing you to it. I'm advising you to follow them."

"What about Kate Mallory?"

"Contact her office and explain that you want to talk to her about *Dad and Dave World*. She's a focused politician. It's part of her job to be involved in something as big as this in her constituency."

Tim smiled. "I've got this feeling about her."

"What feeling?"

"A positive message that she'll see me."

"Tell me where this positive message came from."

"I think I've grown a third eye."

Cynthia smiled. "The third eye is a myth. It is nothing more than extreme sensitivity to the spiritual nature of the universe. The Tibetan monks are said to have it because they live in the highest mountains in the world with no clutter, no noise, no distractive influences; nothing but clean clear air. They are free to receive messages from the planets, and to connect with the spiritual influences of the universe."

"I don't live in Tibet, Cynthia."

"That changes nothing."

"If I don't live in Tibet, how come I'm getting messages?"

"The pain of tragedy opened your mind. The Sun in Scorpio is powerful and intuitive. In your chart, it appears as twins; it energises your mind, and because Scorpio was rising when you were born, your Sun is twice as powerful. You are being nudged into doing something satisfying and important in Wide Bay, and I'm pledged to help you."

"Then I'm in luck."

"There's no such thing. We are all given opportunities; either we pick them up or let them pass. If we use logic to deny first impressions, we lose the chance we've been offered. Luck is so-called because it's supposed to be good fortune bestowed by chance."

"I know where you're coming from, Cynthia."

"And I know where you're going," she replied. "Are you ready for the next step?"

"If you say so."

"You're a fascinating creature," said Cynthia. "You're daring to question the establishment. You feel it's responsible for the injustice you've suffered, and you want to get even."

"I'm afraid that's the truth."

"The truth is nothing to be afraid of. People like you suffer injustices every day of their lives, and they never do anything about it. You're willing to take chances to even the score, to follow through—that's unusual."

"It's how I feel."

She waited for a beat or two. "You used a false name for your first visit to me. Your real name is Tim Cameron."

"You checked."

"It wasn't hard; you've been in the news."

"I can't be Tim Cameron and do what I want to do. I'd be called a vengeful nut like I was before, and I'd be stopped before I start. I have to walk softly, and as Tim Cameron, I can't do that."

"The false name you used to come here is fine for the moment."

"I suppose you know why I used it."

"Kit Walker, yes, the name used by the Phantom in comic books when he wants to be incognito."

He explained, "Kit Walker is the name of the Phantom's father."

"And your father is special."

"So is my mother. They were taken from me, Cynthia. I can't get them back, but I feel there's a debt that has to be paid."

"The establishment doesn't agree with you. I do. There's a lesson to be learned here, but like all lessons of value, it has to be delivered with care."

She fixed her eyes on him and spoke slowly. "The results must mean something, and not just to you."

"I don't understand."

"If you're to show the world that you were unjustly treated, you have to make sure you don't appear to be a hot-headed victim. People must believe you've fought for something that life owes you. There can be no satisfaction for satisfaction's sake. Do you know about the rules of Karma?"

"April said you'll tell me more."

"You don't need to know any more. Not yet."

"When will you update me?"

"One step at a time—you're not playing hop-scotch."

"So, what do I do, now?"

"Leave the Sunshine Coast as soon as possible and relocate either to Maryborough or to the nearby resort of Hervey Bay. The object it to find out why the Forbes theme park is beckoning you."

"How will I know?"

Cynthia smiled a cheeky smile. "Your third eye will tell you."

Tim tried for smart. "You mean, be receptive to its messages."

"If that's what you want to do."

Tim's reply was eager. "I'm sure they'll be recruiting for the for the Forbes theme park in Maryborough, Cynthia."

A broad smile lit Cynthia's face. "You're getting more messages already."

"You're teasing me."

"Far from it." Her tone was serious. "A job in the theme park won't automatically get you close to Mackenzie Forbes."

"I realise that. I'll still leave tomorrow."

"The course is set. Follow it."

He gave her an enlightened look. "I've never been on a journey like this."

"This is your chance to discover a world you didn't know existed. Are you familiar with the words of Walt Whitman?"

Tim answered immediately. "'Now voyager sail thou forth to seek and find.'"

"I'm speechless," said Cynthia.

Tim smiled. "This could be the start of something big."

"Those words have been put to music," said Cynthia. "I believe Judy Garland wanted to sing them in *A Star is Born*, but there were copyright problems."

"You're a fan?"

"She was one of Destiny's children; she didn't belong on this planet."

"And you think I do?"

"I know you do."

Tim stood and walked over to her. "You know you're part of whatever this is, don't you?"

"Oh, yes."

"Does that sit well with you?"

"It does."

"It could get messy."

"Karma is never cut and dried."

He turned, moved through to the door, looked back once, and smiled a knowing smile. She moved with him to the door, watched him open it and walk down the hallway. Then she closed the door and returned to her desk.

A few minutes later Enid came into the room. "He left more money. I told him you didn't want it, and he told me to take it instead."

"That's fine."

"I'll put it in your bank."

"Keep it for petty cash."

"You know who he is, don't you?"

"I do."

"He's mixed up in that Anzac Day tragedy."

"He's not mixed up at all, Enid. You'll be seeing him again."

Enid waited a second. "That's nice. I like him."

Cynthia looked up. "I do, too. He's a very extraordinary young man."

TIM PACKED AS SOON AS he got home. He reasoned that he'd still have to be Tim Cameron on his driver's license and his passport. His bank account was weighty, he'd have no trouble transferring funds and opening an account in the name of Kit Walker. He knew he'd have to wait for credit cards to be forwarded to his new address, so he drew enough money for expenses and a rental deposit in Maryborough.

After a busy afternoon, he sat on his balcony and watched the rays of the setting sun splattering over the waves. He'd miss the peace and the seagulls, but his lazy days beside the sea were over for the time being.

He was now Kit Walker; a man with a mission and his own third eye. Okay, according to Cynthia, third eyes were something else, but he still believed he'd grown one.

He called April Dawn and told her he was going away.

"Don't tell me why over the phone. I'll come over."

"I'd like that."

She arrived as twilight was falling and sat on the balcony with him. He told her where he was going and why.

She approved. "I love it that you're doing something positive."

"You started it."

"You look wonderful."

"So do you."

"Do you want to do it in the bedroom?"

"Is it too chilly to do it out here?"

"It won't be chilly for long."

Afterwards, they moved to the bedroom, April stayed until the sun was rising the next morning. While he was making coffee, she dressed, came to him in the kitchen, and said, "I don't have time for coffee, I have a busy day."

"I'll miss you."

"Hardly. You're not only good looking, now that you're getting over that awful hurt, you're absolutely gorgeous."

"You're very special, April, and it's not just the sex."

She smiled. "I don't put out for everybody."

"I've known that all along."

"Take care. Just do what you have to do."

A thought jumped at him. "Am I going to see you again?"

She sighed. "You still don't get it, do you?"

"Get what?"

"I didn't say goodbye. All I said was, take care."

"Okay, I will."

She held him for a long moment, kissed him, and left.

He drank a cup of coffee, dressed, loaded his bags into his car, drove to the real estate office, paid a late cleaning fee, checked out of the unit, and headed for the highway to Maryborough. It was six-thirty a.m.

WHEN HE ARRIVED FOUR HOURS later, he booked into a motel and scouted around to get the feel of the place. There was no doubt about the *Dad and Dave* factor: it was out and about; everyone's favourite topic. The town was buzzing. Because he didn't want to advertise that he wasn't short of money, he leased a modest but comfortable furnished cottage close to the Mary River, paid up for a month, and told the real estate agent he was hoping to score a job with the theme park.

The agent gave him the thumbs up and said, "You're a cert, mate."

He was all set. There was something about the town that grabbed him. He knew what it was without thinking. He was sure his third eye was blinking at him again. It was getting to be a habit. After scouting around for the rest of the day, he was convinced that he was in the perfect place for his next step.

BOOK TWO

THE KARMA JOURNEY BEGINS

10

MACKENZIE FORBES HAD NO TIME for palatial mansions. He had it summed up:

Give a man too much luxury and pretty soon he wants more. Give him more, and he stops being a man; he turns into a limp dick; swigging champagne and scoffing pansy tucker. Next thing you know his brain rots from over-indulgence, and he's gone!

Mackenzie's residence was built on several acres in the southern hinterland of the Noosa Resort on the Sunshine Coast, a short distance away from the Noosa Airport for light aircraft, and no more than fifteen road minutes north-west of Tim's vacated apartment.

Access to the Forbes residence was along a private road on the eastern edge of Lake Weyba, a large expanse of shallow water that entertained hungry ducks and sea birds. Mackenzie referred to his place as 'The Homestead.' It looked like one; Aussie to a T. It sprawled impressively over a large block of land with wide verandas, white walls, plantation shutter doors, full-length colonial windows, and a pool under palm trees with a spa. The five bedrooms were big and airy; the huge dining and living rooms had fireplaces; the kitchen was functional, with lots of spacious cupboards, and a wood-burning stove than Natalie Forbes loved.

She also loved Mackenzie. She'd been his wife for over thirty years. For as long as she lived, she would love him, she would always love him; unerringly and unconditionally. She loved him for who he was; not what he was. Natalie knew he strayed, but she also knew she was his anchor. Other women had tried to lure him away, and they probably always would, but he always came home, he always would. The chains of her anchor were too strong, and they held him to her, unbroken by jealousy, or the carnal temptations of temporary affairs. Natalie was a woman who had fathomed the deepest mysteries of love, the worth of it, and what it really was. That knowledge kept her safe and happy.

Weeks ago, when Mackenzie told her of his plans for *Dad and Dave World*, he'd been as enthusiastic as always about everything he did. But Natalie had sensed a tiny element of doubt, and she identified it. Mackenzie was no longer in the first bloom of youth. His years were beginning to mellow him, as they habitually mellow men like him; men of substance who can sense the wispy signs of debilitating old age lurking on the distant horizon.

Natalie asked for details of her husband's latest venture and listened intently to his elaborations. When he'd finished, she opened the door to her feelings.

"Do it, Mack, and do it soon, while your ideas are still fresh enough to trigger other ideas. Don't waste a moment. Start tomorrow. Make it happen and make it big."

It was exactly what he wanted to hear. "You'll be with me?"

"All the way."

"I'll turn into a maniac."

"You always do."

There was a tinge of doubt in his voice. "I've never done anything as big as this; not ever."

"What's been keeping you?"

"It could turn into a monster."

"Then keep it caged."

A trick question. "Any suggestions on how I do that?"

She smiled her understanding smile. "Do what you always do, Mack. Surround yourself with fabulous people; people you trust, and people who trust you. Get them hooked, make them excited and take it from there."

"You're always right about everything, Nat."

"I know, isn't it lucky?"

"Should I involve Josh?"

"He's your son, Mack."

"He likes running his own race."

"He's never been asked to run in a race like this; give him a chance."

'Okay, it's a deal."

He looked at her. "I won't be home, much. I may have to relocate for days at a time."

Natalie nodded. "I'll only be an hour away in your fancy airplane."

"You don't want to relocate, too?"

"Who'd look after The Homestead?"

Mackenzie officially launched his project the next day and his brainchild came to life, quickly turning into a hungry giant that was on track to change his life and rule his world with a will of its own—*careful what you wish for, Mack.*

THE DAD AND DAVE CONNECTION

THE SUN WAS GOING DOWN when Tim drove to his rented house in Maryborough, parked his car in the garage, unloaded his luggage, made two trips up the seven steps to the front veranda, unlocked the front door; walked in, and looked around.

He'd inspected the place with the real estate agent, liked it, and after a quick walk-through, he'd signed the lease. Now he was taking time to inspect it more closely, he sensed a familiar feeling. The place reminded him of the house he'd grown up in.

It was nowhere near as big, but the furniture and atmosphere were first cousins.

He checked the rooms, opening doors and windows; then stood in the kitchen half-expecting to see his mother standing by the stove.

When he opened the casement windows above the sink; there they were; the mock-orange trees, first cousins to the trees that grew outside the Manly kitchen. They were in bloom, and their sweet perfume floated in through the open windows.

He closed his eyes and breathed in the sweetness. He knew it then—his third eye nudged him. He had made the right decision. He was where he was supposed to be, in the right house in the right street in the right town, and on the right mission.

Cynthia's advice had been golden.

He unpacked, hung his clothes in the bedroom closet, stashed his smalls in the big chest of drawers, stacked his toiletries in the bathroom, took a shower and went for a thirty-minute walk to case the nearby CDB. By eight-thirty he was back home, happily asleep in his wide comfortable bed.

He awoke at six-thirty to the chortlings of a crowing rooster somewhere down the street. He showered and dressed, then drove to the CDB for a breakfast of buttermilk pancakes, bacon, eggs, and coffee in a place called the *Muddy Waters Café* in Maryborough's heritage-rich Wharf Street, right beside the Mary River. After browsing through a copy of the Fraser Island Chronicle, he caught the attention of one of the locals, who had him pegged as a visitor.

The casually dressed man—sixty-something, with a keen face, and bright inquisitive eyes that he fixed on Tim said, "Mind if I join you?"

"Be my guest." Tim shook the man's proffered hand.

"George Armstrong," said the man.

"Kit Walker," Tim replied.

"Are you here to work at the theme park?"

'I'm hoping to."

"The recruitment office is just down the street in the Customs House Hotel."

Tim nodded. "I'm on the way there as soon as I've finished breakfast."

"Do you know Maryborough?"

"I'm an out-of-towner."

"You know you're in Mary Poppins country, doncha?"

"Mary Poppins?"

George Armstrong spoke with pride. "Pam Travers who wrote *Mary Poppins* lived right here in this town; born and bred. "

"I didn't know that."

"People come here for the Mary Poppins Festival every year."

"There's a festival?"

'Not sure if Pam Travers would approve; she was feisty."

"Feisty?"

'She fought with Walt Disney when he made the movie. She didn't like what he was doing with her story. They fought all the time; goes with the territory with creative people. Mackenzie Forbes is feisty too."

"That's what I like about him, Mr Armstrong."

"You've met him?"

"No, but I want to."

"You want a job with him because he's feisty?'

"One reason, yes."

"You look kind of familiar, what do you do?"

Tim didn't want to be familiar; that wasn't part of his plan, and he didn't want to talk about himself or trade information with a curious local. He bought the question off.

"I'm ready to do whatever Mr Forbes wants me to do."

"Best way," said George Armstrong.

Without being over-familiar, Tim chatted on about Maryborough, and what Mackenzie's theme park could do for it, then looked at his watch, and rose from his chair. "I understand the recruiting office opens at ten o'clock."

"On the dot, Mr Walker."

"Then I'd better get going."

"Best of luck, mate,"

Tim smiled. "And a spoon full of sugar to you, Mr Armstrong."

12

SNAKE GULLY STIRS: FACT OR FANTASY?

ALL KINDS OF PEOPLE WERE milling about in the recruiting office. Tim remarked on how busy the place was to the young woman sitting at a desk, handing out application forms.

She handed him one, gave him an interested look and said, "You're not a local, are you?"

"I'm planning to be."

She gave him a bright cheeky smile. "Things are looking up."

He studied the application form, and filled it in. In the space requesting details of qualifications, he wrote *Marketing and Events Graduate, London, UK.* He quickly completed the rest of the questionnaire and handed the form back.

'That was quick," said the young woman, looking him over. "You're a fast worker."

Tim caught the move. "I'm not into wasting time."

Her reply suggested much more than she said, "Neither am I.

Tim took a seat while the young woman moved through the room collecting more forms and answering questions. She then handed the completed forms to a smart, efficient-looking middle-aged woman, who opened a door that obviously led to an inner office. She took the forms and closed the door again.

Several minutes went by.

Tim waited patiently, exchanging casual glances with the young form collector, who was busy explaining the questionnaire to other hopefuls. Ten minutes later, the middle-aged woman opened the door again, and called: "Mr Kit Walker?"

Tim stood. On the way to the door. he passed the young woman, who smiled again and said, "Give 'em the works, spunk bucket."

He was ushered into the office. As she closed the door, the older woman said, "I'm Dottie Austin, Mr Josh Forbes's assistant, he'd like a word with you."

She indicated a desk. At it, sat an impossibly fresh-looking eager beaver, with a bright face and clipped wavy brown hair. Tim was sure he was looking at Charlie Brown. The eager beaver stood, offered his hand across the desk, and in a chirpy voice tinged with mischief, said. "I'm Josh Forbes. Mackenzie's my Dad."

Tim took his hand. "Hi there, Josh."

"Your form says you're a Marketing and Events graduate from London. Are you a Brit?"

"I'm an Australian. I studied in London."

"That's awesome. Are you serious about working for us?"

"That's why I filled out the form."

"Take a seat, then. Man, this is a real break. Dad's been sweeping the radar for someone like you, he's pretty particular, and he hasn't been able to find anyone he liked."

"That's interesting."

Josh took another look at Tim's recruitment form and noted his Maryborough address. "Have you been here long?"

"Two days. I came here hoping to sign up on your Dad's team."

"He's got to meet you. Do you have time today?"

"You mean to meet your father?"

"Is that okay with you?"

Tim's third eye blinked.

"I'm all yours," he said.

"Let's not waste a second."

Josh got up from his chair and spoke to Dottie Austin. "We're off to the Snake Gully site to meet Dad. I probably won't be back until late. Call me if anything urgent comes up."

Efficient Dottie nodded. "Have a good time."

As they crossed the outer room to exit, the young woman handing out the recruitment forms spoke to Josh. "Are you going somewhere?"

"Construction site; back later today."

Tim took yet another cheeky look from the young woman and felt a little tingle of interest that increased with her bright-eyed reply. "You're a fast worker for sure."

"Only way to play," answered Tim.

Josh led the way out of the building. "I see you caught Diane's eye."

"Diane?"

"The hot chick with the forms. Her name's Diane Petersen. She a specialist."

"Specialist?"

"She's a stud catcher. Are you interested?"

"Now that you mention it."

"If she likes you, she's very cooperative."

"Are you speaking from experience?"

"How else would I know?"

"Thanks for the heads-up."

Josh grinned. "We'll take my wheels to the site, you're not nervous, are you?"

"Not especially."

They rounded the building to enter an undercover car park; Josh walked up to a shiny red Dodge Viper. "Be my guest, man. You're in safe hands."

Tim was impressed. "I take it this rocket's all yours?"

"Dad gave it to me when I joined the team. He told me that if I dud him, he'll take it back."

"Which means you have no intention of dudding him."

"And not because of this pile of tin. My Dad's a legend."

Josh hauled out his mobile phone, punched out a few numbers, held the phone to his ear and spoke—with appropriate pauses. "Hey, Dad, I got someone special I want you to meet. Yeah, that's what I said, he's awesome . . . a marketing marvel, Dad . . . all the way from London, and I'm bringing him out to the site . . . You gonna be available? . . . Marketing marvel, yes, Dad, like I said. We're leaving in a minute."

Josh clicked the mobile off. "All set."

Tim sat back in the Viper's soft leather seat, clipped the seat belt in, and waited for the machine to come to life. Josh eased it onto the street and drove it though the CBD onto the Bruce Highway. His foot went down, and Tim felt the car shoot instantly into overdrive.

"The trip is about thirty minutes on cruise control," said Josh, "fifteen if I open her up; your choice."

"Let's take the slow ride; I'd like to check the scenery out."

'Good move. This is a great part of the country."

Josh was right. The landscape was lush, pretty, and green. As the Viper purred on, Tim looked out on a tree-littered country that was laced with a string of green-edged water holes, a playground for all kinds of birds, water dragons, and fish.

As they neared the site, Tim's ears picked up the sounds of action before it came into view. Several minutes later, the Viper turned off the road into a grassy clearing with a huge sign that said, 'Snake Gully Construction Site. No Admittance, unless on business.'

The Viper crept to a stop beside a line of parked cars, trucks, utilities, and covered vans. When Tim opened the door of the car, he got the full blast of the construction site—a man-made orchestra of excitement—graders, bulldozers, low-level cranes, and a sea of hard-hatted workmen; all of them going at it. There were half-finished buildings, and roughly graded streets waiting to be sealed. *Dad and Dave* flags fluttered on flagpoles that stabbed the air.

Right beside the entrance to the site was a long half-finished train platform, still under construction. Josh indicated it with a wave of his hand. "This is the Snake Gully Train Station, and just over there is where the entrance gates will be. Inside, we'll have another train station for the smaller train that circles the town. For that job, Dad's bought two of the vintage coal-fired Puffing Billies that used to run sugar cane from the farms to the refinery in Bundaberg, and he's having special carriages built. What do you think?"

Tim was honestly gobsmacked. "Too incredible."

'This is just the start, man. Follow me, the office is over here."

They picked their way through the action to a nearby building bearing a sign that said, 'Construction Office.' The building had the look of an Australian Federation cottage with a wide front veranda, gingerbread scrolls on the posts, curved awnings over the windows, and a chiselled front door. Tim followed Josh up the steps to the veranda.

"This is going to be the Snake Gully Information Centre. Right now, it's the site office—it's where the geniuses hang out; architects, engineers, electricians, foremen, heaps of blueprints, plans, white boards, and big decisions; it's a real buzz!"

Josh opened the chiselled door and swaggered into the front room, where a man and two women sat behind a low counter.

"Hi, Josh," said one of the women. "He's expecting you."

Josh opened an inner door to what was obviously the main planning room and held it open. Tim walked in and got his first look at Mackenzie Forbes in the flesh. He was standing beside a desk neatly piled with files and papers. He was about six feet tall and straight; his lean frame held no flab, and his open face was like a banner that announced who he was; a man who didn't make excuses for anything, a fearless human being whose confidence was etched in the expression on his tanned face. His hair had thinned a bit, and it was streaked with silver. His dark eyes radiated immediate interest. They zeroed in on Tim, gave him the once-over, then flashed up to anchor on his face. Mackenzie Forbes held out a hand, wrapped it around Tim's, but said nothing.

His eyes did the talking, and Tim felt as though he was being fed into a computer. The hand that was still holding his, tightened its grip and held it for a while longer before letting it go.

Tim met Mackenzie's eyes with no hint of modesty. "It's good to meet you."

A faint positive expression crossed the great man's face. "You, too." He then looked at Josh and said, "This is your marketing expert, right?"

"Right on, Dad—all the way from London."

Mackenzie turned his eyes on Tim again. "Doesn't matter where he comes from. I'm more interested in what he can do, isn't that the idea?"

Tim answered, "What do you want to know, Mr Forbes?"

"What's your name?"

"Kit Walker"

Mackenzie nodded. "I see, Kit Walker, the Ghost Who Walks?"

"You got it, Dad—Just like the Phantom."

Mackenzie's lips held a little smile. "Kit Walker, eh?"

"Coincidence," said Tim.

"Look, let's get something clear," said Mackenzie. "For starters, Kit Walker is not your name. Am I right?"

Tim was momentarily caught off balance. "Why do you say that?"

"Your name is Tim Cameron. You're the fella who got caught up in all the bloody bullshit that went around over the Anzac Day terrorist hit that took out your mother and father. You look a bit different, the face fuzz has gone, and your hair is shorter but that's who you are. Have I got you pegged?"

Tim saw no sense in a denial. "Yes."

"Awesome," said Josh.

Mackenzie went on. "They hounded you, didn't they? You weren't supposed to say anything. You were supposed to sit back and let them make excuses about ethnic privileges and injustice and everything that hangs around in the same bag. I saw the television interview where that up-herself tart ripped into you about your Dad and Anzac Day. I thought it was the most unpatriotic beat-up I'd ever seen."

"Thanks for that, Mr Forbes."

"My name's Mackenzie; everyone calls me Mack."

"Thanks for that, too."

"I can understand that you don't want to use your right name, fella, it keeps the bugs from biting. But let me tell you this, there'll be no bugs biting if you come to work for me. You can use the name your Dad and Mum gave you, and you can be who you are around me and my son here, but you're Kit Walker if you feel it's better for everyone else."

Tim was gratefully relieved. "Thanks. I appreciate that."

"Last thing you want is a lot of curious sticky-beaks asking questions and getting in your hair. What happened to you and your folks is too private to be public property." Mackenzie took a breath. "Tell me, son, and I've got to ask this—how are you bearing up?"

"I'm on top of it, and I'm staying on top of it."

"I love a bloke with balls. You'll fit in well here, we'll look after you, you're in Australia, mate. It's my country, and I don't take to anyone who knocks it. That's why I'm building this theme park. I want kids to know what it was like for people like me who grew up here. Now I'll tell you what Tim, you and me and my son here are gonna sit right down and talk a while. You can tell me how you think the marketing should happen for my project. How's that?'

"Just fine."

"Awesome," said Josh.

"My problem is that I'm a loudmouth," said Mackenzie, "and I realise that loud is not the way to get this project happening. It's okay in Maryborough, because it's good for the town, but I've got to get the message out there. It's not about the money, it's about the project. I want people to come here to experience the Australia that too many dickheads are kicking in the arse. If we're gonna call Australia home, then we better bloody well know what kind of home it used to be, and what it still should be."

Tim felt like cheering. "I'm right in your corner!"

"Do you have some time right now?"

"As much of it as you want."

"Awesome," said Josh.

"Let's get down to business," said Mackenzie, who turned to Josh. "It might be an idea to put a sock in *'awesome'* for a while. You sound like a talking cockatoo. We all know everything's awesome we just don't need to be reminded all the time."

"Sorry, Dad."

Mackenzie cleared a space on his desk, took to his chair, and waited for the two young men to sit facing him. "Where do we start?"

Tim explained. "I've got the broad picture. I need details."

"Like what?"

Tim took off on a wave of enthusiasm. "I'll need to know as much about this project as you know. I need to be briefed on every aspect of the operation; details of the butter factory, the electricity and sewerage plants, the hotel, restaurants, food, and the theme rides; how everything has been planned; how the actors and employees are going to function; how much accommodation in Maryborough is needed; how the Snake Gully Express is going to run and when; how many visitors are being catered to; how supplies will reach the site, and how much cooperation the council is willing to give."

"Stone the crows," said Mackenzie. "You don't muck about, do you?"

"In the marketing world, knowledge is everything. If you stuff up, sooner or later you're caught out."

Tim continued, "The public will need to be sold on the park's nostalgia. They'll have to know that they're walking into Australia's past; more than that, they'll have to believe it."

"Awesome," said Josh.

For a good ten seconds, Mackenzie sat there in silence. "You're bowling me over. Are you finished?"

Tim took the punt. "You're going to have to start behaving yourself with the media. You can't keep telling them they're a bunch of dropkicks, even if you think they are. You'll have to play their game, get into their good books and win them over."

"That's a bloody hard ask."

"Absolutely essential."

"How do I go about that?"

"By listening to me. I'll set up the interviews and turn you into Santa Claus."

Mackenzie's eyes narrowed. "Santa Claus?"

"Dispensing good cheer and happy thoughts."

"Awesome," said Josh.

Mackenzie gave in. "You're sure that will work?"

Tim was all reassurance. "Always has and always will."

"Sounds great, Dad," said Josh.

Tim made another point. "You'll have to be happy in the Dad image or it won't work. Is that going too much against the grain?"

"The Dad image?"

"It's the *Dad and Dave* theme park, isn't it? People are going to associate you with it, and you can't be a bully. Is there anyone around we can tie to the Dave image?"

"No sweat," said Mackenzie, "We'll get Dusty Rivers."

Tim's eyes lit up. "The Outback Jackaroo?"

Mackenzie filled him in. "He's my best mate! *Outback Jackaroo* was my movie. He played himself in the picture, and he's still associated with it."

"Would he be willing to work with you on this?"

"Like I said, no sweat. He's a bit of a rogue like me, he's got a beautiful wife and two young daughters. The public is still in love with him. The Jackaroo picture might be ten or twelve years old, but every time they play it on television, it rates its arse off."

"Dusty is a hero," said Josh.

Tim was all smiles. "We've got our man."

Mackenzie's face was a neon light. "Looks like I've got my man, too."

Tim shot a look across the desk. "I'm hired?"

"How much money do you want?"

'Whatever's a fair thing."

"You don't want to lose the bulk of the earn to the Taxation Department. Those bastards get plenty from me."

"Me too," said Josh.

Mackenzie threw him a look. "You got a bonus, boy, the Dodge Viper was tax-free."

"Awesome."

"What did you say?"

"Fantastic!"

"Right!"

Mackenzie addressed Tim. "First things first . . ." He did a speedy search through one of the piles of papers on his desk; extracted a thick file and laid it in front of Tim. "Here's a copy of the Snake Gully bible fella; a detailed overview of the entire site and everything in it. Read up on it and take it all in, any questions, ask Mr Awesome here, he knows it all by heart, and he can show you over the site as soon we've finished here. Now to the future. I've leased a building in Maryborough's man street, and it will operate as the new Official Snake Gully office as from tomorrow. We'll be out of the Customs House Hotel as soon as we've done interviewing today's personal, and that will free up Dottie Austin to work with you. She can be your right hand. She's A-one efficient, and she knows the ropes. Awesome here can keep you posted on everything you need to know. How does that sound?"

"Lollipops and roses."

"Use your time while the office is being set up to get to know the town. Move around a bit, get to know the locals, they're nice friendly people, and they'll like you."

Josh piped up, "He's already met Diane Petersen, Dad."

Mackenzie dropped a wicked wink. "Yeah, well, that's a good start."

"Anyone else I should know?" asked Tim.

"There is," said Mackenzie, "I had a trickle of positive interest from one of the local pollies—a Senator Kate Mallory. Might be an idea to contact her to keep her in the loop. She's a Maryborough girl, and she's popular with the locals, she's no dill either."

"I've checked her out already."

"What?"

"I checked you out too, and I boned up on your project. I figured that if I wanted to work with you, I'd have to know what I was getting into. I realised that Kate Mallory could be an ally, so I wanted to know if her positive interest was genuine."

"And what did you come up with?"

"I'll let you know."

'I was right. You're a world-beater."

"Let's just say I'm off to a flying start."

"Josh will show you around the site. There's a canteen, and the tucker's more than decent. You'll get hungry around lunch time. Make the most of it, fella, try one of our Aussie meat pies—baked on the premises. You'll love 'em. It's great to have you on the team."

Tim felt he'd been caught in a whirlwind. It was just noon on his third day in town, and he was already on the way. Things were happening. He was sure his plan was in the pipeline, and Mackenzie Forbes was part of it. His third eye was smiling.

Josh's tour of the Snake Gully site included close inspections of the rising skeletons of the Snake Gully township. They lunched in comfort on meat pies with mushy peas, mash, and black sauce and sipping on billy tea, seated beside a tribe of chattering tradies on benches under the unfinished main street's gum trees. On the edges of the site, rails were being laid for the Puffing Billy train.

Snake Gully was everything Mackenzie had tub-thumped it to be, even though it was still months shy of its projected opening.

By the time Tim and Josh returned to the recruiting office in the Customs House Hotel, it was close to 6:30 p.m. The place was quiet, and the staff had vacated the premises, so they took off to the Muddy Waters Café down the street for a seafood dinner: *Fresh as the sea breeze.*

"I'll whiz you home in the Viper," said Josh. "You don't have a car yet, right?"

"I drove to Maryborough in my own car."

"Sell it. I'll fix you up with one of the company cars, logo and all. You can pick it up at the Customs House Hotel in the morning—howzat?"

"As exciting as it gets, man. It's been one long amazing day."

"Catch some zeds. It's way after nine. We'll be on again tomorrow."

After Josh let him off at his rented cottage, Tim took a long shower. As he was towelling dry, he heard the knock on the front door. He wrapped the towel around his flanks, crossed to the door and opened it just enough to see who was on the other side.

Diane Peterson stood beaming at him. "I'm here to welcome you to Maryborough."

He didn't quite get it. "You mean officially?"

"Not exactly." She pushed the door open, and as she entered the room, she unwrapped Tim's towel, closed the door and hung the towel on the doorknob.

It only took a few seconds for her to step out of her shoes and remove the short dress she was wearing. She was now as naked as he was, and her eyes cruised his body.

"You weren't kidding when you said you didn't waste time."

"I wasn't."

"I can see you meant it, and I won't want breakfast."

The welcome took half the night. When Tim woke in the morning, Diane had already gone. He felt like he'd been sleeping for hours. As an official employee of the great

Mackenzie Forbes, he was ready for another day in Maryborough.

13

MEETING THE WIDE BAY SENATOR

SENATOR KATE MALLORY TOOK TIM'S call in her Kent Street Office at nine o'clock. Josh had already briefed her, and she arranged to see Tim at ten.

Mildly surprised that she agreed to meet so soon, Tim, with his head full of Cynthia's assessment of Kate's astrology chart, shaved close and took extra care with his grooming and wardrobe. He was keen to make an impression, and he was right on time for the meeting.

The Senator's offices were on the first floor of the Kent Street building. He was met at the door by a young man, who shook his hand and said, "I'm Terry Curtis, Ms Mallory's assistant. She'll see you right away."

Tim walked into a pleasant office with pale apricot walls and all the usual office furniture, accessories, and equipment. Kate rose from her chair behind a polished desk and allowed her eyes to take him in. His positive reaction was instant. She was neatly dressed in a cream jacket fitted over a loose cream blouse with a soft collar. Her honey-blonde hair was styled in a soft becoming bob that complemented her lightly tanned face. Her deep hazel eyes rested on him without blinking, and her pleasant forty-two-year-old features still held their youthful freshness. With a graceful extension of her arm, she offered him her hand.

He took it, felt the warmth of it, and said, "Thanks for seeing me so soon."

She let his hand go, sat down, and got straight to the point. "Josh Forbes tells me you're the project's Marketing and Events man; an expert from London."

"I signed on yesterday."

"You've won a friend. Josh is full of praise."

"I'm happy to be on board. It's an exciting project."

"Have you been involved with anything like it before?"

"Not exactly, but I've worked on the marketing for big-budget films, live productions, arena shows, major festivals in the UK, and elite hotel events for British designers in the Paris Fashion Collections."

She registered that, then said, "Do you mind if I ask why you want to work in Australia?"

"I'm an Australian, Senator, this is my country and I'd like to live here."

"Permanently?"

"Permanently."

"You don't miss London?"

"I think *Dad and Dave World* is as exciting as anything I've worked on in London."

"Do you like this part of Australia?"

"I like Australia."

"Maryborough is hardly London."

"If wanted to be in London, I'd be there."

"You sound confident."

"I am."

"Do you have any reservations?"

"What about?"

"About the success of the Mackenzie project?"

"I believe it has been amazingly well-conceived and planned. The detailing is incredible, but that doesn't automatically mean it will be a success. It will need to be presented to the public as the unusual endeavour it is. That will take a lot of understanding and patience, but that's my job. I intend to give it everything I can—without reservations."

"That's very admirable."

"I'm not looking for admiration, Senator. I'm looking to help launch a winner."

"How do you find Mackenzie Forbes?"

"I think he's remarkable in every way. Most of all, he's honest and forthright."

Kate was walking softly. "You don't see him as difficult?"

"I've made it clear that if he wants his project to happen, he can't be seen as difficult."

She flashed a faint smile. "You told him that?"

"Exactly that."

"Is he listening to you?"

"So far, yes."

"You mean for now, Mr Walker."

Tim knew what she was doing. She was testing him, trying to find something that would expose him as a fake, a man who was all talk and no resolve, someone who would take the money and disappear when things got too hot to handle. He'd had enough of her probing. He decided to pull it up and let her know what he was all about.

"No offence, Senator, but I want you to understand that I'm serious about being involved here. I'm not playing games. I'm here because I chose to be, I'm not here to dud this town or anybody in it. I have accepted Mackenzie's offer because I believe in his project, and I'm convinced I can help him. I'm also aware of the delicate position you'll be in if you decide to approve of his so-called way-out project. You're a politician, and it's your job to look after the people who voted for you. I understand that, but this I can tell you—in my opinion— Mackenzie Forbes is on track to give this part of the country the biggest break it's ever had. If you don't believe that, too, I'll get out of your hair right now and there'll be no hard feelings."

Kate took it on the chin. "You don't hold back, do you?"

"Are we finished?"

"Is that an ultimatum?"

Tim paused. "I'm not sure."

Her tone was definite. "Because if it is, you've read me incorrectly."

"How's that?"

She explained, "You're an impulsive young man, and I don't say that disparagingly. You've told me what I wanted to know, and you can tell Mackenzie Forbes that I'll do what I can to make his project happen; that is, with one proviso."

"Which is?"

"I'd need to be advised about every marketing move you make in advance, so I'll know how to handle it. Is that a problem?"

"Not at all."

Tim had been offered the initiative and he took it. "Here's my first move. I plan to launch Mackenzie Forbes as the true-life Dad in the marketing of *Dad and Dave World,* and at the same time, I'll be announcing that the true-life Dave will be Australia's much- loved movie star Dusty Rivers. Let the nay-sayers in the bureaucracy cope with that."

The Senator was impressed. "Has the Dusty Rivers move been confirmed?"

"Not yet, but Mackenzie and Dusty's friendship is solid."

"I'll need confirmation if I'm going to issue a press release."

He smiled a big one. "A positive press release from this office would have heaps of clout."

"Which is why I need to be sure."

"I'll clear it, as soon as I can."

"It's great to meet you, Mr Walker."

"And that's mutual, Senator."

"Are we done?

"For now."

Tim rose from his chair and said, "I'll be installed in the new project offices as from tomorrow. I'll be working with Josh and Dottie Austin if you need to contact me. I'm sorry I don't have a business card yet."

"I have Josh's card, Mr Walker, I'll know where to find you."

"Thanks again, Senator. It's been a pleasure."

He gave her his warmest smile, turned, and left the office.

Terry Curtis looked up from his desk and said, "Did everything go okay?"

"Just fine. Are you the senator's only assistant?"

"The only permanent one. There are two casuals. Senator Mallory doesn't believe in wasting public money."

"Terry, you've just made my day."

"Anytime, Mr Walker."

14

DAD AND DAVE WORLD: THE EXPANDING DREAM

TIM WALKED THE SHORT DISTANCE to the Customs House Hotel. The company car Josh promised, a white 2-door Golf convertible, was waiting in car park.

A note attached to the windshield, read: *Diane has the key.*

Tim headed for the project office, where potential employees were still being interviewed. Diane saw him, crossed to her desk, picked up the envelope that contained the key to the Golf and gave it to him.

"Sexy little car," she said, "if you're into sexy little cars."

Tim took the envelope. "How did you guess?"

"You've got sexy little cars written all over you."

"You're very observant."

"Are you going to be in tonight?"

"I hope so."

"Just reminding you that I don't want breakfast, and I don't do dinner either."

"I'll make a note of it."

"See you, spunk-bucket."

He watched her walk away, noted the sensual sway of her too-perfect butt, and had a mental flash about how wonderful it looked uncovered.

He returned to the car park, unlocked the Golf, opened the door, climbed in, inserted the key, and was about to turn it on when Josh, aboard the Viper, drove the car park, and spotted him, purred the Viper over to him, leaned out the window and said, "Coffee?"

"Sure."

"I've got news. Hop in."

Tim alighted from the Golf, locked it and boarded the Viper. "Where are we going?"

"*Pink Flamingo*. Best in town. Are you into homemade cake?"

"Mad for it."

"You'll be in heaven, bro."

Pink Flamingo wasn't big, but Josh was right about it. They ordered and took a seat.

"Dad's been in touch with Dusty Rivers. He's on for the Dave ride. He lives at Cabarita in northern NSW, but he's coming up to Dad's place at Noosa for the weekend; two days away. Dad wants us to be there to bring him up to speed."

"So to speak."

"Dad's flying down to Noosa tomorrow in his private wings, a Mooney Mark 20. We'll fly down on the Bruce Highway in the Viper on Saturday morning. Are you game?"

"They don't have speed traps on the Bruce Highway to Noosa?"

"I've got radar. We'll head off early."

"Early as you like."

"How did you go with Diane last night?"

"How did you know?"

"She checked with me for your address."

"I owe you."

"Di's a legend. She took my virginity when I was fifteen, and I haven't looked back. She taught me all I know. She's all action-plus; nothing else. Never gets in the way, doesn't make demands, never asks favours, delivers like a wet dream, always says thanks, and brings her own toothbrush. She's a great bird."

"She must be a busy one."

"She only targets studs. You've got to look like you can deliver. If you can't, it's bye-bye, birdie. You would have been a natural. Has she been on your case again?"

"I don't want to overdo it."

"Someone else?"

"I'm keeping it a secret."

"I knew you were a stud."

KATE MALLORY PUT A CALL through to her friend Barney Ericson and brought him up to date on the current happenings at *Dad and Dave World*. He listened without interrupting while she gave out details of the Kit Walker appointment and the proposed move to involve Dusty Rivers. Then it was his turn.

"Have you met this London recruit?"

"I have, and I have to confess I'm impressed. He knows what he's talking about, and I think he knows what he's doing."

"What does Mackenzie Forbes say about him?"

"I haven't spoken to him, but Josh Forbes is doing handstands."

"That's a good sign. That Forbes kid is on the ball."

Kate took a breath. "I've decided to give the project a positive nod if the Dusty Rivers connection comes through."

"Have you thought seriously about that?"

"I have. I think it will be good for Maryborough in any number of ways. The town will prosper, employment has already risen, tourism will get an enormous boost, and with Dusty Rivers on board, the public's view will be rosy."

"Can't fault any of that. Any talk of union problems?"

"Mackenzie plays ball with the unions."

"He knows he must, but as they'll be ripping big money out of his theme park, there's a big chance they won't bug him. The present state government is a union government so there won't be any moans from them."

"In fact," smiled Kate, "they'll be likely to take the credit for of the whole idea."

Barney threw a curly one. "It may look like plain sailing, but don't kid yourself. There's no such thing as plain sailing."

"Can you qualify that?"

"This country's immigration policy has been far too reckless, and it has led to the rise of pro-migrant extremists, who use social websites to bleat their criticisms of anything they don't agree with. The Internet has given them a voice."

"I'm listening, Barney."

"Mackenzie Forbes is a target for some of these people. He's independent. He's rich. He makes his own rules, and he's fiercely Australian in the old sense of this country. His new-wave critics see those attitudes as old-fashioned and discriminating."

Kate was cool. "The public at large doesn't."

"That may be true, but as a senator who comes out in favour of what Forbes is doing, you could be taking risks with rabble-raising minorities."

"I'm aware of that."

"They can be very loud and disruptive, Kate. They can also be persistent."

"I've thought hard about that and I still believe I should support a venture that has so many good things going for it. That's that way I feel as a person, and as an elected politician."

"Did the Dusty Rivers business have anything to do with that decision?"

Kate chuckled. "Come on, Barney, of course it did. It was the ultimate positive move.

"That was a trick question."

"It was no trick answer. My decision is based on a combination of things, including the surprise entry from London. That young man has successfully managed to put me clearly in the picture."

"What did you say his name was?"

"Kit Walker."

"What's he like?"

"Young, focused, and committed to the job."

"How young?"

"Late-twenties young."

"Do you want me to check him out?"

"If it will make you feel better."

"Won't hurt, will it?"

15

THE UNRULY ARM OF THE LAW

ON THE SAME DAY IN the Brisbane Supreme Court, the Crown's case against the Australian Army went before Justice Harold E. Broadhurst. Appearing for the twenty-four-year-old man who fired the killer shots on Anzac Day was Geoffrey Barkley, a prominent Brisbane barrister appointed and paid for by the government's Human Rights Institute. Judge Broadhurst agreed with Barkley's view that the young man's name and race could negatively cloud the outcome of the case—the ruling was that the young man was not named, and his ethnic background was not mentioned.

A strong objection from the Army's barrister, Frank Ward, was overruled. Geoffrey Barkley submitted that his client had gone to Manly's Russell Park to protest Anzac Day's misguided glorification of war, and that he and his two companions were intent on making their feelings heard by staging an innocent disturbance that was misinterpreted by a group of enlisted Australian Army personnel, whose aggressive reaction interfered with the firing of weapons initially intended to underline the association of guns with the violent nature of Anzac Day.

After listening to the supporting evidence of the man's two companions on the day of the tragedy, Justice Broadhurst heard the testimonies of Staff Sargent Andrew Denton and Private Perry Collier, the two enlisted men who had forcefully attacked the plaintiff, causing him to lose his balance and fall heavily onto the bonnet of his car while he was aiming his weapon away from the crowd at the dawn service.

Both enlisted men claimed they acted out of concern for those attending the Anzac Day Service, because it appeared that the young man and his friends appeared to be acting dangerously. Other army personnel who were present at the event gave corroborating evidence, but Geoffrey Barkley claimed his client had been attacked without warning instead of simply being rebuked, and that the unwarranted attack had caused severe injury to his right leg and to the left side of his head when he crashed against the bonnet of the car.

Barkley added that the two enlisted men acted aggressively, suggesting that the ethnic appearance of the three men had aroused their undue suspicion. After more conflicting evidence from witnesses, and objections from Frank Ward, Justice Broadhurst found in favour of the plaintiff, and severely reprimanded the two soldiers for their un-Australian behaviour. He left it at that, knowing that the Army, to save face, would have to dishonourably discharge both Andrew Denton and Perry Collier. Negative reaction from the Supreme Court's Public Gallery was stringently silenced by Justice Broadhurst.

THAT EVENING, A GALA CHARITY dinner for the *Independent Committee for Troubled Youth* was held in the Plaza Ballroom in the Brisbane Convention Centre for eight-hundred VIP guests. Head speaker was Committee President Harold E. Broadchurch, the judge who disciplined the two soldiers in the Anzac Day case, He spoke emotionally about the problems of troubled youth, and the need for public compassion and understanding. The response was effusive, and the applause enthusiastic.

At the head table, were Justice E Broadchurch's wife, Victoria, and eight other close associates of the charity. After the official announcements and speeches had been delivered, the dinner drifted naturally into a more relaxed evening with drinking,

dancing, and frivolous booze-tinged gossip.

Engaged in a cosy tete-a-tete at the table while its other occupants were elsewhere, Victoria Broadchurch took to discussing the controversial Anzac Day case with her friend, Eleanor Winston.

Referring to her husband's judicial findings, Victoria said, "Harry did the right thing. There's too much racial discrimination going on in this country and it's got to stop."

Eleanor's question was, "How is taking it out on the Army going to stop it?"

"Harry says it will set a precedent and prevent similar happenings."

"I suppose he knew what he's doing."

"And you don't think he was?"

"I think it's hard on those two soldiers."

"They attacked the men because of the colour of their skin, Ellie."

"Nobody said anything about the colour of their skin."

"They didn't have to. Their attack was a clear case of racism."

"Who said anything about racism? It wasn't mentioned in court."

"It's what people are calling it on the social sites, and you've got to admit it has all the ingredients."

Eleanor Winston wanted to enjoy the evening, so she wisely changed the subject.

Across at the bar were two ordinary well-paid male public servants employed at the government-sponsored Committee Youth Shelter, which had been erected to house troubled youths.

The men were in conversation over a few free drinks.

"What did you think of the great Harry's speech?" asked one.

"Pontificating old maggot," answered his friend.

"You and I know a lot of those kids who live in the shelter are bludging on the government—like making make the most of a good thing."

"Harry will be boasting to his sleazy mates about well he went over."

"What else would you expect?"

"Wouldn't be all that easy, I suppose."

"It won't be, if the Auntie Harriet stuff ever gets out."

"Who's Auntie Harriet?

"A well-kept secret, mate. Who does it sound like?"

The penny dropped. "Give it to me straight. Are you saying Harry plays silly buggers with the boys in the shelter?"

"Only the willing ones."

"That could be just a nasty rumour, mate."

"Not if there's a Whistleblower."

THE MORNING *OBSERVER* RAN THE Supreme Court story over the front page with a big picture of the un-named plaintiff; head covered and on crutches, leaving the building. The headline read: "*The Army's Lost Cause.*" The copy gave the details without over-embellishment, but the insinuation was that Andrew Denton and Perry Collier would be dishonourably discharged for causing a near-fatal tragedy when they attacked an innocent ethnic citizen at Manly's Anzac Day Service.

The story was picked up by FM spruikers, who stirred the pot, triggering a swag of angry calls to the radio stations. National current affairs commentators who knew what was expected of them, launched into tirades about the Human Rights ripeness of the decision and as drumbeating was the name of their game, they over-played it to the hilt, and the public bought every word.

16

DUSTY RIVERS RIDES AGAIN

THE NEXT MORNING JOSH, WITH Tim as his passenger, roared through the gates of Mackenzie's Homestead in south Noosa, at nine-forty-five after zooming past every car on the Bruce Highway. The trip was an experience for Tim—high-speed comfort every inch of the way.

The boys joined Natalie, Mackenzie, Dusty and his wife, Sally Temple, in the large airy living room of The Homestead. On the agenda was the 'Meet Dusty' event Mackenzie had arranged. Obligatory introductions and small-talk were fuss-free; over in less than five minutes.

The casual meeting came to order.

Dusty Rivers in person was everything Tim expected.

At fifty-two, he looked like the forty-year-old larrikin who took the world by storm in *The Outback Jackaroo*. He didn't claim to be a movie star and didn't ever act like one. In his own words: *"I'm just an ordinary bloke who hit the jackpot by playing me."*

He was open, virile, and direct with a suntan and mischievous manly eyes. He didn't bother pretending to be anything more than who and what he was, a stand-up larrikin comic, with a talent for making people laugh.

Tim liked him instantly.

His wife, Sally Temple, was famous as a New York model when they met on the location of a fashion shoot in New Caledonia where he was grilling seafood on a barbecue for a television commercial to promote an Australian frozen seafood company.

Three weeks later they were married on the Great Barrier Reef resort of Deriobar Cay. She gave up modelling to manage his career and earned industry credit for his success in the movies.

When he was cast in *The Outback Jackaroo,* voice and drama coaches moved in to polish him as an actor. Weeks went by, and it was obvious that Dusty was having no luck with drama coaches—patience was running thin, and money was running out.

When the distraught producers of the film approached Mackenzie for extra finance, he agreed to look at the footage that had already been shot.

The Big Man let loose. "You jokers are making this bloke look like a bloody dickhead. He's an outback boundary rider for Christ's sakes, he's not Hugh Grant. Release this crap and you'll kill the bloke's career and fry every penny of your dough. So, I'll tell you what I'll do. I'll buy you out of the movie. How much do you want?"

The producers took the money and ran, and Mackenzie sat down with Sally.

"You're this bloke's manager," he said, "and you've been around showbusiness long enough to know if this piece of goat's lunch has a chance if it's doctored up a bit. Why don't we work on it for a while?

Sally's answer: "I've tried telling those guys that it would work if they just let Dusty be Dusty."

"Is it as easy as that?"

"He's a natural."

"What about the script? I could write a better one."

"Have you ever written a script?"

"I can spell, and I can think on my feet."

"That's not all there is to it, Mack."

"Okay, you write the words, and I'll fix the story."

"Are you telling me you're serious?"

"Dead set. Wanna give it a go?"

"We'll fight all the time."

"What if we just agree to disagree?"

"You've talked me into it."

"Good on you, girlie. Where do we start?"

The rest is history.

Dusty's follow-up movies did okay, but his heart wasn't in them. He was smart enough to know he was a one-movie wonder. *The Outback Jackaroo* had made him rich, and it was keeping him rich. With Sally's help, he'd made some canny investments. She was happy to be out of the modelling business, but she was always on the lookout for something for her celebrity husband. Their two daughters, fifteen and thirteen, were heading towards independence at a reputable boarding school in New England, Dusty was looking as good as ever, and Sally had the feeling that his talent was being wasted.

Which is why she'd pushed for the Noosa meeting.

Tim's self-acclaimed third eye identified her as a potential ally. At forty-five, she was not the glossy model she had been, but she was an eyeful—gracious, streamlined, and elegant, with a sense of humour that hinted at the presence of edgy intelligence.

The Homestead get-together was more like getting-to-know-you.

Natalie was the perfect hostess without over-fussing. Everyone was alert as Mackenzie began with the announcement that Tim had come up with an idea for Dusty's involvement in the theme park.

Tim took over on cue.

"There's nothing revolutionary about my idea," he said. "Dusty is already public property. He hasn't been over-sold on television in games shows, commercials or interviews—he's the same Outback jackaroo he was when the movie came out twelve years ago."

Mackenzie interjected, "On track, so far."

Tim continued, "The movie sold him as a straight-shooter, and as far as the public is concerned, he's still a straight-shooter. People trust him because he hasn't done anything to sell himself short."

Mackenzie agreed, "Still on track."

Tim wound up, "What I'm planning is to update Dusty's familiar jackaroo image by selling him as a sort of first cousin to the theme park's Dave. His stand-up comedy skills will have free rein. He'll be featured in a series of five-minute video grabs shot on-site at Snake Gully during the park's construction—information on the creative progress of the township and everything in it."

The group sat listening in silence as Tim continued, "There'll be no limit to what he will be able to talk about. We couldn't have a better ambassador and we'll save a fortune in advertising.

Dusty's was the first voice. "You've won me, cobber!"

"Too perfect," said Sally.

Tim went into further detail, listing the technical assistance, the budget, a possible time frame for the shooting, Dusty's wardrobe, the pre-booking of the airtime on commercial channels—city and state-wide, press releases and still photography. There was one final detail. The scripts.

"Done deal," said Dusty. "Sally wrote my friggin' movie!"

"Awesome," said Josh.

Tim looked at Sally. "Do we have a deal?"

Sally beamed. "We do."

Mackenzie was in the sky. Natalie was smiling.

Tim took his next step. "There's something else."

Everyone waited.

"It's obvious from the critical barbs from some quarters that *Dad and Dave World* will catch flak from stirrers who'll trash it because it looks like a rich man's try for big money at the expense of the gullible public."

Nobody said anything but it was clear that everyone agreed. Anticipation in the room seemed eager so Tim went on.

"Let's cut them off at the pass. Here's the sketch of my idea. Dusty and Sally have two young daughters, Kate Mallory has two. Suppose we audition for four more and coach them into a singing group that plays a series of spectacular *Dad and Dave* stage musicals in Brisbane, the Gold Coast and all over the state as a promotion for the park."

Silence.

"We'll call the shows, *The Girls of the Golden West.*"

Minds ticked over.

Mackenzie said, "What's the point?"

"Try this," said Tim. "We donate all the profits of the production to the Queensland Country Women's Association to help the children of farmers disadvantaged by the ongoing drought."

That did it.

Natalie was first. "I'm a paid-up member of the QCWA and I'm a yes."

Dusty looked at Sally. "Can you make a show like that happen, honey?"

Sally baulked. "You don't just put a show together with untried amateurs and expect it to work. I'd like to think about it."

Mackenzie weighed in, "How about we pump the idea up a little?"

"Like how, mate?" That from Dusty.

The answer came. "Let's lobby for corporate sponsorship."

"Why would we need it?" asked Natalie.

"Think about it," said Mackenzie. "It would give the big boys a chance to soften their corporate images by involving them in a community project that's got a ton of feel-good clout. They can make big noises about being good guys instead or the mean-arsed wowsers everyone thinks they are."

Dusty joined in. "How could the corporate suits resist? And how can the government? How about we lobby them, too?"

"Awesome," said Josh.

"The idea needs a lot of work," said Sally, "and serious thought."

There was more freewheeling conversation. After twenty minutes, the meeting wound down, with *The Girls of the Golden West* still under consideration.

"Looks like we're done," said Mackenzie. "Anything else?"

Natalie: "How about lunch?"

It was served on the veranda outside the meeting room. The vibe was positive and lively, and the food was easy to take.

Dusty was flying. "It's great to be back in the game, and this time, there'll be no mess-ups."

Tim caught the message. "Snake Gully is not Hollywood, mate."

Dusty laid his cutlery on his plate. "They wanted to take over the whole bit, but they couldn't get past Mack. He stood 'em up and won every argument. They wanted to change the script that Sally put together in Australia, but she wouldn't have any of it. Neither would Mack—and look what happened."

"Would you do it again?" asked Tim.

"Not in Hollywood, fella. That town is all tinsel and talk. They didn't know what to do with a straight player like me, so I busted out."

"You're about to bust right back in," said Josh.

17

KARMA'S FIRST SHADOW FALLS

IN THE CHATTY AFTERMATH OF lunch, Mackenzie approached Tim; made an excuse for a private word, then moved with him to a quiet spot on one of the shady verandas.

"You've been busy in Maryborough," he said, "and you were on the road with Josh this morning, so I'm guessing you haven't had time to check the news."

"Which news specifically, Mack?"

"The Anzac Day case against the Army went to court in Brisbane yesterday."

"And?"

Mackenzie reported on the details of the Judge's decision and watched Tim's face fall. "It was generally regarded as a bloody disgrace," said Mackenzie, "but it happened."

Tim was flabbergasted. "Those two Army boys got done on the shooter's evidence?"

"Done and dusted, mate."

"What does that mean?"

"They were discharged from the Army for acting irresponsibly."

"That's ludicrous, Mack."

"The impression was that the Army boys were racist."

"What?"

"The shooters in question were ethnic immigrants under the protection of the United Nations and the Human Rights Institute– untouchables in other words."

"And that's why they were let off?"

"It's why the Army boys were discharged."

"They acted in defence of the crowd, Mack."

"They didn't manage to save your mum and dad, but they sure saved everyone else."

"Was that put forward as evidence?"

"Put forward and dismissed, but that's not the end of it."

"It's not?"

Mackenzie went big. "Those two boys are now in charge of Snake Gully Security!"

He may as well have fired a gun. Tim's eyes went wide. "You gave them jobs at Snake Gully?"

"Bloody judges are supposed to be wrapped up in justice; they're not paid with tax-payer dollars to grandstand like bloody Judge Judy. That judge's decision was a bloody insult, mate."

"I agree one-hundred-percent but what can we do?"

"I've done it!"

Tim was struggling to take everything in. "Can there be an appeal?"

"The Army boys can make one."

"Wouldn't that be expensive for them?"

"Not for me."

"What?"

"I'm putting Dan Anderson's hat in the ring."

"Your kick-arse barrister?"

"I got him on the job straight away."

"He's appealed already?"

"Why waste time?"

Tim shook his head. "Hold on there, Mack. You've just dealt yourself into the case. Everyone knows Dan Anderson is your man."

"They also know I look out for my people, and my people now include those two Army boys. They've got wives and families. Someone's got to look after them."

Tim hit the reason button. "You saw how I was treated when I stood up myself. I was taken to the cleaners—in the press, on television, everywhere."

"What's that got to do with anything?"

Tim faced him squarely. "I work for you Mack! I'm on your payroll. How long before everyone twigs that I'm not Kit Walker? This is a contentious case. The media will be all over it. It won't take much delving to nail me as the son of the two Anzac Day victims."

Mackenzie didn't say anything.

Tim went on, "As Tim Cameron, you've given me a direct link to you and your theme park. I'm one of your executives."

"So?"

"I don't want you or Snake Gully copping the backlash because of any association with me."

Mackenzie took that in, then said, "Calm down, son. First things first. Dan Anderson will kick arse in court and make Justice E Broadchurch look like a dick puller from way back."

Tim said nothing.

"Broadchurch will have to reverse his decision. It's a done deal boy. Case closed. Everyone's happy—Justice is done, and you'll have nothing to do with it. Easy-peasy, no problem, kid."

Tim felt it, then. He was sure his third eye blinked at him. Somewhere a little bell rang, and a soft voice whispered, *Careful, Mack, careful.*

IT WAS SATURDAY. DUSTY AND Sally were staying over at Noosa until Monday morning. Mackenzie delayed his trip back to Maryborough to be with them. Natalie knew that would mean more Snake Gully talk, and happily arranged the catering.

Josh and Tim roared back to Maryborough in the Viper late on Saturday afternoon and arrived home just after nine o'clock. Josh, wound up like a spinning top, talked the whole way, mostly about Dusty's TV project, and how he intended to round up the best production crew on the planet. Tim tuned in and managed to keep the downer of the court case off his mind. It had been a long day.

When Josh pulled up at Tim's cottage, tiredness took him over.

Josh nudged him. "Is Diane on your case tonight?"

"She won't know I'm home."

"I can let her know, mate."

"Not tonight, Josh."

"Your choice, Timmo. Save it for tomorrow."

Josh took off in the Viper. Tim unlocked his door, turned on the lights, checked his phone and heard the message from Cynthia.

"Call me as soon as you get home, no matter how late it is."

He dumped his things and called the private number she'd given him. She picked up immediately.

"Forget the court case," she said. "It's not important."

"I think it might be."

"You're upset, don't be. Nothing has ended."

"It hasn't?"

"Stay close to Mackenzie Forbes. He's your lifeline."

"How so?"

"I've done his chart. I know you don't understand astrology, so I'll keep everything in your kind of language."

"Marvellous."

"He values your friendship and your talent. He'll stand by you, no matter what. He's protecting you with little regard for his own well-being."

"That's all in his chart?"

"That's the simplified version. He's a powerful friend."

"A reckless one, too."

"He knows how to look after himself."

"I hope so."

"He's been doing it for a long time."

"That's something."

"He has a special place in your life. He's intuitive and impulsive, but he's important to you, and so is his theme park. Stay close to both."

"There's something you're not telling me."

"Everything is as it should be."

"I take your word. I always do."

"You're not supposed to know every piece of the puzzle. This is only one piece. It has its place, and it will fit in when it's supposed to. Stay safe."

"Is that all?"

"I've told you all you need to know. Sleep well."

Cynthia ended the call, but Tim was up in the air.

Now that he'd had time to think more clearly about Mackenzie's rescue of the two discharged soldiers, he was edgy and uncomfortable. Had the move been too off-the-wall? Had it suddenly changed the game.? Mackenzie was already a target for the power players in the bureaucracy. Had he made a serious mistake by coming out in support of the two servicemen who acted in defence at the fatal Anzac Day Service? The worry nagged at him. What would be the reaction when it came out that the two victims of the attack were the parents of the Marketing and Events Manager at *Dad and Dave World*, and not Kit Walker. The question hung around, and Tim couldn't get it off his mind.

He'd warned Mackenzie that trouble could be on the way, not just for him but for the Snake Gully project as well. There was little doubt that Harry Broadchurch's judicial decision against the two soldiers had been ordered by the bureaucracy. The pair had been legally taken out of the game in court, and Mackenzie had brazenly brought them back in.

Wrong move, Mack!

To ease his mind, Tim opened the kitchen windows and inhaled the perfume of the mock orange trees outside. They were never in bloom for long, so he stayed beside the open windows for a while longer, hoping that his negative thoughts would drift away on the sweet notes of the blooms in the garden.

It was late, he was tired. He undressed, got into bed, and turned off the bedside light. As he drifted into sleep, Cynthia's words replayed in his mind. "*You're not supposed to know every piece of the puzzle—this piece will fit in when it's supposed to."*

18

KATE MALLORY TOOK BARNEY ERICSON'S call in her Kent Street office, early the next morning. His tone was earnest. "If I fly up to Maryborough later this morning, may we meet at your house?"

"This sounds urgent."

"It is."

"Ten-thirty?"

"Sit tight."

Kate picked him at the airport, got the small talk out of the way, drove him home, and sat opposite him at the white cane table on the veranda with a coffee pot and two china cups between them.

Kate waited for him to speak. He took his time. "Sorry to put an Alfred Hitchcock spin on this, but I need to make you aware of something in person."

Kate was fascinated. "Go ahead, Barney."

"The London genius on the payroll of the Forbes theme park is not Kit Walker, his name is Tim Cameron, and you know who Tim Cameron is."

Kate looked him straight in the eye. "The whole country does. And by now everyone in Wide Bay will know he's not Kit Walker." A long pause followed before she spoke again. "And it obviously bothers you that as Tim Cameron he's on the Mackenzie Forbes payroll. Right?"

"I have concerns."

"Obviously."

"I'd like to know what he's doing in Maryborough, and what his game is."

Kate frowned. "Does he have to have a game? After the negative publicity that's stalked him, couldn't it be that he just wanted to be to be left alone under a new name?"

Barney nodded. "I gave that some consideration."

"And?"

"It didn't worry me until I read that Mackenzie Forbes has given employment to two of the soldiers involved in the Manly terror attack."

Kate calmly poured some coffee, picked up her cup, took a sip or two and did the arithmetic. She worked out that Mackenzie's rescue of the two soldiers could be seen as a move to assist Tim Cameron in his fight for justice in a controversial case that had links to racial discrimination,

"What you're saying," said Kate, "is that I'll be taking risks if I keep *Dad and Dave World* in my good books."

"The underground social sites could make a mess of you. They love playing the racism card."

"It's made-up racism, Barney."

"Racism is racism, Kate. It's the new word."

"I realise that."

He looked at her and waited. "Well?"

"Where did all this racism business come from? Who's behind it, and how much more is there? It's all too pat, too organised to be incidental. It just reeks of another conspiracy to compromise the Forbes project, and everyone connected with it—including me."

"Seems that way to me, too."

"What can you find out? Someone must know something."

"I'll ask around."

Kate put her cup down and took a breath. "I'm not sure I can turn my back on this issue just to avoid four-letter-word salvos on the Internet, the overblown reprimands of political commentators, and the scorn of big-city latte addicts."

Barney parried. "I'm not talking about Internet trashing or political commentators. I'm talking about the persuasive powerbrokers who run the country, people who can influence political commentators and buy the opinions of the social sites."

Kate fixed him with a friendly stare. "I'm an elected member of parliament, Barney. I don't splurge on trendy outfits, wear Dorothy's red slippers, or link arms and legs with well-paid toy boys. I won my seat on promises of a better life for the people who voted for me. I'm aware that many of those people believe that Tim Cameron is worth their sympathy and understanding—and so do I."

Barney took a breath. "Is that your final word?"

"I refuse to be railroaded into making decisions that don't fit with my thinking."

"I admire you for that, Kate."

Kate calmed down for a moment. "Look, Barney, you clearly believe that all this is ridiculous enough to be serious."

"Serious is the word, and believe me, I'll have feelers out the moment I get back to Brisbane. Something's going on, Kate, and I don't like it all. You'll be my urgent call when I've got something to tell you."

Barney's words were a sincere expression of support. He knew that when Kate made up her mind. she was full-on. There was no doubt that *Dad and Dave World* was shaping up as a Forbes minefield, with the eyes of the powerful bureaucracy all over it. He was right—something was going on, and it wasn't pretty.

He was not a happy man.

19

SNAKE GULLY BEGINS TO WALK

THE NEW DAY BROUGHT NEW energy. Tim was at the site early. When he walked into the site office, Dottie Austin greeted him with a smile that could have blasted anyone's troubles straight through the window.

"It's a great day Tim, you'll be thrilled. The waterside and pool—all finished."

Tim spread his arms, 'Come on."

"Up and running."

"Splashdown?"

"Josh is down there with your cheeky photographer who's taking pictures for the press release. It's all ready, do you want to check it?"

"I'll see you when I get back."

"Everything's working," said Josh when Tim got to the pool.

"I've invited the boys for a few trial runs later on. Take a look, Timmo. We've got a live one."

Click Roberts, Tim's photographer—way-out, way-on, and moving around like an animated corkscrew, was on the job snapping images. He'd been booked on his reputation and ability—worth every cent of his fee.

Indicating the slide and the pond, he said, "You've got a red-hot winner here, mate. It's just like the waterhole we went to when we were kids. We didn't have a slide, so we used to climb way up in the gum trees, and dive in—in the raw, too. Bloody hell, did we ever show off for the sheilas."

Tim had a chuckle. "I don't think there'll be any of that happening here, Click."

Click winked a big one. "You never know. When the sun goes down, and the moon comes up, you never tell what else can come up. Par for the course, Timmy, Mother Nature knows what's what!"

"Awesome," said Josh.

A few minutes later, Mackenzie, home from the Dusty-Sally weekend, arrived at the pool and picked up the buzz. Clearly impressed, he spent a good fifteen minutes, casting admiring eyes over everything, but he was distracted.

All looking good," said Mackenzie. "It's great to have this locked away. We're running on schedule, but I'm getting impatient. We should get Dusty's television grabs underway. I know everything's coming together but I'd like to increase the size of our work teams to hurry things up. Is it too early to nail a date for the official opening?"

Tim was cautious. "I don't advise rushing into that; not until we're sure there are no hiccups. Sorry to play the downer card, but once we announce an opening date, we can't back off."

Mackenzie nodded. "Gotcha. That Noosa weekend with Dusty has made me impatient, and I'm raring to go. So close and yet so far."

"Not exactly," said Tim. "I can get Dusty's grabs organised, and I think it's a good idea to increase the workforce."

Mackenzie ploughed on, "Queensland Rail is anxious to get the laying of the rail track from Maryborough finished so they can test run the vintage engine. They're also keen to get the go-ahead with the polished pine overlays on the hard steel carriages."

"I'll arrange that," said Josh.

Click butted in, "Mack, I got a note to say you're due on the Gold Coast next Saturday. They're giving you some fancy award, and I'm on call to shoot you standing there holding it, just like one of those dinky actors at the Oscars."

Mackenzie thought for a minute. "Maybe we can give that a miss."

"Not a good idea," said Tim. "It's a Corporate Award for the Most Enterprising Entrepreneur of the Year, and it's worth its weight in gold."

"Solid gold bullshit," said Click.

Tim stayed on track. "It's important, Mack, you should be there in person, all fired up and showing off for the groupies."

Click had the last word. "As they say in the classics, the bloke that wears the crown is always up to his nuts in limp-dick gigs, boss."

IT WAS PAST EIGHT O'CLOCK when Tim drove home, and he was feeling more relaxed about everything. He saw the pale-yellow Honda parked outside his house and noticed that the lights in his front room were on. He mounted the veranda steps, opened the front door, and walked in. April Dawn, sitting on one of his comfortable chairs, smiled sweetly at him. She was all in yellow with a yellow band in her hair.

She smiled up at him. "They gave me a key at your town office. I told them I was your grandmother."

"I'm sure that fooled them."

"I've been waiting for over an hour. You look beat."

He walked over to her. "You look fantastic."

"Your Aunt Charlie asked me to check on you after she read about that awful court case. Everyone's talking about it."

"So I believe."

"Are you hurting?"

"I'm okay."

"They'll get theirs."

"True."

"The night's a pup. Why don't you take a shower and freshen up? After you're done in the bathroom, put on something you can take off in a hurry. It's summertime, and the living is easy. I've made a shaker of martinis with fresh pomegranate juice instead of vermouth. They'll do wonders for what ails you."

He was suddenly wide awake. "Who said anything ails me?"

"Forget it. Be quick.

"Fifteen minutes later, he was seated beside her in a loose T-shirt, white shorts and open sandals—sipping on a pomegranate martini.

"You're gorgeous," said April.

He smiled. "Happy too, we trialled the water slide at the Snake Gully site today; it's a sockeroo."

April's eyebrows rose. "Are you going to show me?"

"Now?"

"Now."

"Okay, if you don't mind a thirty-minute drive."

"Time will fly. Finish your drink and let's go."

Snake Gully, half-finished, looked misty in the moonlight. Dim work-lights showed the way to the waterslide and the gleaming pond. Fully grown willow trees and flowering heliconias grew on the landscaped banks of the pond, and the high, curvy waterslide hung over one end of the pond like a giant corkscrew.

April was in raptures. "It's *Snow White and the Seven Dwarfs*. I love it."

"The water is filtered through a special screen," said Tim, "when it hits the slide, it bubbles and froths like ginger beer."

"I've got to see that," said April.

With no second thought, she ditched her yellow dress and everything else. Tim took the cue, shucked his gear, and they sank naked into the water together.

She lolled in his arms in the centre of the pond and said, "Is the slide working?"

"If you want it to be."

Tim switched on the under-cover escalator and they rode up together. When they reached the top, he pulled one of the rubber mats away from the pile, placed it at the entry of the slide, and sat on it with his legs outstretched. She straddled him, face-to-face, lowering herself onto him, a perfect fit. His lips found her breasts—his hands, wrapped around her waist and held her tight. The moonlight played over her body and tinted her shiny blonde hair blue. Beside the pond, the trailing fronds of the weeping willows waved softly in a light breeze.

Tim reached for the slide's starter button. He pressed it, and a fountain of water gushed out over the mat. Still holding April tight, he leaned forward. The mat, sliding easily into the gushing spray, hit the downward curve of the slide and the ride took off, twisting and splashing, heading for the pond below. April's joyful screams tore the air. Frantically clinging to him, she stayed firm in his lap while the surging tide carried them down in a bubbling cradle of water. At the end of the ride, the mat speared into the pond in a tumble of beautiful bodies and churning water. Tim's climax came with no effort at all.

April, in heaven's spell, planted a wet kiss on his lips, and said, "Are you going to encourage the paying customers to try this?"

"We'd need a bigger pond to cope with the traffic."

"Are we going again?"

"The night's a pup; you said so."

THEY HAD AN EARLY BREAKFAST of goodies at the Muddy Waters Café. The clock said seven-thirty, and April was ready to take to the Bruce Highway.

"I'd love to stay, but I've got things to do."

"Give my love to Charlie."

"She'll be chuffed to hear you're safe and happy."

April finished her coffee. "How's your plan with Cynthia?"

"In the incubator."

"Is she keeping you on the case?"

"Absolutely."

"Then stay cool and listen to her."

"Goes without saying."

She gave him a long soft look. "You know, if ever I decide to fall in love, it's going to be with you."

"That's nice because if ever I decide to fall in love, it's going to be with you."

"We both live in Disneyland, you know that."

"Is that bad?"

"No, but it's worth remembering."

Tim hit her with bright eyes. "How could either of us forget."

20

THE DARK WORLD OF THE SECRET SIX

THE REST OF THE WEEK rolled on in a flurry of happenings. Forty full-blown tradies from all over Wide Bay had been added to the Snake Gully workforce. The rail link to Maryborough was on target, the vintage steam engine and the polished overlays on the steel carriages had been checked; the Snake Gully buildings were rapidly rising, Sally Temple's scripts for the Dusty video grabs were finished, and Dusty was set to start shooting.

Josh and Tim, supervising everything, were on site, continually checking and approving. Mackenzie was playing Santa Claus all over the place, and Maryborough was turning into a bouncy boutique metropolis that had hijacked everyone's attention. Visitors to the site were gobsmacked; and for once, the word was aptly applied.

News of what was going on in Wide Bay filtered into the shady world of the faceless bureaucrats, the un-elected tribespeople of the ruling class; formidable ego-driven bullies who wallowed in taxpayer-funded zones of decision-making. They were the heavies that ordinary Australians didn't know— and knew nothing about. The lived like the lords of the manor, they were rarely seen, never identified, never interested in acting for the best interests of the country, and never caring about anyone but themselves.

No matter who was voted in or voted out, no matter who the elected Prime Minister and the ministers of his cabinet were; no matter what the media said or didn't say, this lot remained above it all, protected by an ancient Westminster law that allowed them to rule the roost. Adherence to their wishes and instructions was often questioned but rarely challenged.

In the world of super politics, these characters channelled the Star Wars heavies of The Force. By comparison, Darth Vader and Jabba the Hutt were a pair of sissies.

In their midst, a darker handful of bureaucrats, six in all—four men and two women; referred to as *The Secret Six*, plotted and schemed to make sure that nobody challenged their supremacy by changing rules or out-flanking them in the public eye.

Mackenzie Forbes and his giddy plans for the revival of the vintage years of an old-time Australian lifestyle were not appreciated by *The Secret Six*.

They knew only too well that if the world that Mackenzie was hell-bent on re-creating ever managed to win over the voting public, new rules could be introduced, and their domination could easily be eroded. That could never happen.

At a secret meeting, masquerading as a vintage Moët & Chandon dinner in an exclusive location, the subject of Mackenzie's bid to infiltrate and overtake the minds of the people on the street, was under serious discussion.

Snarling sentences, over-fuelled by mouthfuls of elegant designer tucker and elite champagne were tossed around like lollipops at a kid's picnic.

"Forbes is the tallest of the tall poppies, and he's dangerous."

"Unstoppable, a menace and charlatan."

"He's got Kate Mallory on his side, for what it's worth.'

"She's Wide Bay's favourite senator; holds the voters in the palm of her hand."

"How do we know Mallory is in his corner?"

"Frontpage news in the Wide Bay Gazette. Her support is public knowledge."

"That's too incredible."

"Forbes is challenging our verdict in the Anzac Day Shooting case."

"*Why wouldn't he? He's got that young Cameron trouble-maker on his payroll.*"

"*Along with those two Army trouble-makers.*"

"*Hasn't he upped the ante by joining hands with Dusty Rivers?*"

"*Christ, yes! That makes two cowboys on the loose!*"

"*Forbes has been selected for a major award for something important on the Gold Coast next week.*"

"*How important is important?*"

"*The media will be there in force, and so will he. He won't miss this opportunity.*"

"*Grandstanding of the first order.*"

"*That can't be allowed to happen!*"

"*It will happen. It's been officially announced.*"

"*How many more games has this yobbo got up his sleeve?*"

"*We're in trouble—I'm talking real trouble.*"

"*Real trouble always needs a real solution.*"

"*And serious thinking.*"

The discussion proceeded on a sour note that more bottles of vintage Moët failed to sweeten. "*The party's not over till the fat lady sings.*"

21

THE RETURN OF THE OUTBACK JACKAROO

DUSTY AND SALLY RIVERS, IN preparation for the job in hand, had leased a place at Hervey Bay, a popular holiday resort no more than a short drive east of Maryborough. The Bay locals were buzzing. Having a living legend like Dusty Rivers bedded down in the vicinity was big news. They handled him with care; no pushing for autographs, no invitations to backyard barbecues, no crowding Sally when she went shopping at the supermarket, and no expecting him to be on tap for a beer or two at the local pub. Dusty was prime merchandise, a dinkum Aussie VIP, and a *'bloody good bloke.'* Hervey Bay was off its face.

As a genuine gesture of respect, the manager of the Hervey Bay Picture Theatre scheduled a special screening of *The Outback Jackaroo*, with Dusty and Sally in attendance as special guests. It was supposed to run for two nights; it ran for two weeks. Dusty matched the box office takings dollar for dollar, added a decent bonus, and donated the cash to the Hervey Bay branch of the Queensland Country Women's Association to be handed out to needy kids.

Dusty's stocks hit a Hervey Bay high. His fame had been reignited.

He spent time on the wide veranda of his leased property with Sally, leafing through her scripts for the Dave shoots, reading them out loud and having the time of his life.

"This is not like making a movie," said Dusty, "where you've got to keep thinking about where your friggin' lights are, where the camera is, being treated like trash by the director, and remembering how you said the friggin' key line for the close-ups. This is a piece of apple pie, and I'm in like Flynn."

"You're a new man, honey," said Sally.

"And all fired up."

"We start shooting your TV grabs next week."

"Bring it on." Dusty was in the clouds. "I'll be on the site all day tomorrow; a last-minute check. After that, I'm hot to trot."

22

THE GIRLS OF THE GOLDEN WEST

SALLY STOOD IN THE HALF-FINISHED main street of Snake Gully taking everything in. Her special point of interest was the Snake Gully Picture Theatre, which was close to being finished. Included in the video recordings of the re-mastered Australian films, which were scheduled to be played when the theatre opened, was at twenty-minute take on the vaudeville careers of vintage Tivoli comics, George Wallace, Roy Rene (Mo), and Hal Lashwood. Sally had seen it, and it had stayed in her mind waiting to be forgotten as such things often are.

She walked into the theatre foyer, past the replica of an old-time ticket box, cast her eyes over the re-mastered posters of *The Sons of Matthew, The Overlanders, Forty Thousand Horsemen, and Bush Christmas,* entered the theatre, sat in one of the leather seats in a row of other leather seats, and lost herself for a good fifteen minutes while her imagination went into overdrive.

She had promised Tim to consider his idea for *The Girls of the Golden West.* Agreeing that the concept had merit, she felt it needed something more than pretty girls singing. The '*something more*' came to life for her in the leather seat of the Snake Gully Picture Theatre. She could see it all!

Tim's golden girl chorus line originally featured Kate Mallory's two daughters teamed with Dusty and Sally's two, plus four more to be selected at auditions.

Sally's revised plan was to hold auditions to fill all eight roles from the ranks of talented student singers and dancers—

trained and rehearsed, costumed to kill, and shown off as polished stars.

Her added wow was Dusty, cast as a vintage Tivoli comic, featured alongside the girls in comedy sketches and old-fashioned song and dance routines. The Tivoli, Sydney's once-upon-a-time-home of much-loved Aussie vaudeville, would be born again!

The Girls of the Golden West would preview live on the Snake Gully Live Theatre stage, then be filmed as a musical for distribution Australia-wide, with proceeds still going to the families of farmers in distress via the Queensland Countrywomen's Association.

Sally was out of her leather seat, high tailing it down the street to the Snake Gully Project Office. Josh caught her as she entered the front door. She grabbed him and blurted out the bones of her idea.

"Take it easy Sally," said Josh, "Tim and Dad are checking the signage on the main train station. Take a seat in Dad's office. I'll deliver them to you in one of the work buggies. Follow me!"

When he heard Sally's idea, Mackenzie hit the sky. "This could turn into something." He shot an eye at Tim. "Is it do-able as a marketing idea?"

Tim's reply: "Plannable for sure."

Josh: "Christmas on a stick, Dad."

Mackenzie was in. "Let's get it happening."

The quartet sat down. Mackenzie launched.

"You're on first, Josh. Get some help to comb through the list of every corporation we do business with. Send out urgent emails to their CEOs inviting them to a Golden Girls Sponsorship Social at the Brisbane Convention Centre as soon as you can arrange it. We'll sell this as the best Aussie charity ever. We want corporation cash and we're not taking no for an answer. Order an open bar, fancy tucker, and audio presentation stuff. Let's belt their ears while we get the bastards pissed. Soon as you can, kid, on the double."

"Done deal, Dad."

Mackenzie turned to Tim. "We'll lean on the government for support. That mean-spirited mob find it hard to part with hard cash, but we'll give them the chance to do something for busted farmers."

"I'm on it," said Tim.

Josh gave Tim a nudge. "I've got a mate I can lean on in the state government public service; a piece of cake, mate."

Mackenzie turned to Sally. "Looks like we're all set, Sal. Tell me you're happy."

"I'm happy," said Sally.

Mackenzie eyed Josh. "Are we in the saddle, kiddo?"

"Whip crack away, Dad."

Mackenzie's eyebrows shot up. "What's happened to awesome?"

"Just giving you a break."

"About time."

"Awesome."

The high circulation Southeast Queensland News, commenting on the press release relating to the *Girls of the Golden West* treated it as front-page news.

"Is there anything else Mackenzie Forbes can throw at Dad and Dave World? This latest development is like topping a wedding cake with so much icing that the cake is double-heavy. The question may well be, 'How much is too much?' but that's not the question being asked in Wide Bay, where the population has every reason to believe they're experiencing some kind of miraculous happening. Whatever, the flags of success are flying, and Mackenzie Forbes, everyone's favourite man-with-a-plan, is riding high.

Not everyone agreed.

Barney Ericson scanned the report and put in another urgent call to Senator Kate Mallory in her Maryborough office.

He broached the subject straight away. "This Golden Girls business is way over the top. Forbes needs to take it easy; big isn't always better. This could be another thorn in your side."

"You don't live in Maryborough, Barney."

"The citizens may be singing and dancing, but out here in the real world, Forbes is seen to be waving a red rag at the heavies in the bureaucracy. He's upstaging them with all these wild ideas, and it's getting more out of hand."

"I'm aware of that, but he's unstoppable."

"I don't want any of his wild ideas to shine a negative light on you."

"I don't see how this one can. It's a people-pleaser."

"What happens when the little Jones girl gets overlooked in the auditions or the Smith kid misses out because she's too fat?"

Kate hesitated for a second. "I suppose things like that can happen, Barney."

"Step back, Kate, see this move from the distance of disassociation. Granted, it has merit, and the public is fired up, but it's alive with traps if it runs off the rails."

Kate revived instantly. "Forbes has insurance, Barney."

"You're way ahead of me."

"He's got the reborn Dusty Rivers on his side. It's called People Power."

"People Power can be very volatile, but there's something you're missing."

"Oh?"

"Tim Cameron is Mackenzie's Achilles heel. That boy is the joker in the deck. He's the racist card, Kate, and if the bureaucracy decides to use him, he's their trump."

"Dan Anderson is sitting pretty to upset Broadchurch's judgement in the Anzac Day case and that's the sleeping tiger," said Kate. "I know I keep harping on the same subject, but I can't help it." Kate paused on the line. "Have your connections come across with anything yet?"

"Murmurs only, but something's in the wind, and it's not a spring breeze."

JOSH FORBES, ACTING ON HIS father's orders, made personal contact with a well-informed employee of the Treasury Department of the State government. The employee made it clear that there would be no financial or moral support for the *Girls of the Golden West* project, or for that matter, for any future plans for *Dad and Dave World*. He'd also found out that the heavies in Queensland Rail were seriously rapped over the knuckles for agreeing to the Maryborough-Snake Gully rail link; for making vintage steam engines from the Ipswich Rail Museum available for purchase, and for working to update the steel railway carriages from New Zealand with expensive timber panelling.

Josh reported back to Tim. "Sorry. No go, mate. The reason given was orders from higher-up."

"Higher-up where?"

"Try the fat cat Canberra bureaucracy—as high as it gets."

Tim reported to Mackenzie, who reacted philosophically. "Why am I not surprised? That bloody mob in the State Government buckle down whenever Canberra opens its mouth. They're living it up on taxpayer donations, and they couldn't give a damn about anything. Most of 'em are trailer trash who were raised on bread and dripping for dinner, and baked beans on Sunday."

"Hardly the point, Mack. You didn't expect them to play, did you?"

When Mackenzie reported the refusal to Dusty, he was unfazed. He smiled, sat back, and sang the first few bars of "Happy Days are here Again," in the key of G:

"Happy days are here again, and the sky above is clean again."

Sally gave it a rave. "We should use that to open our show. The key's too high, though; why not try it in B flat?"

"Nothing flat about me, Sal. I'm on the comeback trail as a dinkum Aussie sideshow star. You never know where this will lead. Maybe Wotisname Webber can write me into a hit musical. How about *Phantom of the Outback*?"

Mackenzie raised his question. "You don't care that we were knocked back on the request for government support?"

Dusty wrapped it up. "We're better off without 'em. If they'd said yes, they'd have wanted to have a say on everything. Forget it, Mack, they can't even run their own show, why would we want them horning in on ours?"

Nothing more was said. So far, so splendid.

ON A BRIGHTER NOTE, THE urgent email invitations to the sponsorship gig had gone out, positive responses were coming in, the Convention Centre space had been confirmed, the fancy tucker was a done deal, the open bar was happening, and the audio presentation unit was on call—complete with spotlights and animated visuals.

The ubiquitous upbeat message was: *"The Girls of the Golden West appeal, featuring special guest star, Dusty Rivers, is all set to bring joy and happiness to the future splendour of Dad and Dave World."*

But as everybody knows, when baby turtles race for the sea, they don't all make the waves.

Mackenzie had the last word. "Overconfidence is a like a red back spider. It can bite you on the arse, and you don't take any notice until your arse catches fire. Let's just play it nice and easy and sneak up on the bastards. Let's make 'em realise that this is one helluva great chance to polish their profiles and leave it at that."

TAKING A WELL-EARNED BREAK in the living room of his leased cottage in Maryborough, Tim was feeling uneasy. His third eye was restless, and he couldn't understand why.

Everything was going to plan. Maybe he was just tired. No. He was way into his job, *Dad and Dave World* was coming to life at super speed, Snake Gully was looking like a real Aussie country town, Dusty's input was A-okay, so what was wrong?

The ringing of his mobile phone interrupted his thoughts, and he answered it in a mildly tentative voice.

"You sound so far away," said Cynthia Del Largo.

He rallied instantly. "Cynthia, hello."

"I need to see you."

"I gather this is important."

"It is."

"Too important for a telephone call?"

"When are you free to come to Montville?"

Tim thought for a few seconds. "Tomorrow afternoon, late. You're only a two-hour drive from here."

"Can you make it by seven o'clock?"

"Close, yes."

"We'll dine in the garden. It's beautiful. Enid does wonderful food."

"Sounds perfect."

"Drive safely."

"I always do."

"Take special care. Don't take risks."

"The drive's a breeze."

"Seven o'clock tomorrow."

Cynthia ended the call. Tim switched the mobile off and nodded to himself. His third eye was right again. It had picked something up, so had Cynthia Del Largo, and it was clearly important enough to be discussed at a face-to-face meeting. His uneasy feeling was still hanging around, but he shrugged it off to check his schedule for the next couple of days. The important Convention Centre fundraising meeting was on track for the night after his meeting with Cynthia, and he eyed the details again.

There was no script, Mackenzie stayed away from scripts. He preferred to shoot from the lip, and that's what he always did.

"You've got to eyeball 'em to make sure they're hearing every word. If you have to drop your eyes to read from a piece of paper, they can get away from you and you can lose them. That's not my speed. I like to get 'em hooked and keep 'em hooked."

Tim looked again at the running schedule, the timing of the foodservice, and the scheduled starting time of the presentation. There was to be no liquor service during the thirty-minute pitch for cash.

"*We don't want anyone over-boozed before my speech, but it's open slather afterwards, as much beer and hard stuff as they want; wine, too, but no rotgut, we're not mean wombats like the government. Give 'em good label stuff. We want them to be satisfied.*"

Tim relaxed. Reassured that all was well, he went to bed and slept well.

23

HOW TO RIDE THE STARS

THE NEXT AFTERNOON TIM LEFT the Snake Gully site at three-thirty, drove home, showered and changed, then headed for Montville just before five o'clock.

He drove through the little mountain village as the sun was setting over the Blackall Ranges, and turned west into the private lane that took him to Cynthia's rainforest cottage.

In the closing summer twilight, the cottage resembled the set for a movie musical. It was a symphony of soft lights and deep shadows. He parked his car, walked down the path to the front door and rang the bell. Enid opened the door, greeted him affectionately, and lead him though the house to the rear garden.

The vision anchored him to the spot.

Enid explained, "One of Cynthia's clients is a theatrical lighting technician."

Tim was looking at the evidence.

The trees and shrubs seemed to have been invaded by a squadron of fireflies. Tiny bud lights in the dark green foliage twinkled and gleamed in the leafy movement of a light breeze. A round table covered by a white lace cloth held white plates, cutlery, gleaming crystal glasses, and candlesticks alive with flickering white candles.

Two director chairs were dressed in dark blue covers, and beside the main table stood a white sideboard that held the food and more flickering candles.

Cynthia was seated—dressed in wispy dark blue with a fine silver scarf draped over her shoulders. She smiled up at him.

He was lost for words, so he just smiled back.

"Enid has created a sublime treat," she said, "baked ricotta with blanched almonds, mushrooms stuffed with ground macadamia nuts, avocadoes from our own trees, braised baby carrots with honey and cinnamon dressing folded into buckwheat pancakes and fresh mulberry yoghurt with crystallised ginger."

Tim took the chair opposite her and said, "Too perfect."

"We don't eat meat and we don't do alcohol; we're drinking fresh pink grapefruit juice."

The meal began, the food was light and beautiful. After the first course, Cynthia raised a tall crystal glass to her lips and looked over at him.

"This meeting was designed to calm you."

"It's working."

"Things are happening faster than I imagined."

Tim registered a jab of doubt. "Should I be concerned?"

"If so, don't give in to it—don't have doubts, don't interfere with anything, let everything happen as it's supposed to." Her green eyes sparkled as they speared into his. "I'll make a request. I want your full attention."

"You have it."

"Imagine the stars are a beautiful white horse. Think of yourself in the saddle as the horse moves through the misty forest. Don't touch the reins, let the horse find its own way. It may appear to falter, but the path is clear, and the white horse will take you into the light at the end of the forest."

"I understand."

"Are you sure?"

"You're telling me that whatever will be, will be."

"A bland cliché, but yes. You have no control over what will happen in the future. Do you still believe you have a third eye?"

He smiled. "Yes, and it's looking right at you."

Cynthia's face brightened. "Is it telling you to understand what I've said?"

"It's telling me how blessed I am to have you as a friend."

"I have never entertained anyone in this garden. I chose to do it tonight because the moon is full in the constellation of Scorpio—your birth sign and your rising sign. The moon is your mother and father; it's shining its warm light on you. If you look up, you'll see it floating up there with the planet Venus by its side—they're constant companions."

"I trust you, Cynthia."

"Ride safely with the stars. Trust them as you trust me, and we'll celebrate together when you reach the end of the journey."

He raised his half-empty glass, and said, "Here's looking at you, kid."

"Ah, yes. *Casablanca* did wonders for Humphrey Bogart. *Dad and Dave World* will do the same for you. No matter what happens, do not interfere, do not doubt the blueprint, it's been drawn up by powerful hands. Leave everything alone and let the Karma play out as planned."

Tim gave her a questioning look. "The Karma?"

"It's riding in the stars with you."

"What do I do?"

"Nothing. Let it happen."

'Nothing?'

"Promise me."

"You have my word."

"Then that's all."

When it was time to leave Tim drove home with a clear head. Cynthia had eased his mind. She'd warned him that his star path was one of surprises. His third eye was confirming it. Out of the blue, an oft-quoted line from an oft-quoted movie mischievously tickled the funny-bone of his conscience:

"Fasten your seat belts, it's going to be a bumpy night."

Up there in the sky, the stars in the Scorpio constellation were beaming brightly. After that night, everything in Tim's world seemed to settle down.

Kenn Lord

BOOK THREE

THE UNEVEN RACE

24

PEOPLE LIKE US AND HOW THEY PLAY

BARNEY ERICSON'S SEARCH THOUGH THE gossip zones of the underworld had borne fruit. Enlightenment came via Tobey Groundwater, a Junior Assistant in the thirty-seventh-floor offices of Geoffrey Barkley, barrister. Geoffrey was no ordinary barrister; his services were retained by the executives of Human Rights Institute who operated under the financial umbrella of the untouchable bureaucracy known as *The Secret Six.*

At the age of forty-eight, Geoffrey had it made. His high-level offices looked down on the Brisbane River curling around the CBD way below. His lease was paid by his fruity court-room commissions, and his lifestyle included family holidays in elegant haunts like *Majorca, St Tropez, the Italian Alps, the Maldives, Acapulco and the Galapagos Islands— never anywhere ordinary like Asia, the Mediterranean, Japan or Aspen.*

Geoffrey's wife, Jennifer was smart enough to behave like the wife of a big-time legal eagle. She never shopped at Target, K-Mart, Woolworths, Dan Murphy or Aldi. She bought designer-label everything and went regularly to the gym.

The trendy couple's two boys played football and cricket at an expensive private school that encouraged interest in the arts and the engineering profession.

Geoffrey was a savvy barrister, one of the brighter sparks of the profession. His verbal mastery of the English language had been taught by an old-time actor who specialised in private tuition for a fat one-on-one fee. In court, Geoffrey was the consummate barrister, always on the ball, never over the top. His neatest trick was to look unaffected and natural, as much like Gregory Peck in *To Kill a Mockingbird*, as possible. He came across as a legal champion dedicated to the outcome of justice.

In Tobey Groundwater's carefully considered opinion, Geoffrey Barkley spelled *inspiration*—he was the man Tobey wanted to be when he was forty-eight.

At twenty-one, Tobey had a lot of living to do, and he made the most of every opportunity to learn as much as he could about everything.

He had the look of an eager yuppie, an astute young man with perfect manners and a friendly disposition that masked an iron will to make it to the top no matter how many challenges had to be met and dealt with before he rose to his place in the sun.

Tobey was never way-out or obvious. His wardrobe was neat, his hair was kept cut and styled, his shirts and ties and shoes were conventional. He was a picture of conformity. His fresh face and willingness to please gave him a valuable edge.

People were attracted to his gregarious nature. He made friends easily and cultivated those he figured he could use. As is often the case, the people he was using were also using him—par for the course.

As Geoffrey Barkley's Junior Assistant, Toby was privy to all manner of information, and always gave the impression that he heard nothing and saw nothing. He arrived at the office every day on time, stayed late when he was asked, and never complained.

The days he liked best were when he accompanied Geoffrey to court, and that's where he came in contact with Barney Ericson. Tobey knew that Barney moved in the upper circles of business, both corporate and commercial, and that sometimes his exclusive Public Relations Company acted in an advisory capacity to important people. Sometimes important people relied on Barney's knowledge to advise them when they tripped up and found themselves facing a judge.

A mutual friendship began when Barney realised that Tobey was in touch with the workings of the Internet ferrets, the nosey parkers who picked up on all sorts of rumours and gossip that were not always reliable, and not always factual. But if they were colourful enough there was always a chance that someone, somewhere, would be interested. Predictably enough, Tobey's most interested someone was Barney Ericson.

Rumours and gossip were Barney's business, and he was willing to cough up hard cash to be well informed about happenings that related to his clients. Tobey's freshness and conventional appearance were the cultivated masks that underpinned his ambition. But youthful Tobey was wiser than he looked.

There was another arrow to his bow. He'd seen enough of the high life to realise that corruption and rorting and political hypocrisy were the enemies of fairness in the lives of ordinary people.

He especially disapproved of the frequent injustice of the courts. His legal ideals were affronted by the result of the Anzac Day case, and he was seriously critical of the ethnic shooters' unpatriotic attitude. Geoffrey Barkley had represented the man who fired the killer shots and got him off. Tobey didn't approve but that was not the end of it. Mackenzie Forbes' hotshot legal eagle, Dan Anderson, had instantly filed an appeal to contest the verdict, and the case was pending. It was going to be interesting for a handful of reasons.

Harry Broadchurch, the judge who found in favour of the killer, was suspected of acting under instructions from someone higher up in the bureaucracy. Because of the sensitive emotional nature of the case, the decision had caused a wave of protest in the media. After all, you don't just turn your back on the killing of a beloved mother and father and forgive the puller of the trigger. Understandably, the Human Rights Institute, cast in the role of ethnic protector, was under pressure to comment.

So far, there was no response. Tobey knew there wouldn't be. The over-juicy underground rumour at the time of the trial was that Harry Broadchurch fiddled around with young men housed in the Institute-administered welfare shelter—and that the Institute had advised him to do as he was told or face an exposé.

That was merely a smokescreen to cloud the real truth of the case. Tobey knew that Harry had in fact, carried out the wishes of the United Nations representatives in Australia when he dismissed the terrorism charges.

Tobey's perceptive guess was that the three shooters were cleared because the UN wanted the heavies in the case to be Tim Cameron and the two army boys—Andrew Denton and Perry Collier—the racist link that compromised Mackenzie Forbes and his standing with the public.

Tobey had further discovered that a hastily laid plan was afoot to whitewash the negative image of the shooters. He didn't know what the plan was or when it would happen, but he knew it would be ingenious and important. Red herrings abounded. The word radicalisation was bandied about as though it had magic properties and it sounded good.

So far, Tobey was in the dark, but it was juicy stuff for a patient mole.

Involved in the Anzac Day controversy were the Wide Bay Senator, Kate Mallory and a cluster of *Dad and Dave World* heavies—Josh and Mackenzie Forbes, Dusty Rivers, his wife Sally Temple, and the park's marketing genius, Tim Cameron, the loving son of the Anzac Day victims. How heavy can it get? Motivated by his disapproval of the Broadchurch verdict, Tobey was watching every blip on his radar screen and listening for every bleep. As soon as he could pin exactly what the whitewash plan for the killer trio was, he'd make Barney aware of it. If there was something rotten afoot—something that could affect the futures of the Anzac Day shooters, Barney had to know about it. Who else was there?

Tobey wanted justice, albeit at the expense of his employer's reputation.

25

SHOW ME THE MONEY

AT 5:45 P.M., THE DODGE VIPER, hardly more than a red blur, was roaring south on the Bruce Highway bound for Brisbane and the crucial sponsorship meeting in the South Bank Convention Centre. Josh and Tim, togged up like a couple of Wall Street money studs, were in good spirits. They were attending the gig as observers only. The headline stars were Mackenzie and Dusty, with Sally added for a dash of feminine charm. Together they were a notably persuasive trio.

Josh was predicting a wipeout. "By the time Dad and Dusty have finished ear-bashing these dudes, they'll be channelling the robot in *Lost in Space*—waving their arms and lost for words." Josh was on a high. "You've never seen Dad when he's got an audience. He even bowls me over. I've seen his act a hundred times, and it still gets me going."

At the Convention Centre, the room was abuzz with corporate leaders summonsed to cop the colourful sermons dished out by the twin hucksters and their juicy bird.

The invitees knew what they were in for. They willingly attacked the smoked salmon, Sevruga caviar, and other tempting items on the perfectly presented buffet, and lined up like good little boys and girls at the open bar where the scotch was Chivas Regal, the gin was Bombay Blue, the beer was Stella Artois, and the champagne was vintage Pol Roger. Female guests were not in over-abundance—a curious wife or two, and a handful of savvy distaff CEOs mingled with the A-listers—one hundred and twenty-five in all; not a bad round-up for such a short-notice affair, and a testament to the magnetism of the almighty Mackenzie, who waited out of sight in a side room with Dusty and Sally.

Geoffrey Barkley, the Human Rights barrister had been invited, but opted out due to his '*busy schedule.*' He sent his wife, Jennifer, to stand in for him. Bursting with curiosity, she stood chatting to Maxine Chambers, better-half of Mal Chambers, CEO of the Western Ridge Mining Company.

Maxine, never one to waste time on small talk, let fly. "What a pity Geoffrey couldn't be here, Jenny, it might have done him good to witness this turnout."

Sensing an ambush, Jennifer was cautious. "Why's that, Maxine?"

"The positive response to this function, announced only days ago, is clear evidence that Mackenzie's rescue of those two Army boys involved in that Anzac Day case has not dimmed his profile one bit."

Jennifer fell into the trap. "What's that got to do with Geoffrey?"

Maxine fired the arrow. "We all know he railroaded those boys in court, Jenny, hardly the right thing to do, considering the circumstances."

It was too late, but Jennifer tried. "Geoffrey didn't hand down the judgement; he just outlined the facts like he usually does."

"He gave Harry Broadchurch nowhere to go. Harry's never been the brightest candle on the table, and he's always been a Geoffrey fan, so he gave in, just like that."

"I'm sorry you see it that way, Maxine."

Maxine's bright smile said it all. "Too late for tears, Jenny, but I still say it's a shame Geoffrey's not here. There's been an appeal against Harry's decision; maybe your husband will do the right thing next time."

Across the room. Tim and Josh were being entertained by Click Roberts, Tim's rogue photographer, who had been booked to shoot the VIPs. Behaving against type, Click had taken trouble with his wardrobe. He had managed to look respectable. His shirt had been ironed, he wore a tie, he'd combed his hair, and his face stubble had been neatly trimmed. Click was as close to *GQ* as he could get. Josh gave him a grin and wrinkled his nose.

"You didn't hold back on the aftershave, did you, Click."

Click beamed. "Old Spice, mate."

Josh winked. "Hello, sailor."

"No way, fella." Click leaped to his own defence, "never played that game. I'm a chick freak through and through, and there's a couple of 'em here tonight that could easily have my flag running up the flagpole."

"Down, boy," said Tim, a friendly remark.

"Gimme a break, Timmo mate, it's just wishful thinking. I don't mind a touch of class now and then. I know It's off the menu tonight, but I wouldn't mind sidling up to the cougar in the lace dress. I wanted to immortalise her in HD, but I got a knockback."

"Nice try," said Josh.

"Like I said, mate, wishful thinking. The bird she was with told me she was that barrister's wife, and that she wouldn't want a pic anyway."

"Which barrister, Click?" Tim's question.

Click frowned. "You don't want to know, mate."

"Which barrister, Click?

Click shook his head. "Me and my mighty mouth! It was that Geoffrey Barkley bloke in that Anzac Day court case the other day. Sorry, Timmo, like extra sorry, mate."

Tim tapped his arm. "I'm a big boy, Click. No sweat."

He meant it.

The room lights dimmed, the stewards attending the bar stepped back, the conversation ended abruptly, the spotlights snapped on to illuminate the podium, Mackenzie stepped into them and faced his audience. Immediate applause lasting a full thirty seconds greeted him. The animated presentation screen lit up, and Mackenzie went into his act.

In a ten-minute oration, he delivered his bid, never once off the track, all bases covered with illustrations and shameless hype. The perfectly planned fantasy of *The Girls of the Golden*

West took flight. When he finished, the applause was genuinely enthusiastic. He raised a hand for silence and introduced Dusty Rivers.

There's no light like starlight. Dusty followed up, outlined his role in the project, and acknowledged Sally as his inspiration and guardian angel. Sally, the glamour girl in full bloom, joined him on the podium and told the room how excited she was to be part of the project. A roomful of bright-eyed gents, primed by tasty tucker and top-of-the-range booze, would have said *yes* to the bride of Frankenstein. Sally had them on the verge of hollering. The women guests simply shook their heads in wonder. Everyone knew they'd been taken to the cleaners, and it didn't hurt a bit.

A voice in the room called out, "Hey, Dusty, why don't you and Sally ice our cake, and tell us when you're going to make another movie."

"No way." Dusty was quick as a flash. "Hollywood is not my playground; Sally's either."

The reply was just as quick. "I'm not talking Hollywood. I'm talking right here in Australia. You won't have to build a set. Snake Gully sounds picture-perfect; what do you say?"

"Can't say anything off the top of my head, cobber."

The voice owned up. "Mal Chambers is the name—Western Ridge Mining. I'm on for the ride with the Golden Girls, and I'd be just as keen to talk about something called *The Return of the Outback Jackaroo*. Think about it and get back, and I'm not talking through Mack's booze. Try me and see."

Click Roberts edged closer to Tim's ear. "Talk's cheap, but Chambers has baited the hook, and it's a friggin' fat worm, old son."

"Not wrong, Click."

It was one of the biggest moments in a night filled with big moments. Mal Chambers found himself in the scene-stealer's chair. He was chuffed to discover that if his offer were picked up, he'd be looking at several eager partners.

Mackenzie caught Dusty alone. "That movie offer came out of the blue, mate. What's your reaction? And I don't need double talk."

"I could be interested, Sally, too. What about you? A movie set in Snake Gully could be right up our ally, mate."

"Best not go off half-cocked. Talk to me when you've let the idea sink in. We've scored big time tonight. I'll move around the room to show my appreciation and tie up a few loose ends. The bar's on call for another hour at least."

DUSTY AND SALLY DROVE BACK to Hervey Bay. Josh and Tim, aboard the Viper, heated up the Bruce Highway in light traffic and made it back to Maryborough on the south side of midnight.

Mackenzie drove to The Homestead to find Natalie waiting up for him. She inquired about the night, asked the right questions, got the right answers, and made him a stiff drink.

"I know you would have done tonight without this stuff, so take a few swallows, I need to talk."

"Sounds great, Nat."

She took him by surprise. "First question—why did you need to hustle for funding for *The Girls of the Golden West?*"

"Big project, kiddo," the logical reply.

"You've had big projects before, and you'd never had to ask for financial support." Her eyes never left him. "It's not your game, Mack."

"This one's a charity, kiddo, you know how they are."

She stayed on track. "There have been charities before, lots of them; what's so different about this one?"

Mackenzie took a long pull on his drink. "Where is all this going?"

"How about we stop horsing around?" Natalie bit the bullet. "Tell me about the trouble in South Africa."

He gave her a long, uncertain look. "How did you find out?"

"It doesn't matter how I found out. Tell me about it, and I mean all about it. We've never locked each other's problems in the closet. Let's not start now. Come clean, Mack. Best way—always."

When he came clean, it went like this.

Diamond prices were falling all over the world. They'd fallen before and come back, and they'll fall again, name of the game. In the past, he had always adjusted, tightened his belt, waited for as long as it took everything to level out, then it was back to business. This time there was no belt to tighten. *Dad and Dave World* had thrown the belt away. Expenses had been extraordinary. Staff costs had blown out; even more so when forty new tradies were employed to help melt the time it was taking to get Snake Gully up and running. He was building a small town from the bottom up—a gargantuan ask. It was what he promised, and against the foot-stomping tantrums of his critics, it was coming good. So far, he'd been able to keep things happening. The cruncher came when the South African Government hiked up the mining tax. To meet their demands and the strain of the falling diamond market, his company was forced to cut costs. Two hundred workers were listed to hit the skids. The union bosses hit meltdown—and in a gesture to ease their pain, Mackenzie refused to send his workers to poverty row. The result was that he was operating in the red, and he didn't know how long he'd be able to stay afloat.

On top of all that was the problem of the racism slur that had surfaced with the employment of the two discharged soldiers involved in the Anzac Day shooting. That had put him in an awkward position with the Human Rights Institute, more so when he arranged for his killer barrister to represent the two men when their appeal lobbed in the courtroom. In old-fashioned speak, that was the straw that broke the camel's back, and it dimmed the gleam of his diamonds. They were still his best friends, but Marilyn wasn't singing his song.

"My real worry, Nat, is that I may have to throw *Dad and Dave World* open to investors."

She threw him a long hard look but said nothing.

"After tonight's win, there'd be heaps of takers."

"That's unthinkable!" Natalie's reply hit the mark. "You can't do that—you'd be putting yourself in a terrible position. You've always been a one-man-band. If you take on investors, you'd have to answer to a board."

"I'd still be in control."

"In name only. You'd wear yourself out fighting." Natalie was making a strong stand. "It's too risky. Chances are that sooner or later you'd lose control, and Snake Gully would no longer be Snake Gully. It would become a cash cow for the money men—the predators who wait for giants like you to stumble. They'll fill it with Big Macs, Coca-Cola, and KFC, charge inflated prices for everything, and they'd never be able to handle the Wide Bay Council like you do. You can't let that happen, honey. You can't do that to Maryborough; it would be like dropping a bomb. That town trusts you; you can't let it down, and I don't want to listen to you crying yourself to sleep every night if you have to do it."

"Easy, Nat."

"Don't 'easy' me, baby. Don't. You may be the big man-of-the-world out there where you can stand tall and straight, but deep down you're a sensitive and caring person. That's what sets you apart." Natalie stopped for long enough to ask her inevitable question. "How long can you hold out?"

"Hard to say; a few months."

"Long enough for Snake Gully to open and start earning money?"

"With any luck."

"Make your own luck, Mack. Can you speed up the operation?'

"I've already done it. I'm running for a big splash opening on Australia Day."

"Have you announced that?"

"Not yet, but it's what's I want."

"You'll have to let everyone know soon."

"As soon as I've sorted everything out."

He finished his drink and put the glass on the table.

"It's not all lost, yet, but the warning lights are definitely on. One favour. I want this to be our secret. If anyone gets wind of it, morale goes out the window, and so does all the enthusiasm we've drummed up. We've got to keep the flag flying. You and me, Nat, like always."

"What about Josh?"

"No."

"Give him a chance."

"Not yet, and not Tim Cameron, either. They've got enough on the plates, and I don't want them roughed up."

"They could well be your secret weapons."

"Then let's keep them secret for a while longer."

"Fair enough if that's your call."

Natalie said no more; there was nothing more to be said, but her mind was in a whirl. She didn't want to think about what would happen if the Snake Gully dream couldn't come true, and if it couldn't, she didn't want to think about what would happen to the powerhouse she was married to. More importantly at the moment, what would happen if Mack's financial vulnerability became known to the bureaucrats who had him on the hit list? With one almighty heave, she swept such thoughts out of her consciousness.

She didn't want to know, and for once in her life, she didn't want tomorrow to come, but come it would, and if trouble came with it, she'd have to be there for him.

JENNIFER BARKLEY DROVE HER LATE-MODEL Mercedes-Benz into the driveway of her too-perfect family abode, waited for the automatic carport door to open, drove in, alighted, walked along the tiled entrance that led to the broad living room, dumped her keys and handbag on a padded chair, and walked twenty steps to the door of the media room. Geoffrey was watching television. She waited for him to see her, then watched him switch the television set off. He stood up, and she said four words.

"You've got a problem."

He looked at her. "How's that?"

Jennifer walked back to the living room and took a seat.

Geoffrey followed, took the chair opposite her, and sat back in comfort. "What's the story?"

"Anything but good news, Geoffrey. I spent almost three hours in the company of the town's movers, shakers and doers; all of them behaving like a bunch of Mackenzie Forbes and Dusty Rivers groupies—and I felt like an outcast."

"Why? I thought the affair was some kind of charity fundraiser."

"It was—for the latest Forbes project, but right now, Forbes cannot be set apart from Tim Cameron and your performance in that Anzac Day court case."

Geoffrey sat forward. "You mean that was mentioned?"

"Alluded to, yes, and the overwhelming feeling was that those Human Rights bureaucrats you're in league with are nothing more than a collection of meatheads living high on taxpayer-funded salaries, and in the collective opinion of the room—they've all lost the plot—you, too."

Geoffrey sighed. "I was afraid of that."

"Be very afraid, Geoffrey. You and your bureaucrats can talk ethnic privileges until the cows come home, but the truth is that it cuts no mustard; not when privileges like that are used to excuse the murder of two innocent people at an Anzac Day Dawn Service."

"Murder is a little over-the-top, isn't it?"

"What else is it? It was an act of terrorism, and it was deliberately planned and carried out by three despicable characters protected by the ethnic label they wear like a badge. And they were all saved from retribution by you."

Geoffrey tried. "Brake-up there, Jen."

It was a wasted try.

"Saved by you, and that mealy-mouthed Harold Broadchurch. Is he on the take form the Human Rights vigilantes, too?"

"He's a judge; he's above reproach."

"Is he, now?" Jennifer lowered her voice to a canine snarl. "It was whispered into my little pink ear tonight that above-reproach Harry gets his jollies by playing dirty daddy to accommodating little boys."

"That's bloody rubbish, Jen." Geoffrey was adamant.

"Juicy rubbish all the same, Geoffrey."

"An unfounded rumour."

"Rumour or not, it's a whisper, and it's juicy enough to stop being a whisper for much longer. Dirty Harry walked into the lion's den when he let your ethnic client off. He then compounded the issue when he victimised the two soldiers who acted to prevent a full-scale tragedy by slapping them with a racist insinuation."

"Steady on. Racism was never mentioned in court."

"I said insinuation, Geoffrey, an insinuation that was obvious enough to start the ball rolling—right at your nine-pins."

Geoffrey let that go. "There's an appeal in the wings, you know."

"On the nose, you mean!" Jennifer was warmed up. "Even if the appeal flies into a dismissal, it's too late. The cat is out of the bag. You and your mob of Human Rights twits have got a big problem, and if you can't do something about it, your arse is grass—as they say." Jennifer paused for a second or two. "I don't know about you, but I feel like a drink, several drinks in fact. For the first time in my life, I feel like a criminal."

Geoffrey had nowhere to go. "All right, I'll call Jane Armitage first thing in the morning."

Jennifer was outraged. "Jane Armitage! Is that what you said?

"You heard."

"What the hell has Jane Armitage got to do with this?"

"She's head of the Institute."

"Since when?"

"Appointed yesterday."

"My God! That's ridiculous. She's the worst kind of academic, pretentious as they come. Pretentious, odious, and absolutely deplorable. Her young son was autistic. Instead of looking after him, she shoved him into a mental home, and the poor little kid drowned himself in a treatment bath. What kind of human rights label can you hang on that?"

"That was years ago, Jen."

Jennifer shook her head. "Oh, shut up, Geoffrey. If you've got to suck up to that bloody vampire just to keep us in champagne and truffles, then I'll take beer and baked beans any day."

"I don't really think you mean that."

"Try me! after you play her nasty games with all the other public servants in the Institute, you won't be worth the price of a discount special at KFC. Grow a spine, Geoffrey, take Armitage and her mob of hypocrites and drop them into the nearest wheelie-bin. If you won't do it for my sake, do it for our two boys. I'd like them to have a chance to grow up to be young men—the kind of person you used to be, before you decided to sell yourself, and your incredible talent, to the highest bidder."

"Why don't you just nail my knees to the floor."

"There'll be plenty of that treatment going on elsewhere now that Armitage is wearing the Human Rights crown. I wouldn't want to be Mackenzie Forbes or any of his associates for all the gold in Fort Knox. I hope he knows what that bitch is capable of, and I'll sure as hell pray he'll be watching his back."

Geoffrey was done like a dinner. "I've got the message, Jen. Jane Armitage will be my first call in the morning."

"And I'll be standing right behind you!"

26

THE AWFUL TRUTH

IT WAS CLOSE TO FOUR-THIRTY p.m. Tim was seated beside Sally Rivers in the main hall of the Maryborough School of Arts, and the place was jumping.

News of the impending talent search for *The Girls of the Golden West* had been broadcast in the Wide Bay *Journal*, and it was consumed with fervour by the parents of every young girl in the eighteen-to-twenty age bracket in Wide Bay and beyond.

Prospective cast members were required to fill in forms downloaded from the Internet, stating details of experience, ability, training, and willingness to be part of what the WB *Journal* trumpeted as "the showbusiness chance of a lifetime." Completed forms were then emailed to the *Dad and Dave World* website. Successful applicants would win a chance to audition for roles alongside the famous Australian movie star, Dusty Rivers.

As expected, the Internet caught fire.

Tim and Sally, scanning scores of printed email applications, were backed up by a musical director, a voice coach, a music chart expert, a drama coach, and a dancing school coach, all of whom had been on the job since midday. The collection of successful auditionee forms was piling up.

"We'll be up for days of non-stop auditions next week," said Sally, "and we'll have to be lethal."

"That's the way the ball bounces," said a voice. Nobody disagreed.

At the height of the activity, Josh Forbes entered the hall, approached Tim, and spoke to him in a low voice.

"Kate Mallory just called the office and wants to know if you're free for an urgent four-way catch-up with Barney Ericson."

Tim looked blank. "Who's Barney Ericson?"

"A-list Brisbane Public Relations dude. Front row spin doctor. Loads of contacts. Heavy. Clean as a whistle."

"An associate of Kate's?"

"Friendly advisor; not on her payroll but trusted."

"When's the catch-up?"

"Right now. At her house. The Viper's idling outside."

"Kate, Me. Barney Ericson—and you?

"With bells on."

"Let's go."

FOUR WHITE CANE CHAIRS CIRCLED the white cane table on Kate's wide veranda. A coffee pot, cups and saucers, and glass tumblers were set on the table. Greetings, hellos and introductions were dealt with fast. Tim sat opposite Barney; Josh sat opposite Kate.

The buzz was business. Barney led the charge, addressing Tim and Josh.

"A few days ago, I met with Kate to discuss her support of *Dad and Dave World,* and she voiced concern for recent happenings associated with the park. I picked up on her worries and made some inquiries. I'm keen to share the results of those inquiries with both of you.

"Go ahead," said Tim.

Barney began, "In my opinion, *Dad and Dave World* is not just a theme park, it's a thorn in the side of renegade bureaucrats who feel challenged by the popularity of the project, and I think they're working on ways to bring it down."

"No way," said Josh. "Why would they want to do that?"

"Because they can. Life just goes on for most people. They live from day to day without noticing what's happening.

Laws are passed, freedoms disappear, but so what? Everyone cops it sweet—what else is there?"

Barney took a breath. "Then one day, *Dad and Dave World* comes along, and the man who conceived it talks like a leader, a man who can change things; the hero on the white horse—but not in the eyes of the bureaucrats who run the country. They are suddenly extremely upset."

Interested silence all round before Barney took off again.

"What most people don't know is that the United Nations in New York have operators in this country, and they dictate the UN's stringent immigration policies—policies that have been set and can't be changed despite objections from thinking people who don't want them."

Josh looked aghast. "Come on, Barney—the UN? are you kidding?"

"Take a look at the number of mainstream Australian politicians and bureaucrats who jet off to the United Nations in New York every other month. It's like a sycophant's pilgrimage."

"Then if what you say is true, it's more like a suck-up," said Josh.

"That's one way of putting it," Barney replied. "It still happens. When a high-profile incident negatively involving ethnic immigrants occurs, the UN is upset. The terrorist attack in Manly came out of the blue, and the UN hit the panic button because it happened on Anzac Day, one of Australia's most emotional and sacred days."

"Hold on a minute," said Tim. "What do you mean by 'came out of the blue'?"

"It wasn't supposed to happen."

"Whoa there," said Tim. "Are you saying that those three hoods broke one of the stringent UN rules—no attacks on Anzac Day?"

"I'm saying that's exactly what happened."

Tim shook his head. "That's incredible."

"Hear me out," said Barney. "I believe the UN stooges in Australia fuelled the media bitching of you that came in the wake of that attack. You lost a mother and a father to ethnic bullets on Anzac Day, and that angered a lot of people. The solution was to close all the legal doors, then turn you into an emotional wreck who couldn't handle what happened. Look at the way you were badgered into losing your cool in that television interview."

"That was a setup?"

"It took you out, and put the case to rest, didn't it?"

"I suppose it did."

Kate had a word. "All this sounds like supposition, Tim, but something funny is definitely going on. Barney and I are trying to work it out. I think it may have been triggered when Mackenzie caused an upset when he stood up for you and rescued those two soldiers after the Anzac Day court case.

"I realised that move could have been hasty."

Josh picked up. "It's turned out fine with those two guys but you're the reason they're in Snake Gully, Tim, and everyone knows it."

"True story," said Josh.

Kate poured coffee. The break lasted no more than two or three minutes while the milk and sugar bit happened, then Barney took the floor again.

"You're the fly in the ointment, Tim. Mackenzie put you on the payroll and made you a major player on his team. You took the initiative and pushed this theme park further into the limelight. That didn't go down well with the UN and they got desperate."

"How do you mean?

"They told Harry Broadchurch to let the Anzac Day shooter off to compromise you with a racist slur."

Tim sat up. "Broadchurch was bought?"

"He's a UN man. He pulls favours all the time—a nasty little creep; appointed by the State's Attorney General, who's another a closet member of the Down Under UN team."

"Shit!" said Josh, who quickly added, "Sorry, Kate."

"Forget it," said Kate. "I'm on your side,"

Barney began again. "Meanwhile, Snake Gully was never out of the news, and in the eyes of the UN, Mackenzie hit the danger zone when his best mates, Dusty and Sally Rivers gave him added clout. The heavies in New York knew it was time to move. They worded the bureaucrats down here to appoint Jane Armitage as the decision-maker on the board of the Human Rights Institute."

"Their nastiest move, yet," said Kate.

Josh gave her a questioning look. "I'm getting lost here."

Kate answered, "Armitage is one of their most lethal backroom operators. She's there to keep things going their way, and she's pure poison. She was moved into the front line because she takes no prisoners, and shoots to kill."

"Hot damn, Kate," said Josh. "This is James Bond without the fun."

Barney continued, "Armitage's job is to upset the Snake Gully apple cart. She can buy co-operative members of the media, and open back doors in the government. Her budget is open slather. She comes across like someone's favourite Auntie Maud, even when she's sticking the knife in and twisting it with a smile on her face."

Josh shook his head. "Man, this is heavy stuff."

Barney nodded at Josh. "If she can make a clown out of your dad, a racist freak out of Tm, a nasty white elephant out of Snake Gully, and succeed in putting it on the market, she's done her job. She's been given the brief, and it begins with the white-washing of the ethnic shooters—watch this space."

Barney's speech took an upward curve.

"I'm hoping that it may not be all peaches and cream for Armitage—I'm holding a wild card—I have a mole in Geoffrey Barkley's office. He's informed me that Barkley has refused to act for the plaintiff when the Anzac Day appeal goes to the court. He's letting people assume it's because he won't tangle with Dan Anderson, Mackenzie's firecracker, but that's not it. Barkley has grown a conscience, and there's another twist."

Silence again.

"Harry Broadchurch won't hear the appeal. He'll be replaced with another UN judge, who'll cloud the issue by confining the ethnic trio in a minimum-security prison awaiting a final decision on their fate, which will never include arrest."

"Do you believe that?" asked Tim.

"It will be a buy for time. Out of sight, out of mind; then who knows?"

Tim's question: "Can we do anything about that?"

"We can't, but Dan Anderson can. He's handling the appeal."

Tim frowned. "But can he handle the crooked UN judge? Those three goons can't walk free, Barney."

"Dan's a hard player, he'll be doing his best."

"Some game," said Josh.

"This is not a game," said Barney. "Your father, with his way-out ideas and savvy team members, is upsetting the Down Under UN. It's a cold war and they're desperate to re-write the rules. That's far too complicated for the average Jack and Jill, who are more interested in the political ins and outs of *Game of Thrones,* but I need to make this perfectly clear. I don't think the war has started yet. Let's wait for the next move."

On Kate's veranda in the failing light of late afternoon, the coffee was cold but there was a welter of thinking on call.

Josh asked the question, "What do you think the next move is gonna be, Barney?"

"If I knew that, kid, I'd know how to stop it."

Kate spoke up. "What about your mole, Barney? Has he come up with anything else?"

"Give him time, Kate."

Tim's turn: "So, we sit it out. Right?"

"What else?" said Barney. "At least we're all in the picture."

"Yeah," said Josh, "and we'll be staying in it!"

WHEN THE DISTURBING MEETING ENDED, Tim drove home. He did his best to relax, changed into something easy, poured a glass of white wine, took a seat, and called April Dawn. When he heard her pick up, he said, "I'm missing you."

"You're too busy to be missing me."

"How do you know?"

"Snake Gully is all Golden Girl news. People are rapt."

"When am I going to see you?"

"That depends."

"It's important."

"Do you work weekends?"

"I work every day. When am I going to see you?"

"Friday night?"

"That's tomorrow."

"I'll be there at six. Where do we eat?"

"How about the Snake Gully Bakery? They make the best meat pies."

"With peas?"

"Smashed peas, and they make proper bread and butter pudding."

"With sultanas?"

"Of course."

"I think I'm falling in love with the Snake Gully Bakery."

"The Snake Gully Bakery is a moral to fall in love with you."

"I hope so."

"You're too good to be true, April."

"And you're too gorgeous to be on the loose. I'll be on your doorstep at six o'clock, so you better let the Snake Gully Bakery know they won't be seeing us until eight-thirty—at least. I'm not driving all the way up there just for meat pies with peas and bread and butter pudding with sultanas, no matter how good they are."

"Why haven't I met you before?"

"I was saving you up. Now be a good boy and go to bed. After all, tomorrow is always another day."

He heard the click when she ended the call and finished the last of his wine.

On the way to bed, he had a sudden thought that stopped him in his tracks.

Cynthia had said there was always something more. What more could there be?

27

THE CALM BEFORE THE STORM

THE SNAKE GULLY BAKERY WAS bouncing like a beach ball in heavy surf. Josh had talked Mackenzie into opening the place as soon as it was finished to give it a decent run-in before the official opening. Snake Gully workers and their families were putting it to the test and having a ball. The tables and chairs were polished wood, and illumination came from vintage kerosene lamps electrically wired on dimmers to give the room a cosy glow. Under the spotlights on the corner stage, the Snake Gully five-piece band played solid gold country hits that kept the room rolling.

Seated at a corner table away from the band, Tim and April were each digging into a serve of bread-and-butter pudding with sultanas. In enamel mugs on the table, chilled homemade ginger beer laced with Bundaberg rum was the finishing touch. *G'day, Aussie!*

After making his way through the crowd, Click Roberts suddenly materialised at the table. He gave Tim a knowing look and said, "How are ya, cobber, or don't I need to ask?"

Tim mouthed a reply but Click wasn't hearing. With his eyes registering every inch of April's feminine allure, he made his move, "I s'pose it'd be too much to drag up a spare chair and expect to be seated."

April answered, "Is that a request or a promise?"

Click didn't miss: "Maybe I can just stand here and worship from afar."

Tim grinned, made the introduction, and said, "Take a seat, Click, and no close-ups."

Click grabbed the nearest empty chair, twisted it at the table and sat down. Tim threw an amused look at April. "Click is Dad and Dave's official photographer."

"True story," said Click. "I specialise in immortalising steamy April dawns, and unmade beds on cold winter nights; all in the name of art."

April played along, "And I bet you've got spurs that jingle jangle jingle."

"Not only at Christmas."

"That's a shame, 'cos this little bauble is all booked up."

Tim got a friendly word in. "Tomorrow is Mackenzie's big day on the Gold Coast, Click. You're on duty. Shouldn't you be having an easy night?"

"Easy nights are not my speed, mate." Click punched the air with his fist." I'll have that gig nailed up, no sweat."

"You'll be five hours on the road. Drive carefully."

"No need, old son. I'm flying down with Mack in his Mooney Mark 20 Rocket."

"I didn't know."

"Last minute changes. He wants to be home early tomorrow night."

April's interest peaked. "Am I missing something?"

Tim outlined the importance of the award and Click did the rest.

"It's the Gold Coast Oscars—biggest blast of the season. Every dude with an office and three secretaries will be there, so will all the wanker journos and dropkick TV spruikers. And Mack's the drawcard. As soon as he said he'd be there in person, they had to rent a bigger room."

"Who told you that, Click?"

"True story, Timmo. It was booked for one of the hotels. They've moved it to the friggin' Casino. Mack only found out today."

Tim's brow furrowed and Click noticed.

"What's the matter, mate? It's a big deal. Bullshit baffles brains every time, man."

The Snake Gully Band played on, so did the crowd. Click spied what he referred to as an award-winning bullseye on the other side of the room and took off.

April caught Tim's downer. "You're upset."

"Thoughtful."

"Something's rained on your parade."

"It's only a shower."

"Is Mackenzie getting too much?"

"He's turning into Captain Marvel."

"He always was."

"I guess that's true."

"So, how's your shower now?"

Tim didn't answer straight away. Sitting in the back of his mind, niggling at him, was Barney Ericson's rundown on the potential danger of Mackenzie's growing hold on the general public. He put it into words.

"It's just that sometimes bigger isn't always better."

"Depends on what the deal is."

"Sometimes it's best not to know."

April winked. "Is the water-slide open?"

That did it. Tim laughed. "Not tonight."

"So, we turn on the sprinkler and make out in the back yard at your place."

"Why do you always have this incredible effect on me?"

"Because that's the way I play."

"I should stop asking questions and cop it sweet."

"Why don't you?"

"Do you want to dance?"

"Only if it's foreplay."

28

LADIES WHO LUNCH

IN THE UPPER AVENUES OF Brisbane's executive players, *Dad and Dave World* had ceased to be treated like a joke. Mackenzie's charity project, *The Girls of the Golden West* had turned the tide. It was socially correct to be included in whatever Mackenzie was doing; an attitude that had taken over the designer-minds of executive wives, some of whom had become enthusiastic Snake Gully supporters.

Western Ridge Mine's Maxine Chambers and her friend Jennifer Barkley, who had pushed her husband Geoffrey in the right direction after he'd blown the Anzac Day case, often lunched on Brisbane's South Bank in Simon Amberson's chic restaurant, singularly identified as *Aspire*.

Simon owned, operated, and cooked in his establishment. His room seated one hundred diners at glass-topped tables with the river in the background. The chairs were white with padded backs and seats in shades of autumn gold, apricot and ochre.

The floor was covered in ochre tiles, and the diner's chic glassy cocktail bar came complete with high backed chairs that faced the river.

The snappy bartender's name was Walter, and Walter specialised in cocktails; anything and everything from Fluffy Ducks to Moscow Mules. He preferred being referred to as a mixologist—a cocktail connoisseur. In the matching league, Simon was a food connoisseur; a walking encyclopaedia of ingredients tossed and mixed in the creation of his delectable dishes. His menu never varied. His patronage did. Simon's fantastic nosh appealed to anyone who could afford it.

Simon was infallible.

Maxine and Jennifer sat in *Aspire* at their regular table for two with a view of the river. They never looked at the menu—the menu was Simon's job. They never looked at the wine list. That was Walter's job. On this occasion, he eschewed the wine list to shake up two tall glasses of chilled Long Island Tea—one for each of the lunching ladies. *Perfect.*

Jennifer held the floor. "Thanks for accepting my invitation, Maxine. I felt I should connect after we chatted at the Golden Girls thing."

"Lovely," said Maxine. "We've all heard that Geoffrey has decided not to represent that Anzac Day shooter at the appeal hearing. Who changed his mind?"

Jennifer smiled a pearly smile. "You did; indirectly."

Maxine waved a hand. "I simply said what needed to be said."

"I'm so glad you did."

"You heard my husband's offer to Dusty Rivers the other night. It wasn't party talk."

"Mal really wants Dusty's movie to happen?"

"I'll put it this way, Jenny, he's interested in preventing this country from losing its original identity; a huge change of heart for him. A year or so ago, he was one of those make-Australia-a-Republic supporter, but not anymore."

"Wonderful."

"You approve?"

"Everyone approves, Maxine."

"I believe Mackenzie Forbes is responsible. One of those commercial television channels ran a viewer poll a night or so ago. asking for people to indicate who should be Australia's next Prime Minister."

"I had no idea."

"Mackenzie leads the vote by over seventy per cent, and he's not even a politician."

Jennifer flashed her pearlies again. "It hardly matters. If Mackenzie ever became the Prime Minister, he still wouldn't be a politician—he's not the type."

"The bureaucracy will not be happy," said Maxine. "Neither will Jane Armitage—their resident vampire "

"Even more so," said Jennifer. "Geoffrey knows how I feel about her. It's time someone moved her out. Maybe if Mackenzie Forbes ever gets to be PM, he can have her deported."

Simon's waiter appeared at the table with the first course, and suddenly, Jane Armitage was not on the planet.

29

A SKY LOAD OF TROUBLE

AT THREE P.M. ON SATURDAY, MACKENZIE'S deep yellow and white Mooney Mark 20, gleaming in the afternoon sun, sat parked beside the runway at Maryborough Airport. Since Mackenzie had flown it back from the Noosa meeting with Dusty and the team, it had been checked and serviced for the hour-long flight to the Gold Coast.

The flight had been approved, logged, and recorded, and it was due to land at four-ten p.m. at the Gold Coast airport. The weather report was excellent.

Click Roberts arrived at two-thirty, loaded his fancy camera, equipment, and carry bag, then retired to the men's room to spiff up for the flight. Click, who habitually took everything in his stride, was excited. When he emerged from the men's room, one of his mates who worked at the airport gave him the once-over.

"Hot damn, Click, you're looking spiffy. Don't tell me you're flying to London to see the Queen."

"Fuck the Queen," Click replied, "I'm on a special assignment with Mack Forbes. He's getting a big wanker award for being a smart-arse in big business, and I'm the official photographer."

"How about that? Isn't that Mack's fancy Mooney Rocket on the tarmac?"

Click preened. "Right on, old son. Guess who the passenger is?"

"You're flying with Mack?"

"By special request. Done deal."

"Bloody hell, Click, you've come up in the world."

"Sky-high, old son. Pity the poor goons who have to fly Jetstar Economy."

"No doubt about you, man. With any luck, you'll be able to upgrade to a few class act roots instead of the scrubbers you usually get."

At that point, Tim Cameron drove to the entrance of the terminal, alighted, and removed an overnight bag from the boot. Mackenzie alighted from the passenger seat entered the terminal with Tim and walked over to Click, who stood to attention, clicked his heels and said, "All set, Mack. Let's fly to the moon."

Mackenzie gave him a nod. "Are you all loaded?"

"Loaded and ready, boss."

Tim had a last word to Mackenzie. "I know this is a chore, but the Gold Coast is turning it on for you. Kate Mallory flew down on a domestic flight this morning. She agreed to do the special introduction."

Mackenzie was impressed. "Kate's done that? It's just some tin-pot award they hand out every year."

"Not anymore, Mack."

"Maybe I should be taking Josh—or Natalie."

"I did suggest that."

"Too late, now." He shook Tim's hand, "I'll spruce up when I get there and fly the flag like a champ just for you, and that's a promise."

"Be yourself. Mack, that's as good as it gets."

The three of them walked out to the plane. Click loaded his luggage and Mack's overnighter then hoisted himself aboard while Mackenzie took the pilot's seat in his prize rocket, warmed it up and taxied to the runway.

Tim watched the sleek little machine glide along the runway, take off and rise into the blue sky, then walked into the terminal and called Josh.

"Your Dad's in the air."

"He's going to be a blast, Timmo. I got a call from the *Sunday Edition* in Sydney. They're sending someone up to cover the night and they want to use some of Click's pictures. Dad will brain them."

"Tell me something I don't know."

Mackenzie's Rocket cruised smoothly south in a cloudless sky. He stayed close to the seaboard to take in the stunning sub-tropical landscape of south-east Queensland. Floating by down below, the pretty towns of Gympie and Nambour on the right, gave way to the spectacular seascapes of Double Island Point, Laguna Bay, and the sandy stretches of the Sunshine Coast. Mack flew low over The Homestead, his lakeside mansion at Noosa, revved the motor a few times to let Natalie know he was on course, then rose again to fly over Mt Coolum to head south for the Glasshouse Mountains.

Click, on his first-ever flight in a private plane, was goggle-eyed and speechless.

Mack edged left to expose the green and gold wonders of Bribie Island and gave Click a word of advice. "Save your bucks and invest in a house or a block of land down there, fella. It'll be a worthwhile move. Values are on the way up, and they'll go higher."

Click got a decent eyeful of Bribie's long stretch of ocean beach on its eastern edge and on its western edge facing the narrow-bridged passage that separated the island from the mainland. "Looks great, boss," he said.

And that's when the first loud crack of the engine filled the small cockpit.

Mackenzie, thinking he'd hit a high-flying bird, expected to see blood and feathers all over the windscreen. "Jesus," he said, "What the hell was that?"

A second loud crack followed. The engine spluttered, and the plane lurched to the right, slightly resisting Mackenzie's efforts to hold the course steady.

Click, completely confused, registered the uneven movement in alarm.

"What's the problem, Mack. What's happening?"

The reply came on an urgent voice. "Damned if I know. Something's not right."

The next crack was followed by a loud rattling in the engine, and the Mark 20 kept pulling to the right, harder this time.

In the cabin, Mackenzie leaned left, trying to hold his course. Below them to the west, was the northern curve of the beach and settlement of Deception Bay, to the east was Moreton Island. Without warning, the plane started to lose height. Mackenzie struggled to hold it steady as it pulled against him to head in the direction of the houses on the beachfront esplanade at Deception Bay.

He managed to stay way above the curve of the beach but looming dead ahead was the densely populated Redcliffe Peninsula, at whose northern point sat the sleek seaside residences of Scarborough and Queen's Beach.

Coming up further ahead, was the busy sprawl of Sutton's Beach and its waterfront high-rises and hotels. Mackenzie's gleaming yellow and white Mooney Mark 20 was out of control and heading straight for the high-rise unit towers of Suttons Beach, with Mackenzie desperately trying to swerve west in the direction of the sea to avoid a disaster.

"Shit a brick, fella," he yelled to Click, "we're going to be in big trouble if I can't straighten this bloody plane. I'm aiming for the sea but it's a hard pull, mate. I hope you can swim; I'm going to try ditching in the water."

Mackenzie's eyes closed tight. His struggles were paying off. The Mark 20 was starting to respond.

Then Click yelled one shattering word: "Windsurfers!"

Mackenzie's eyes flew open. "What?"

"Windsurfers, Mack; six, seven. No—ten of 'em! They're sailing out over the bloody water at Suttons Beach just north of us, and you're heading straight for them! Swerve. Swerve!"

"I'm trying, damn it, but I can't get anything happening!"

"We're gonna hit 'em, man. They're gonna go down with us!"

Click had nailed it. The Mark 20 was in a death dive, with ten muscle-bound windsurfers as the target. A terrible panic hit the two men in the plane. Suddenly, the rattle of the dying engine hit a decibel high. In the flick of an eye, one of the surfers looked up and immediately reacted to the danger. He flipped around, and almost smashed into his nearest buddy.

People frozen in shock on Sutton's Beach saw the team of windsurfers desperately trying to glide out of the way as the Mark 20 cannoned towards the sea. The scene was a flurry of sweeping movement. If it hadn't been for the threat of approaching disaster, it would have been beautiful. Short moments later, the tip of the Mark 20's right wing slammed into the water and splintered. Still attached to the body of the plane, the wing snapped back, crashed through the cabin, and hit Mackenzie on the side of the head. He lurched heavily against Click, who felt his right arm break.

Seawater poured into the cabin as the plane began to sink. Click pushed open the cabin door to his right and slid to freedom, wildly trying to stay afloat with a broken arm. Unbelievably, the Mark 20 had missed the windsurfers.

The first of them dropped into the water, grabbed Click and held his head up. The water was suddenly alive with more surfers, paddling all around the dying plane.

"Get Mack," yelled Click. "He's been hit. He's not gonna make it. Get him, get him out. Holy shit! Get him out!"

On the beach, the watching crowd saw what happened next. Eight surfers ditched their boards, hit the water, spread out into a human chain, and passed the wounded Mackenzie, stretched out on one of the surfboards, from one to another, down a line to the beach. The remaining two, supporting Click, brought up the rear.

Click, holding tight to his lifesaving windsurfer on the edge of the water, was barely conscious. His vision was blurred, and he was shaking. He looked up and said, "Did you get him. He was still in the plane. Did you get Mack out?'

The reply came from heaven. "Stay cool, dude, we got him. Your mate's okay."

Amid a surge of activity in the crowded street above Suttons Beach, three ambulances arrived with a small fleet of police vehicles. One of the policemen surveyed the situation and made a comment. "Those guys in the plane were in luck. There's a high tide running out there. If it hadn't been pulled out, they'd have gone all the way down in deep water for sure."

PERRY COLLIER, THE EX-ARMY MAN, on weekend duty at Snake Gully Security, took the call that came through from the Redcliffe Police, noted the details, and alerted Josh, who was busy at the Butter Factory.

"Did the coppers say how Dad is?"

"He's in intensive care at the Redcliffe Hospital. That's all they said."

"What about Click?"

"Broken arm, and shock, that's it."

"No details on the crash?"

"It went down at Sutton's Beach."

"No way, man, no way! Anyone else hurt?"

"No. Your dad was pulled out of the wreck by a mob of windsurfers."

"Okay. Alert everyone at the park, they've got to know Dad and Click are all right before the crash hits the news. I'll get to Mum and Tim—he can contact that function on the Gold Coast. Thanks, man."

JOSH PHONED THE NOOSA HOMESTEAD and told his mother the news. There were no hysterics, no useless questions, nothing but clear-headed understanding. Mack had crashed and he was injured; that's all she wanted to know; all she wanted to do was to get to him as fast as possible. She called a hire car service, and twelve minutes later she was on the road to the Redcliffe Hospital with an overnight carry bag in case she needed to stay.

THE ORGANISERS OF THE ENTREPRENEURIAL Awards on the Gold Coast called Kate Mallory at the Surfers Paradise Marriott and passed on details of Tim's phone call. They decided that the Awards ceremony would go ahead with the presentation of the minor prizes, and Kate agreed to accept the major award on Mackenzie's behalf.

She got in touch with Barney Ericson in Brisbane and put him in the picture. His first question was, "Are they saying it was an accident?"

"They don't know, Barney. The report I got was that Mackenzie and his photographer had been injured in a small plane crash on the Redcliffe Peninsula, that's all."

"No other details?"

"Not yet, but it will be all over the six o'clock news."

"I don't like it one bit, Kate, not one bloody bit."

"I don't either, Barney."

"Are you staying overnight on the Gold Coast?"

"At the Marriott, yes."

"I'll drive down early in the morning. Can you meet me for breakfast?"

"Seven-thirty on the terrace."

TIM AND JOSH, IN FULL southward flight on the Bruce Highway in the Viper, made it to the Redcliffe Hospital in record time. Natalie Forbes had been there for two hours. Josh took one look at her face as she sat in the waiting room outside the Intensive Care Ward. He knew the news wasn't good. He sat down beside her.

"Let's have it, Mum, how is he?"

Her poise was under tight rein. "A bad head wound, and potential brain damage. He's in a coma."

"Will they operate?"

"Not yet. They're draining the wound."

"So, what do we do?"

"We sit tight."

"That's it?"

"We sit tight and wait."

Tim had a word. "Mon Komo Hotel is no more than five minutes away. I'll book us in and come back. It could be a long wait here."

It was a long night. At one-thirty a.m. on Sunday morning, Bruce Moore, the young Redcliffe doctor in charge; sharp, efficient, and totally in control, spelled it out for Natalie.

"We're doing everything we can, Mrs Forbes. He's comfortable and in good hands. There's not much you can do here. Go to your hotel and try to rest."

"Should he be moved to a bigger hospital?"

"He's in no condition to be moved. This is one of the biggest and best hospitals in the state, and I can assure you, we've got everything under control."

"Are you able to stay in charge?"

"I'm making myself personally responsible."

"That's wonderful, thank you."

"One more thing, Mrs Forbes, your husband's photographer is in a room downstairs. His broken arm has been set, but he's still in shock. He's under sedation, and we're keeping him under observation for two or three days."

Natalie, satisfied and resigned, went to Mon Komo with Josh and Tim, settled into her room, and stretched out on the bed in the dark. Twenty minutes later, she was asleep.

In Josh's room, Tim downed a cup of coffee and said, "I'll rent a car and get back to Maryborough."

"In the morning?"

"Right now. Your place is here with your mother and father. My place is up there in Snake Gully."

"Dottie's up there, Tim. She's on top of everything."

"In the office, yes, but there's a workforce that will need supervision and direction come Monday, and with you and Mack out of action, I don't want anything running off the rails."

"There are foremen, Tim."

"Foremen can't watch everything, mate."

"Okay. I'll stay in touch."

"Say hello to Click—might be an idea to keep him away from the nurses."

Josh laughed out loud. "You've got him pegged."

Tim had his last word. "No matter what happens, we'll ride this out together, kid. I've been there, and I know how the cookie crumbles."

THE TELEVISION NEWS BULLETINS ON Saturday night went for broke. Reporters on the scene at Suttons Beach treated the story like *Saving Private Ryan*. The drama was bolstered by graphic amateur video footage shot by scores of Steven Spielberg wannabes—Mackenzie lying under bloodied towels on a surfboard, muscle-god windsurfers paddling to the rescue on surf skis. Click Roberts, in shock and distressed, being treated in the ambulance—stunned reactions of watching crowds, several interviews with eyewitnesses, plus shots of Suttons Beach besieged by sticky-beaks, and abundant shots of the surfer-boy heroes who referred to their part in the drama with genuine modesty. Their best quote of the day, *"It was no big deal. We just did what we had to do, and we'd do it again. Windsurfing is no video game, and it's not supposed to be played with busted aeroplanes."*

Television news bulletins also featured something incredible—three or four minutes of amazing footage, videotaped by an amateur expert who had created an action masterpiece:

The wounded Mark 20, is seen in the cloudless sky, glistening in the afternoon sun, moving unevenly above the group of windsurfers. It shudders as it loses altitude, and when it begins its descent, the windsurfers soar around it in lyrically graceful flights, dipping and diving like crazy as they skilfully endeavour to avoid collisions with each other and the doomed plane. From the vantage point of the beach, it appears that the Mark 20 is on course to slice the surfers to pieces, but it doesn't happen. By some miracle, the plane, surrounded by flying wind riders, dips sideways into the sea. In one electric moment, one of its wings snaps and slams back into the cabin in what appears to be a fatal hit for the pilot. Seconds later, the surfers, having ditched their harnesses, sails and boards, surround the sinking plane. Click is caught and held with his head above water. Mackenzie is pulled out of the wreck and lifted onto one of the surfboards. The dramatic human-chain rescue follows, with people on the beach rushing to help as Mackenzie, bleeding and surrounded by the crowd, is lifted gently from the water.

The clip played from go to *whoa*, and television-studio message banks seized up.

Word hit the streets. Still-image grabs from the video swallowed the front pages of the Sunday press, and short video clips smothered the Internet. The savvy cameraman who shot the footage slapped it with an instant copyright claim, but it was too late. The vultures were all over it, and the coverage went viral.

The next day, Suttons Beach and its environs were inundated. People simply had to see where the Mackenzie miracle had happened.

Not far away on the Redcliffe Esplanade is an emotional tribute in pictures, words and sounds, to the Bee Gees, the local heroes of the music world. For some time, the Suttons Beach miracle looked like giving the Bee Gees a run for their money.

30

POST-FLIGHT CONFUSION: WHAT REALLY HAPPENED?

KATE MALLORY'S BREAKFAST WITH BARNEY Ericson at the Surfers Paradise Marriott had nothing to do with bacon and eggs. It was black coffee and concerned conversation.

"This Suttons Beach thing is beyond imagining," Barney told Kate. "It's been hyped into a media bombshell. It has put Mackenzie Forbes and Snake Gully on the lips of every person in the country—if not the world. I assume you saw last night's coverage."

Kate replied, "It was played on the audio-visual screen at the Awards event and totally rocked the room."

"All of it? That amazing video of the crash?"

"That got a standing ovation."

Barney tapped the table with his fingers. "I'd like to give the whole deal three cheers and a medal for the publicity it's scored, but there's something getting in the way."

"Like what, Barney?"

"I'm not sure that crash was an accident."

"That occurred to me."

"There will have to be an inquiry. Here's how I think it will go—an investigation will be ordered by bureaucrats and conducted by aviation experts. They'll blame some fault with the engine during the flight—a minor collision with a flying screw from a busted weather balloon or something. Who knows? The experts will do as they're told and come up with an excuse that the public will buy because it sounds official, and it's printed in a newspaper."

Kate's concern was evident. "What happens if Mackenzie doesn't make it?"

"Who knows, Kate? He's still in a coma in the Redcliffe Hospital."

"Is he safe there?"

Barney nailed the tone of the question: "A plane crash is one thing; wiping out a patient in intensive care in a reputable hospital is something else."

"Your cold war is heating up, Barney. Is this the something else you thought was going to happen?"

"If it is, it's missed the mark and the vigilantes in the bureaucracy won't be happy."

"A mild observation, Barney."

"It looks as though their grand plan was taken out by a bunch of windsurfers. If those boys hadn't been around, Mack's plane would have splashed down into a high tide, and we'd be looking for wreaths in the florist shop."

A Marriott waiter approached the table and excused himself.

"Mr Ericson?"

"Yes."

"There's a phone call from a Mr Tobey Groundwater at the desk. Do you wish to take it? Our supervisor will apologise if you don't."

Barney was on his feet in an instant. "No need. Thank you."

"This way, sir."

Barney followed the waiter to the desk. Long minutes later, Barney returned to join Kate, who said, "Tobey Groundwater?"

Barney smiled and sat down. "My all-knowing mole and I've got it all. I called him last night and told him where to find me if he'd heard anything."

"Are you going to tell me what he said?"

"Steel yourself, Kate. An Irishman by the name of Declan Mulqueen arrived on a flight from London to Sydney this morning. He's presently on a flight from Sydney to Canberra, and he's big trouble."

"Who is he?"

"A crusty, sixty-year-old spin doctor, one of the best. He spins for the Labour Party and the globalists in the UK; works for big money, knows all the tricks, and how to pull them. He's deadly, passionate, and brilliant, and he's not here to play canasta with the backbenchers. He'll be on amazing money, and he'll deliver."

"For Jane Armitage?"

"According to Tobey, Mulqueen is her answer to the problem of the ethnic Anzac Day renegades. The UN wants them whitewashed so the Mackenzie Forbes project can be hit with the racist death blow that takes it out."

"What about the crash?"

"Tobey is not t buying what's being said about an accident."

"He's thinking what we're thinking?"

"He says the word is that the miracle that saved Mackenzie's life was never meant to happen. He's also picked up a whisper that Mackenzie's mines in South Africa are in trouble. If so, he could be financially vulnerable, and the UN will have Snake Gully where they want it."

Kate frowned. "What will happen to it?"

"The UN will buy it, or flog it off, and find some showbusiness huckster to run it."

"Which means it won't be the theme park it's supposed to be," said Kate.

"It will be Fake Aussie honky-tonk, with Dad and Dave played by Mickey and Donald clones. It will still be big, and it will make money, but not for Wide Bay and not for your voters in Maryborough."

"And Dusty Rivers?"

"He'll be on call to do what he's promised with the Golden Girls, but after the first season, the new owners of Snake Gully will boost the budget for the movie Western

Ridge Mining wants him to do. He'll take the offer, be a bigger star than ever, and they'll cash in."

Kate threw a spanner: "You're wrong about Dusty. He'd never dud Mack."

"He may not have a choice."

"What about Tim Cameron?"

"Mulqueen will bury him in a sea of made-up empathy, give him a medal, and pay someone to write a loving song about his mother and father."

"I wish you hadn't told me any of that."

"I wish I hadn't needed to."

"Do you trust Tobey Groundwater's information?"

"He's infallible."

"I hate it, Barney. What are we going to do?"

"Pray for a miracle, baby. We'll need the parting of the Red Sea."

DUSTY RIVERS AND SALLY TEMPLE caught the Saturday evening news bulletin in their leased abode at Hervey Bay. After initial expressions of shock, Dusty watched the unfolding coverage of the Suttons Beach crash in mute disbelief.

When it ended, Dusty vacated his chair, walked out to the wide balcony that ran along the front of the house, and stood gazing at the early evening charm of the resort. In the sky behind him, the setting sun splashed the sea with an orange glow that he saw through clouded eyes.

He registered Sally's silencing of the television set. Seconds later, she joined him on the veranda. He turned away from the view to speak to her.

"I don't get it, Sal. I just don't get it. How did that crash happen?"

She reached for his hand. "You saw it all, Dusty."

"That's not what I mean. Something's wrong, Sally, it's all wrong."

"You can't make things easier by telling yourself that, honey."

"Mack loved that Mark 20. He resisted buying it because he thought a bloke had to be a poser to fly himself around in a private plane, but when he learned to fly, it turned into his pride and joy; that's how it was."

"No question."

"Then you know what I'm saying." Dusty disengaged his hand and spoke slowly. "Sally, Mack would never have taken that flight without a detailed overhaul of his plane. It was the same whenever he went anywhere in it. It was a ritual. He had a guy at the Maryborough Airport who looked after it for him, so what happened?"

Sally paused before she replied, "I hate where you're going with this."

"It's nagging at me, and I can't let it go." He faced her squarely. "Is it possible that someone wanted to take him out?"

"Don't go there, honey, just don't."

"Sorry, Sal. I have to know."

"Who's going to tell you? Mack's in a coma."

"Click Roberts isn't. He was with him on the flight."

"He's still in shock and he can't tell you anything more then he's told the media. He can't tell you what caused the plane to stall and crash."

Dusty got the point. "But Mack can."

"He's in the Redcliffe Hospital in a coma, he can't tell anybody anything."

Dusty took a deep breath. "Then he'll have to get over it, won't he?"

"Come on, baby, you're spinning daydreams."

"Mack's in a coma, but his friggin' mind will be working overtime to cut him loose. It'll take more than a coma to beat him."

"I wish I had your confidence."

"Have faith, Sal. If it can move mountains, it can cut Mack loose from a coma, and when it does, I'm going to get together with him, and we're going to find out who cooked up this fancy little plot to take him out."

Dusty, full of fire, burned on. "Look at it my way, Sally. Whoever planned that crash has made a mistake. Mack didn't die, and when he finds out that someone messed around with his fancy Mark 20, he's gonna be asking questions, and he won't back off until he finds out who it was. Someone will be in the hot seat."

Sally played along. "Any ideas who the someone is?"

"I'm working on it."

AT THE REDCLIFFE HOSPITAL, CLICK, mildly relieved and relaxed, was still under observation with his arm in plaster but hazy on the details of the crash.

Mackenzie, after four days in Intensive Care, was still in a coma and reports were still non-committal. The deep cut on the side of his forehead was regularly dressed; the swelling was subsiding, and he was comfortable. Natalie and Josh were sharing the visitor schedule; a twenty-four-seven exercise. Bruce Moore, who was still the doctor on Mackenzie's case was unable to comment on his condition. After four days Mack was not deteriorating, but the longer a patient stayed bound by a coma, the chances of a full recovery were on a downward slide. Time was not cooperating.

31

THE BAFFLING QUESTIONS

THE MIDWEEK EDITION OF THE *South East Queensland News* ran a story that focused on the sporting benefits of windsurfing and spunked it up with full-length pictures of four of the Sutton's Beach heroes. A breakaway piece on page one reported that an in-depth inquiry into the Mark 20 crash conducted by 'an official aviation engineer' who had inspected the wreck after it had been exhumed, revealed that a small piece of metal had broken away to become jammed in the engine. The steering had been negatively affected, and power failure caused the Mark 20 to lose height. The resulting crash was inevitable.

Click Roberts, a passenger in the plane, was quoted as saying that Mackenzie did what he could to keep the plane from crashing into the hotels and high-rise units on the beachfront at Suttons Beach. His efforts paid off and the plane hit splashdown in the sea. There was a picture of Click with his right arm in a sling.

MACKENZIE'S RESCUED SOLDIERS, PERRY COLLIER and Andrew Denton, on a mid-morning security break, sat munching on tasty fat sausage rolls at the Snake Gully Bakery. Perry, eyes focused on the front page of the Sunday edition of the *South East Queensland News* finished reading the breakout piece on the cause of the Mark 20 crash. He looked across at Andrew and shook his head. "This report on Mack's plane crash doesn't make sense. It couldn't have happened like it says here. That plane was kept regularly serviced. There couldn't have been any piece of broken metal anywhere."

"Maybe they didn't run the whole story."

"Whatever, they got it wrong," Perry was adamant. "When I was in the Army, I spent three years in the Aviation Brigade before I switched to Engineer Support. We learned all about small planes. This report is all wrong."

"Newspapers don't always get it right, buddy."

"This is supposed to be the official explanation of a crash that could have sent Click and Mack to the graveyard, and I'll say it again, it's all wrong!

When Perry couldn't get the report out of his head, he found Tim in his office and made mention of what he saw as an error. After questioning Perry in detail, Tim followed up by contacting the news reporter who wrote the piece.

The reporter claimed he was told that the wreck had been inspected by an aviation engineer appointed by the government, that the report was on file, and that it had been checked.

Perry still wasn't buying. "That's not right, Tim. The reporter was conned. I reckon I know what I'm talking about."

Tim was aware that Mack's plane had been held in its own small hangar at the Maryborough Airport. Now totally involved, he drove there with Perry on a fact-finding mission. They were directed to the freelance mechanic paid by Mackenzie to keep his plane sky worthy. Bill Simpson was an official looking grease monkey in his late twenties.

In answer to Tim's inquiries, he said, "I checked everything thoroughly on Friday, the day before yesterday's flight. I had a job in Brisbane, and the machine was A-okay when I checked it. Mack insisted that his plane had to be maintained in top condition twenty-four-seven, and it sure didn't need the other check it got."

Tim's third-eye bleeped. "What other check, Bill?"

"Mack sent an aviation engineer to give his machine a once-over the morning of the flight."

"Where was he from?"

"He told the airport staff he was from the government. He flashed official credentials, so they told him to go ahead with the inspection."

"And that's what he did?"

"He finished the check just after lunch and left."

"Did you read today's report in the South East Queensland News?"

"Yeah. I thought they made a mistake, so I rang the Suttons Beach police this morning to find out if I could take a look at the wreck myself."

"And?"

"The copper said it had already been sold for spare parts."

"So soon? Isn't that unusual?"

"Not always. Nobody claimed it and the cops didn't want it hanging around."

"Did you check on the engineer Mack sent to the airport?"

"Straight away. I rang the Aviation Department at Brisbane Airport and they told me that they had no record of any engineer checking anything at Maryborough Airport. They had notification of the flight, but nothing else."

"Did you think that was strange?"

Bill hedged a bit. "Look, mate, I'm just a two-bob grease monkey. I didn't want to get involved in official government business, neither did the staff at Maryborough Airport. We had nothing to do with anything. I signed off on Mack's plane on Friday afternoon, and it was in top condition, that's all I can tell you."

Tim was floored. "Okay, thanks, Bill."

"Is there anything else you need me for?"

"If there is, I'll let you know."

Bill gave Tim a worried look. "You think there's something fishy, don't you?"

"If there is, it doesn't concern you; rest easy, man."

When they got back to Tim's car, Perry Collier, who'd listened closely to Bill Simpson's story, said, "I knew that newspaper report had to be made up. What are you going to do?"

Tim knew his hands were tied. "Right now, there's nothing I can do, but there's something you can do."

"What?"

"Keep everything to yourself."

"I'll have to tell Pete. He'll think it's funny if I say nothing."

"Keep it simple, then."

"Let me lay it on the line, Tim. Pete is my right arm. If you need us for anything, we're both on call. We operate as a team—it's Snake Gully or bust. Can I say something else?"

"Sure."

Perry gave out. "It looks like that dodgy government engineer could have sabotaged Mack's plane. There are heaps of things he could have done to that motor to make it crack up like Click said. I think that plane was well and truly fixed to crash."

"There's no evidence, mate. Mack is in a coma in the Redcliffe Hospital, and until he recovers, he can't tell anyone anything about any engineer who inspected his plane."

Perry hit a downer. "He might never be able to tell anyone, Tim. Sometimes, if and when coma patients recover, they don't remember anything about what happened."

"Mum's still the word."

"Got ya, mate."

32

THE IRISH CONNECTION

DECLAN MULQUEEN HAD NO INTEREST in channelling a fashion icon. He entered the Canberra Airport terminal dressed like an average blue-collar worker, broadcasting his arrogance, and treating the disapproving stares he was collecting with contempt.

He propped himself and his wheelie bag some distance away from the other disembarking passengers near the exit door and waited.

The young man who been observing him with interest approached him and said, "Mr Mulqueen?"

"Who are you?"

"I'm from Jane Armitage's office."

"Where's your ID?"

The young man reached into his inner pocket, extracted a wallet, pulled out a card and handed it over. Declan Mulqueen took it, read it, and handed it back.

"Robert McMahon, is that you?"

"It's my card, yes."

"Are you an Irishman?"

"I'm an Australian, Mr Mulqueen."

"Good lad."

Robert McMahon smiled. "My grandfather was Irish."

"Where from?"

"County Clare."

Declan smiled back. "Jane Armitage has done her homework. I'm from County Clare. I grew up with the Cliffs of Moher and Bunratty Castle as my best friends. I suppose you knew that."

"Yes. I did."

"How long have you worked for Jane Armitage?"

"One-and-a-half weeks"

"How long did it take her to find you?"

"Excuse me?"

"It would have been in her best interests to locate a public servant with an Irish connection, someone who could make it easier to deal with a crusty old Irish shit-stirrer like me. What do you know about the Cliffs of Moher?"

"I've been there."

"Bunratty Castle?"

"I've been there, too."

"Did you know that an Australian racehorse called Bunratty Castle won the 1968 Caulfield Cup at twelve to one?"

"He led all the way. My grandfather told me about that when he took me to Ireland."

"Is Canberra where you live?"

"It is now. I was based in Sydney."

Declan Mulqueen grew a savvy smile. "I see. You're a fresh face on the political register in Canberra, and you're at the airport to meet someone who could well be your grandfather. Who's to know that I'm here to put an innocent spin on a potentially awkward problem that's been trumped by the racist card—why all the secrecy?"

"You were not born yesterday, were you, Mr Mulqueen?"

"You didn't answer my question."

'It's a sensitive issue that needs to stay sensitive."

"Will we be working together?"

"Yes."

"My first name is Declan. Feel free to use it."

"I have a car in the car park."

"The VIP car park?"

"The public car park; the car park you use when you're at the airport to meet your grandfather."

Declan nodded and smiled. "Shall we go?"

"Do you have to collect luggage?"

Declan reached for the handle of his travel bag. "I travel light."

Robert McMahon led the way to his nondescript car, stashed Declan Mulqueen's bag in the boot, then took the driver's seat beside him, revved the car, drove slowly to the airport exit and noted Declan's question.

"How long does it take to get where we're going?"

"Twenty minutes."

"Tell me everything you know about this assignment and include your opinions."

"What's so special about my opinions?"

"They're special because a bright young man like you must have them."

"I do."

"Then lead on."

"I thought you dealt in facts."

"Facts can be variable, opinions too, but if you trust the person who expresses them, it's a different matter."

"Are you telling me you trust me?"

"Irishman to Irishman, yes."

"So soon?"

"I trust my first impressions. When do we start working together?"

"I haven't been officially assigned, yet."

"You will be as soon as we get to wherever it is. Now tell me everything you know about this case. I want it all, and I don't want poppycock. I want to know why it's important enough to warrant the kind of money I'm being paid to solve it. Once I know what I need to know, I'll be able to put Jane Armitage on the yellow brick road."

Robert smiled. "The Wizard of Oz?"

"Do you know that Frank Baum, who wrote the book, had Irish heritage growing all over his family tree?"

"I didn't, no."

"Now you know why the Wizard was a just a trick."

"I'm going to love working with you, Declan."

"A few words of warning, Robert."

"Yes?"

"I'm no Scarecrow, and I don't like Munchkins getting in my way."

"I'm sure they won't."

"Make no mistake. There are always Munchkins, and they always get in the way. I'm here to win, and I want to win on my terms, so let's start with the Munchkins who caused all the trouble on Anzac Day."

"Not just trouble; it was big trouble."

"That's why I'm being paid big money to fix it, and fix it I will. I'm all ears, Robert, start talking.

"You don't want to take notes?"

"I never take notes. I want it all, boy."

33

TIM'S COTTAGE: THE TWILIGHT AFTER THE CRASH

TIM ARRIVED HOME FROM THE park at four o'clock on Sunday afternoon. He'd had a busy day, his mind was buzzing like a mob of bees in the hive, and he was glad to be alone in his cosy abode. The phone rang. Expecting it to be someone from the site, he answered in his best official voice.

"Tim Cameron."

"You're tired and stressed."

His voice changed straight away. "Hello, April."

"Are you tired and stressed?"

"Resigned."

"Do you need to talk?"

"Yes."

"I'm on the way. What's for dinner?"

"I haven't made plans."

"I'll bring something."

"I'll dim the lights and put candles on the table."

"You look gorgeous in candlelight."

"You do too," said Tim.

"Do we screw before or after dinner?"

"Both."

"I wasn't kidding."

"Neither was I."

"I'm in Noosa. I'll be in Maryborough just after sundown."

"Hurry, sundown."

At seven forty-five they lay together in Tim's bed. It was raining, and April watched the raindrops slipping silently down the windowpanes. Without looking at him, she asked a question.

"Do you want to talk about what happened at Suttons Beach?"

"Mack is still in a coma."

"Have you spoken to Cynthia?"

"She called and said, *que sera-sera.*"

April turned her head and smiled. "Most people think that's just a song that Doris Day sang in a movie—they don't know how true it is."

"Whatever will be, will be."

"Do you accept that?"

"I promised I would."

"I'm here if you want to talk."

"You brought an icebox," said Tim. "What's in it?"

"Trawler-fresh seafood."

"We won't have to cook."

"What do you want to do instead?"

He stretched out. "I want to pretend we're together in the rain."

"Why pretend? It's only gentle rain."

"I've never done it in the rain."

"I've always wanted to."

"We'll get wet."

"That's part of the fun."

At six o'clock next morning, they showered together, ate streaky bacon, scrambled eggs, sourdough toast, and drank grapefruit juice and plunger coffee for breakfast.

"I should be able to make it back to Noosa by noon," said April, "I have an assignment to finish by this afternoon."

"I'm glad you came; thanks for that."

"You don't have to say that word to me."

"You're always gentle on my mind, April."

"You're worried. Don't be."

"Whatever happens from now on, happens to both of us."

She kissed him gently on the lips and said, "Nothing's over yet. Tell yourself that. It's not over."

34

THE BRISBANE SUPREME COURT HEARD the appeal against the Anzac Day shooting decision handed down by Justice Harold E Broadchurch.

Tobey Groundwater's radar was on full alert; he was in *Mole Heaven*. Barney Ericson was hanging out for information and he was working around the clock to track down as much as he could grab.

He'd rightly guessed that the appeal was under the umbrella of Jane Armitage and her mob of Human Rights rough riders. As he'd expected Harry Broadchurch was booted out and replaced with a by someone who was more in tune with the UN's wishes.

In court, Mackenzie's killer barrister, Dan Anderson, successfully argued for a retrial of the Anzac Day killer and his low-life buddies, but the proviso was that they undergo a period of personal re-adjustment to render them mentally competent to understand and submit to the laws of the country. The chosen location for this task was a little-known radicalisation centre close to the Army Jungle Training Base at Canungra, in south-eastern Queensland.

Dan Anderson questioned the judge's decision but submitted to the explanation that the Canungra Human Rights post was remote. It had restricted access, with no chances of social contact with anyone—save the centre's well-drilled staff, who were skilled in the treatment of ethnic inmates. Positive evidence of such success was presented by Jane Armitage's barrister, and accepted by the judge.

Dan Anderson was pissed-off but had nowhere to go.

The whisper in the underground, and in the gossipy legal world, was that the Canungra solution was a blind to railroad the public into thinking that the controversial Anzac Day attack would be open for a retrial when the perpetrators had been socially re-conditioned and ready to face the music.

Tobey Groundwater was wide awake to the deception and said so to Barney Ericson.

"It's all gobbledygook," Tobey said. "It's an-out-and-out whitewash that's been grandstanded to keep the Human Rights Institute on the straight and narrow in the eyes of the voting public."

Barney was wide awake too. "What you're telling me is that social re-conditioning, or not, these three hoods will be trained in the art of sleight-of-hand to come across as proof-positive that they're capable of becoming worthwhile citizens, and they will never have to face trial for the murder of Mary and Jack Cameron. With Armitage's help, the three of them may even find a place in the print media or as commentators on television."

Tobey caught the irony. "A forgone conclusion."

Barney's anger got the better of him. "This is all clever claptrap, Tobey, it's all too smart to be thought up by any of the public servants in the Human Rights Institute. Where are all these moves coming from?"

Tobey's answer was immediate. "Declan Mulqueen, the imported Irish spin doctor is in charge of everything. He has carte blanch. It's in his contract and he's a genius; that's why the UN brought him in. Before questions are asked, he's killed the answers. He briefed the barrister who squashed Dan Anderson's well-researched objection to the Canungra solution, and Dan doesn't go down easy. Mulqueen's brief was all double-talk, but the Judge bought it and ruled it as fact. The atmosphere in court was head shaking."

"How long is Mulqueen around for?"

"Until he's finished."

"Finished what?"

"Watch this space."

"Keep me posted, Tobey."

"Goes without saying."

"The situation's not good, is it?"

"It's what I expected."

"What's your call on what happens next?"

"I'll keep you posted."

"How do you think we're looking?"

"Don't ask, Barney.

35

MACKENZIE: DO OR DIE

THE PRAYERS MACKENZIE GROUPIES WERE sending up to the outer limits were answered on Friday morning, seven days after the Suttons Beach crash.

Mackenzie Forbes regained consciousness in the Redcliffe Hospital, took a breath, blinked a few times, looked around the room, and said, *"What have they done with my bloody Mark 20?"*

The youthful Doctor Bruce Moore ended his week-long vigil close to tears.

The media went berserk. The headline on the SEQ News roared. "Mack's Back!"

In Snake Gully, the Bakery Bar erupted. Tim ordered a Happy Hour that lasted four.

At the hospital, Natalie and Josh were on the verge of collapse.

Dusty and Sally turned on the booze at the Hervey Bay pub, and the locals had a ball. At a community rage at Suttons Beach, the band in the rotunda played and replayed "Stayin' Alive," the big one for the Bee Gees.

At the Redcliffe Baptist Church, the minister said, *"This is what the Second Coming is going to be like."*

The ten windsurfers arrived at the hospital with the surfboard that had floated Mackenzie to safety. It had been signed by all of them, tied up with ribbons and presented at the door of Mackenzie's room.

The card said, " *When you're fit to fly, fly with us. You're the Captain of our Clouds."* The nurses misted up.

Wide Bay and Maryborough copped a public holiday.

Mack was back for sure. In his opinion, he was back with a vengeance.

It wasn't that easy. His condition had been diagnosed as acute concussion that had caused his temporary unconsciousness. There was no serious brain damage after the wound had been drained, but that didn't mean he was ready to take on the mental strain of Snake Gully and its fast-approaching opening.

At the Redcliffe Hospital, Dr Moore explained that although Mackenzie's head wound had been relatively minor, it had done slight damage to his brain, and he had to be kept rested and quiet for the approaching few weeks. It was okay for him to return home if the room could be kept relatively dark. Bruce Moore's further advice was seriously delivered. "There can't be any stress, he can't be plagued by decision-making or anything that causes undue agitation or worry. No alcohol. Good plain food. No wandering around the house. No undue excitement. No television. No radio talk shows. He knows he was in a crash in the Mark 20, but he doesn't know details, and he shouldn't be pressed to recall them."

Natalie smiled a resigned smile. "How long is all this for?"

"Six to eight weeks at least. Make sure it's rigid. No letting up. After that, he should still take it easy. He'll be well on the road to normality, but not if he breaks the speed limit."

"He won't," said Natalie.

"I'm sure he won't, Mrs Forbes. Eight weeks is not a lifetime, and if you want him to be the man he was—the man he deserves to be, keep him focused."

"He's in good hands, doctor."

Dr Bruce Moore's smile lit the room. "This country needs men like him, Mrs Forbes, and I'm proud to have been able to give him back to you."

NATALIE FORBES, AT HOME WITH Mackenzie in Noosa, spelled out the stringent conditions of Mack's rehab over the telephone to Dusty Rivers, who called a general catch-up in the Snake Gully Operations Office. In attendance were Josh Forbes, Tim Cameron, Sally Temple, Dottie Austin, Andrew Denton, and Perry Collier.

Dusty had the floor. "Mack has been told to keep out of the mainstream, at home, for at least eight weeks and Natalie will make sure it happens. She has told me that he still wants the official opening of Snake Gully on Australia Day. He gets his wish. No sweat! It's hell or high water! It's November now. Australia Day is January 26. We're going to be flat strap, but we'll have plenty of help to make sure we pull it off."

Perry had a question. "It's common for coma survivors to lose all memory of what happened. Does Mack remember anything?"

"He doesn't," said Dusty, "and he shouldn't be pushed. As of now, everything is go for the big opening—I'm talking The Golden Girls, my TV clips, all the amenities, the Snake Gully Express, the character actors, the TV commercials, the press releases and all the hype and rah-rah we can dig up."

Dottie Austin had a question: "What about the bushranger stunt?"

Dusty's answer: "A bit of a question mark at the moment because we haven't been able to nail it, but as for the rest of the stuff, we all know our jobs and we know we're on the spot! We deliver! We make it happen! We come through. We win!"

Dusty stopped for breath.

"And there's something else. Mal Chambers, the Western Ridge Mining heavy who wants to finance my next movie, called me yesterday. He told me that the South African mining world has taken a hit. The diamond market is down, and increased taxes have caused cash-flow problems in Mack's mines. Rather than sack his workers, he's kept them on, and there's a financial squeeze at Snake Gully. Mal's company is willing to stand by in case Mack needs cash. If so, they'll boost the coffers with a no-interest loan until the park opens and starts to earn money. That's not for the grapevine by the way, and it should stay that way."

Dusty's tone changed. "There have been sneaky rumours that Mack's plane may have been sabotaged, a possible inside job that involves shady sections of the bureaucracy and the government. These rumours have not hit the mainstream, but they're hinting that the Mark 20 crash was deliberately brought on to rob Snake Gully of its driving force. We can't do anything about rumours like that right now, but they'll keep. The sure way to handle them is to make sure that Snake Gully is an even bigger success. Let's tackle that problem after the opening day is locked away, but if any information breaks out anywhere, let me know on the double! If it's war, these rumourmongering troublemakers want, they're on!"

You could have cut the room's atmosphere with a knife.

Perry and Andrew remained mute.

Dottie Austin, said, "We're with you, Dusty."

Sally said, "All the way."

Tim said, "Done deal."

Nothing more needed to be said. Nobody moved for at least two minutes, then Josh, with misty eyes blazing, stood, and said, "Go, Dad!"

36

THE BUREAUCRACY STRIKES BACK

DECLAN MULQUEEN FLEW ONTO THE Gold Coast with Robert McMahon. They were travelling light. They loaded their overnight bags into a rented car at the pick-up spot and exited the airport car park. In the driver's seat, Robert headed north to connect with the western highway to the rainforest village of Canungra, the hinterland holding spot for the three Anzac Day renegades.

Declan asked the obvious question. "How long are we on the road?"

"Just over an hour."

Declan looked out the window at the bustling holiday resort, wrinkled his nose at the fresh sea air and said, "This doesn't look like a jungle to me."

"It will after we turn west."

"Then it becomes the wild west, is that it?"

"I wouldn't call it wild, Declan."

"What would you call it?"

"Canungra is a pretty little town on the edge of the rainforest."

"A bit like Ennistimon at home?"

"Nothing like it at all."

"Then I've got something to learn."

Canungra turned out to be a surprise for Declan Mulqueen. It was a sunny town with friendly country people, shops, a school full of schoolkids, green parks, little creeks, water holes, an absolute sky-load of fresh sweet air, and a spiffy looking pub with a handsome windowed top floor.

They checked in—neat rooms, all mod cons.

Declan made a wish. He needed to see where the Human Rights Institute wanted to send the three reckless gunslingers in an effort to guide them towards law-abiding Aussie citizenship. He sat with Robert at a high table in the pub's long narrow bar. In front of him on the table were a glass of water and a bowl overflowing with salted peanuts, which he picked up, one by one, to crunch.

Through the bar windows, he could see the cars and trucks rolling up and down the street and townspeople sauntering by and thought how relaxed and natural everything seemed. It was mid-afternoon; except for a couple of occupied tables and bar stools—the bar wasn't busy.

Robert got the impression that Declan was not with him, so he tapped his arm and said, "Are you okay?"

"I'm rarely anything else."

"You're not talking."

"Only a dolt talks when he's thinking, laddie."

Robert took the hint and they sat in silence for a while longer.

Declan finally spoke, 'Would you call this a typical Australian town?"

"One of the smaller ones, yes."

"I'm told there are Army barracks."

"Jungle training, yes, in and around the rainforest."

"And some sort of jail."

"Not exactly a jail, a Correction Centre; not far away."

"Is that where our shooters are being radicalised?"

"No. There's a special place."

Declan's eyebrows shot up. "Oh? Why's that?"

"They need specialised attention, Declan. That's all I've been told."

"Tell me about this special place."

Robert went into graphic detail. The Institute had purchased what was once an old-fashioned two-storey guest house in a little valley just out of town. It had been completely done over with a couple of administration offices on the front lower level and three small self-contained suites opening out onto a long wide veranda at the rear. One end of the veranda was closed to accommodate a canteen and a bar, with steps that lead down to a spacious covered garden with outdoor tables and chairs.

Upstairs were another two self-contained suites, six separate rooms, two bathrooms, and a wide veranda facing front. The building had kept its original name, *Happy Valley*.

Declan shook his head. "And that's where our three miscreants are being accommodated?"

Robert answered with a positive nod, then heard Declan's hearty laugh for the first time. It rolled out and filled the bar of the Canungra Pub.

A couple of customers looked around; one of them called, "Must have been a good one, mate!"

Declan called back, "Would have killed the cat, brother."

Robert sat back and grinned. "Have you got the picture, Declan?"

"When do I get to see it for real?"

"Finish your peanuts."

The manager of the pub provided the car, and the drive took ten minutes.

Happy Valley was exactly as Robert described it. The administration staff, all seven of them, were expecting the visit, and they had been briefed. The inspection lasted thirty minutes. The admin staff were business-like and efficient. The inmates were working in the garden, in the kitchen, sweeping the veranda, or washing walls.

They could easily have been singing, "Whistle While You Work. "Perfect; too perfect for Declan, who sidled up to Robert and murmured, "When do we get to see Cinderella cleaning the stove?"

When the two of them got back to the Canungra Pub, Declan opened up. "I grew up with fairy stories in County Clare, but I'd never seen a real one until today. Robert lad, for once in my life, I'm in awe. Where did they find the administration staff?"

"University graduates."

"They've all got suntans."

"The beach is only an hour away in a fast car."

"They all talk social poppycock."

"They're academics."

"What do they do about conditioning someone who's not fitting in?"

"They open a book."

"Do you approve of all this skulduggery?"

"It's my job."

Declan fixed him with a steely stare. "That is not what I asked you, laddie. I thought we understood each other."

"We do."

"Don't disappoint me. Tell me the truth, now, set me at ease. I have to do what I'm paid to do. I have to come through because that's what I signed on to do. I have to spin this case, Robbie, I have to honour my code, and that's it. That's my job, and it's your job to help me. But all that aside, I need to know how you feel so I'm asking again—do you approve of all this skulduggery?"

"No, Declan, I don't."

"Do you think they might have a bottle of Tullamore Dew Irish Whiskey hidden away in this pretty little pub?"

"I can ask."

"Are you an Irish whiskey drinker?"

"Not really."

"Would you like to learn?"

"Why not?"

"We don't need to overdo it; we just need to elevate the mood a wee bit. Moments like this are too rare. They shouldn't be wasted, and we can use the time to work on ways to give Jane Armitage what she wants. After all, they're her gold bars."

Two hours, and a third of a bottle of Tullamore Dew later, they had the spin mapped out. Here's how it went:

The three renegades would be all cleaned-up and neatly attired. They'd be fit and healthy from working in the garden and washing walls, and they would be shining examples of *"Happy Valley"* magic. No longer resentful or angry but fully blessed by their newly found appreciation of Australia as the country that adopted them. They would be full of remorse and anxious to be responsible citizens.

In their new guise, Declan would arrange for them to be interviewed on *Second Guess,* a respected prime-time current affairs show aired across the country on Sunday evening.

Second Guess's TV presenters were masters of their art, frequently caught by the close-up camera wearing expressions of empathy and concern—wonderful stuff that had worked for years—a practised talent that left Meryl Streep in the soap box.

The three outlaws will be trained to face the cameras—*James Dean times three*—briefed, suitably modest; belittled by what they had done at dawn on that Manly Anzac Day, honestly sorry, and eager to live their re-made lives in peace and unity—appropriately supported and trained by the most experienced man in the business and guaranteed to walk free in their adopted country.

Robert was honestly impressed. "Sounds incredible, Declan."

"I've had lots of practice."

"You know it's corrupt."

"The world is corrupt."

"I realise that."

"We're only passengers on the ship, laddie."

"Did you ever want to be anything else?"

"Once, yes I did."

"What happened?"

"The world happened. It has a habit of doing that."

"And each man kills the thing he loves."

Declan smiled a sweet smile. "Oscar Wilde, yes. He had the world worked out."

"And he paid the price."

"Which is why I prize him but never want to be like him."

"When do you want to start the training sessions."

"As soon as we get home tomorrow."
"I'll let everyone know."
"Good lad."

37

A LAST-MINUTE TURN-UP THAT RANG A BELL

WITH THE PRESSURE MOUNTING IN the official Snake Gully Office, something totally unexpected happened. Dottie Austin, checking through recent applications for employment, came upon well-presented résumés filled out by four applicants to play the bushrangers who saddle up to rob the Snake Gully Express.

Dottie was excited. Maybe this was the missing link for the opening day spectacle, the break she'd been waiting for. The bushranger attack as conceived was a spectacular action-filled stunt that needed detailed attention and expertise. So far, the right applicants to pull it off had eluded the search.

Miraculously, the four new applicants met the bushranger requirements exactly. They were fit and agile—with horse riding ability, advanced acrobatic skills, and judging by the tone of their applications, they showed a keen sense of humour. Finally, it looked as though the stunt could well be included in the Australia Day opening; now less than eight weeks away. *Relief in spades!*

Dottie scanned the résumés more closely. The four guys had all worked at theme parks on the Gold Coast—in acrobatic police thrillers, stunt fights on a water slide, and as cowboys in a stadium show. The leader of the pack, Sam Winston-Smith, was a young athlete who choreographed the routines. On the spot, Dottie decided to contact him to arrange an interview. But before she did, she had a word with Josh—she was reluctant to speak to Tim because the stunt called for a trick gunfight. What with the resurgence of the Anzac Day tragedy, she felt that the key trick may need to be toned down for his sake.

Josh set her straight. 'I've spoken to him, Dottie, I said we'd drop the stunt altogether if we couldn't cast it, but he's okay if we can include it at the last minute. I said we could put a funny spin on it, like the guys falling over each other; messing up the robbery and stuff."

"He approved of that?"

"The gig has been in all the promotional stuff; it's been talked about in Dusty's clips and featured in the advertising. It we can get it happening with these four dudes it would be awesome. They'll be perfect stooges for Dusty's arrival as the sheriff on his white horse when he rides in with his lasso twirling."

"And Tim's cool with that?"

"He's a professional, Dottie."

"Okay, I'll go ahead and check these boys out, then call them in for an interview."

THEY CAME ON LIKE THE Fabulous Four—looking every bit as good as their résumés. Young, spiffy, keen, and eager, tossing off their names in turn—*Tom, Tony, Alan and Sam— Gigs Incorporated at your service.*

Sam did the talking. Tony and Tom backed him up, Alan said nothing.

Dottie, anxious to get everything tied up, said, "Are you all available for a permanent engagement at the moment?"

"Ready and raring to go, lady," said Sam. "Do you want a demo? We can pull one off right now if you've got the space."

Dottie, thinking positively, replied, "There's no need. You're all qualified, I can't see why we can't book you right away. I checked on your Gold Coast stunts. You got a full-on rave."

Sam was chuffed. "Okay, then let's make it legal."

Taking their relevant details, Diane Peterson, the Office's resident blonde, was a picture of efficiency. With that part of the interview over in minutes, Dottie immediately attended to the official details—payment of fees, stunt timetables, rehearsal schedules, costume fittings, and security rules—all over in twenty minutes.

Diane handed out the Snake Gully employment guide that included all the site's attractions and behaviour rules, then added, "Any questions—I'm your contact. All happy?"

"Happy as it gets, chick," said Sam.

Diane smiled one of her best Diane smiles. "Accommodation is tight in Maryborough, do you boys have somewhere to stay?"

Sam answered, "The other boys have found a house to rent together. I've got a room at the Brolga Guest House."

Diane's eyebrows rose. "No kidding. The Brolga is always booked solid and as of now the house rental business in this town is chockers. You boys have sure hit the jackpot."

Sam gave her a wink. "We can be persuasive when we have to be."

"Positive is as positive does." said Diane.

Sam hit another wink. "Confidence is a virtue, chick."

"My philosophy to a T," said Diane.

Dottie, working on the employment form interrupted, "I need one more detail. You're all engaged under your business name of *Gigs Incorporated*. Do you have a frontman?"

Sam piped up, "Meet the leader of the pack, I take care of everything. You can check it all out with me. Where do I sign?"

Five minutes later it was all done, and *Gigs Incorporated* left the office with a well-paid stunt fee all locked away.

Dottie was a bundle of pleasant achievement. "That's it," she said, "and it came right out of the blue. Who'd have thought?"

Diane was all smiles. "I love guys with leadership ability, don't you?"

At nine p.m. that evening, Sam heard the gentle knock on the door of his comfortable furnished room on the top floor of the Brolga Guest House. He opened it, and Diane Peterson said, "I'm here to welcome you to Maryborough."

Next morning, Sam ordered breakfast-for-one in the spacious Guest House dining room. His eyes were sparkling, and his satisfied smile lasted until the last sip of designer coffee.

To the naked eye, Sam appeared to be one happy Space Cadet, and an even happier bushranger. *Gigs Incorporated* had arrived.

DIANE, CHECKING IN AT THE office on time as usual, said good morning to Dottie, and added, "Sam's not the smarty pants I thought he was. Just like I suspected, he didn't get into the Brolga Guest House on spec at all. He made the booking over six weeks ago, the same day as he rented the house for the other boys."

Dottie was barely interested. "Who told you that, love?"

"The Brolga manager is a friend of mine. He owns the guest house."

Dottie looked up from her desk. "Sam Winston-Smith's contact on the Gold Coast told me that the boys had their eye on us for a while, but they were pencilled in on another booking. I assume Sam booked ahead in case the other booking fell through."

Diane smiled a big smile. "So, we all got lucky."

THE PACE AT SNAKE GULLY was frantic, but like a well-oiled machine, everything was happening as planned. Tim and Josh, driving the action, were in confident control. Sally had the Golden Girls working towards the perfection of her spectacular musical in the Snake Gully Live Theatre. Dusty being Dusty was in harness as the show's Funny Man. It was all happening. The clock was ticking, and the days were whizzing by at super speed.

At the Homestead, Natalie had nursed Mackenzie into the confident zone of neat total recovery, and he was looking good. She had kept him away from the madness of the Snake

Gully site to get him mentally fit and prepared for the Australia Day juggernaut.

Out in the real world, the *Dad and Dave* buzz was deafening. The media was in countdown and Maryborough was the city that never sleeps.

The Christmas and New Year holidays had turned the town upside down. Hervey Bay was booked solid. Snake Gully was all set to ride into history as the Aussie miracle that was on track to turn Disneyland into last year's tinsel on the Christmas tree.

In Hervey Bay, Dusty Rivers took in the hype for the approaching *Second Guess* television exposé, then called Natalie Forbes in Noosa.

"They're hard-selling that *Second Guess* story on television. It's all over the friggin' channel. Be a good idea to make sure Mack doesn't see it."

"I'm way ahead of you," said Natalie, 'I've made sure he doesn't know anything about anything. I don't want him interfering."

Dusty laughed. "He can interfere all he wants when he's permanently back in business. How's he doing?"

"Reading Nigella cookbooks and thinking up ways to improve the catering in the pub on opening night; harmless stuff but it's keeping him happy. How are you doing?"

"Gangbusters! Sally's moving mountains. Can I tell you something, Nat?"

"Fire away."

"That bloody plane crash wasn't all bad. It's pushed everyone into overdrive at the Gully. They're so friggin' hot to have the place at full speed for Australia Day that they're pushing boundaries, and it's all for Mack. It's fantastic; they want the opening to ring bells for him—that's everyone—everyone on the team!"

38

DECLAN MULQUEEN'S FULL-BLOWN MIRACLE

THE SPECIAL EDITION OF *SECOND CHANCE*, television's mega-hyped Current Affairs ratings champ was being pumped to feature the episode entitled, *All the Right Moves*, a detailed account of the re-conditioning of the three ethnic shooters who ran amok with bullets and guns at the Brisbane suburb of Manly on Anzac Day.

Watching the show take to air in the television studio's private viewing room, Declan Mulqueen and Robert McMahon barely moved, and breathed evenly.

Declan's training had been lengthy and full-on. He drilled, explained, drilled again, relentlessly detailing all the behaviour necessary to seduce the cameras and to be fully equipped with the business of professional interviews.

To make sure everything was fully understood, he took the role of the compere, videotaping his interviews in of one of Sydney's state-of-the-art audio-visual studios. He rehearsed his charges until everything came naturally; every question calmly answered, every accented syllable correct, every word carefully framed—*every eye movement carefully choreographed.*

Robert was his only assistant. For the period of the coaching, all five were booked into fourth-floor units in a George Street apartment building. Under Declan's instructions, the three men were prohibited from leaving the building—meals were ordered in.

The same arrangements were adhered to by Declan and Robert who sat in Declan's unit after the third week of tutoring to discuss the situation, which had suddenly been elevated to a state of urgency. Five representatives of the United Nations in New York had arrived in Australia to cast their beady eyes over the Human Rights Institute and the Mulqueen project in particular. Declan was unfazed.

"The only interest I have in the UN is that they're paying me."

"They may want to meet with you."

"Then they should have said so before."

"You won't meet with them?"

"Certainly not. Now, give me your verdict on what we've achieved, and no loose words."

"Ninety per cent positive."

"Tell me about the ten per cent."

"They're responding, they're following your directions perfectly; they're sounding good, their answers to your questions are on the button every time, but I'm not sure they're honest. It could be an act."

Declan nodded. "Clever little customers, aren't they?"

"I'd have to agree."

"Their progress since the first week—when they were trying us on, treating the training like a sandwich short of a picnic—has been easier to take."

"Does it matter if they're still trying us on?" asked Robert.

"As long as they get it right on camera, who cares? On the big night, I'll wind them up like cuckoo clocks, and let them go. I think we've killed the cat, laddie."

Robert nodded. "We've got a week to polish them—new clothes, nothing too flash, simple haircuts, and an Aussie catchphrase here and there."

Declan grinned. "How about, '*all good, matey*?"

Robert grinned. "*No sweat.* We could take them out on the town once or twice, shoot a few happy snaps with ordinary people—good stuff for the print media in the lead-up; maybe a selfie or two to flash on the show."

Declan looked confused. "Selfie?"

"A pic you take of yourself by holding the Smartphone at arm's length."

Declan shook his head. "Sounds like kids' stuff. Will it help?"

"It's idiot's delight, Declan."

Everything was on track. By the end of the week, *All the Right Moves* was ready to play on prime-time television all over the country.

Second Guess producers were so rapt they decided to give it pride of place—the top story of the night. It was promoted in the lead-up week and all through Sunday's six-p.m. news. The host/compere was Jess Davis; softly spoken; forty-nine, compassionate and feminine, but with eyes that could turn from warm to cold in a split second. Jess was no easy front person; she had undone more than a few con acts in her day. When she pulled her iron-fist-in-a-velvet-glove routine, she was the Queen of the Spiders.

On the big night, Jess's hotly anticipated interview with the three stars of the shootout was preceded by a cosy info-chat with the Human Rights Institute Regent, Jane Armitage, who came on like Julie Andrews making an Oscar speech.

She may have been the vampire from hell, but she looked calm and regal in a softly draped cream bodice and a string of pearls with matching earrings, neither of which came from Kmart. Her chestnut hair was combed into a becoming bob, and her voice was soft but assured. Jane Armitage was hardly human; she was more like an elegant robot, designed, created, and kept in her box to be taken out to make problems disappear by sprinkling them with stardust.

Jess Davis was out of her league at once. She listened respectfully to the smoothly stated Armitage pleas for leniency—*These three young men had been driven to violence because their emotionally arrested lives in the cold-hearted and soulless world they came from, had given then no chance to develop as caring human beings. They had been granted residence in Australia, but on the day of the unfortunate Manly incident, their in-bred anger and ignorance* stood in the way of their assimilation, and their tragic upbringing took over.

Her closing words were:

"*We have successfully re-made them into responsible members of the community. They are full of remorse, and they are ready to exist and progress, living beside other Australians as examples of how our natural compassion and understanding can mend broken human beings.*"

Jess Davis, the Spider Queen, was gone.

She threw to the commercial break with a tremulous voice and wet eyes. Her following interview with the three re-made Aussie citizens in the wake of the commercial break was a finely tuned performance full of integrity, sincerity and hopes for the understanding of the watching hordes on the couches of the country. The final scene of *The Razor's Edge* had nothing on this.

Jess Davis' closing words said it all, "*I think we can honestly say that we've kept our promise to give you all the right moves.*"

Declan Mulqueen had done it again. Seated beside him in the private studio of the television station, Robert McMahon cast a sideways glance in his direction, and simply remarked, "Brilliant. I'd say genius, but you'd be offended."

"I just did the job I was paid to do."

"You're a legend, Declan."

"You don't approve."

"That's beside the point."

Declan waited for a beat or two. "Are we still friends?"

"Does that matter?"

"As a matter of fact, it does."

Robert meant it when he said, "I'll miss you when you go home, mate."

"True friends are friends forever, kid."

SECOND GUESS HAD DROPPED A curly one on the approaching Australia Day opening of Snake Gully, where the collective response to *All the Right Moves* was anger and outrage; all for the off-handed way Tim Cameron had been side-swiped as a non-caring racist individual who was content to trade justice for compassion.

The emotional bubble bounced all over the place in the aftermath of the broadcast, but the lights of Snake Gully had taken to burning through the night, with teams working twenty-four-seven on eight-hour shifts in the race to make Australia Day happen.

No matter what, the race could not afford to be compromised by a controversial television show that reeked of manipulation.

Tim caught the telecast in the Centre Office where was he was putting in the long hours with Josh and Dottie Austin. Before either of them could get too over-heated, he put the brakes on. "It's a television show," he said, "we don't have time to get upset, let it go through to the keeper."

'All the same, Tim," said Josh, "you could have done without that."

Dottie waved a hand. "Everyone knows that show over-steps the mark all the time. By next Sunday they'll have another load of rubbish for everyone to get steamed up about, and we'll be another week closer to Australia Day. Let's get on with it."

THE NEXT AFTERNOON, DUSTY, HIS head filled with *Second Guess,* checked his watch. He was on call at Sally's dress rehearsal for the *Girls of the Golden West* at 4 p.m., and it was twenty minutes past noon. He knew Tim would be at the Snake Gully Office, and without making an appointment, he took the hour-long drive to the site and walked into the Centre Office. Diane Peterson was busy checking the costumes for the train-robber bushrangers and looked up.

"Wow, Dusty, this is an unexpected thrill, what can I do for you?"

He gave the costumes the once-over and said, "What's with the outfits, Di? Are we doing *The Magnificent Seven* this week?"

Diane was ready to play. "Try the magnificent four, Dusty. This stuff is for *Gigs Incorporated*, the guys playing the bushrangers." She held up a pair of super tight spray-on jeans. "What do you think?"

Dusty's smirk said it all. "It that what you call free advertising?"

Diane sighed a saucy sigh. "The cowboy who wears 'em has been practising. He pulls 'em on, then takes 'em off—slick as a whip crack—he's got the moves down to a fine art."

Dusty's smirk stayed put. "Yeah, well. I'm here to see Tim. Can do?"

"In Mack's office taking a break. He's free now but he's been flat out with Josh and Dottie all morning."

Dusty opened the door of Mack's office, walked in, and closed the door. He got straight to the point. "We've all seen that pile of bulldust that went to air last night, and we're all pissed-off. What are we going to do about it?"

"We let it fly by, Dusty."

"Just like that?"

"Why give it more attention than it deserves?"

Dusty moved to a chair, sat down, and let fly. "Look, mate, that insult last night wasn't just aimed at you, it was a backhanded slap at this theme park."

"I realise that."

"Nothing more than a follow up to Mack's fake plane crash. That rumour is still out there, and I can't get it out of my head. It's the crash you have when you don't have a crash. Mack kept that plane in top shape."

"I checked everything out with Perry Collier, one of the Army boys who are just as suspicious as you and I are."

"So, what do we do?"

"We can't do anything without proof, Dusty."

"Someone must know what happened. There's a whistle-blower somewhere."

"Whoever it is, is being protected."

"Then let's get the bastard."

"The timing's all wrong. We've got an opening coming at us at super speed and we've got to pull it off—your words, mate."

Dusty leaned forward in his chair. "I know that but look at it like this. There was a move to hit you with a racism slur, and it looks like there was another one to take Mack out, so how do we know there's not another one to take Snake Gully out?"

"I've thought about that."

"And?"

"You could be right."

"Do we just let it happen?"

"We keep our eyes peeled and the radar switched on. We've got a multi-million-dollar opening coming right at us. You, me and Josh are the drivers, and we can't be side tracked."

Dusty backed off. "Sorry for the panic attack, man, but I have this nasty feeling that our big fancy opening could be shaping up as a sitting duck."

"If so, I've got Andrew and Perry and the Security Team on stand-by. Relax and do your best to enjoy it all, mate."

DURING THE LEAD-UP THREE weeks to the opening, *Dad and Dave's* two Army boys—Andrew Denton and Perry Collier, temporarily billeted at the hotel, took turns on twelve-hour shifts, working with three four-man teams of security guys on the grounds, and three teams of three in the security office. They toured the grounds on electric buggies. In the office, video screens receiving recorded images from the outdoor security cameras were constantly monitored.

On a midnight coffee break the night after the *Second Guess* exposé, Andrew broached a subject that had been bothering him.

"One of the boys in the Bakery bar picked up some loose talk about Tim Cameron and the Anzac Day blokes on *Second Chance* last night."

Perry threw him a look. "What kind of loose talk?"

"It was hinted that Tim's supposed to be racist because he wanted those guys charged with the killing of his mother and father, and the talk picked up on it."

"That kind of talk has been around a bit, and I mentioned it to Josh."

"It worries me that we may have a troublemaker on the team. What did Josh say?"

"He said to brief the security boys and tell them to keep their sensors tuned. We should take his advice. We don't have time for some stirrer getting into everyone's ears, and we know exactly what to do if one pops up.

AT NINE-FIFTEEN A.M. ON the morning after the *Second Guess* exposé topped the national prime-time ratings, Barney Ericson landed his Cessna at the Maryborough Airport, took a cab to Kate Mallory's office in King Street, and sat with her for what he referred to as 'an urgent brief.'

He opened up. "Let's talk about the Mulqueen show last night."

Kate, alert as ever, complied. "It was a beat-up, Barney, all wrapped up in hearts and flowers, and as fake as it comes."

"Sydney radio is full of it, and the public is buying. Jane Armitage is the country's latest saint."

Kate asked her question, "Am I in trouble?"

"Has anyone from the local press called you?"

"Not yet."

"They may. Rabble-rousers in the underground have been re-activated—thanks to *Second Guess*, they'll link you to Tim Cameron's moves to victimise the wronged shooters, and because Tim is Snake Gully, they'll be trashing you as his friend, bleating for Mackenzie Forbes to be closed down, and dropping the racist card all over the place."

"Mack is recuperating at home, Barney, if there's trouble they'll have to deal with Dusty Rivers, and I don't like their chances."

Barney hit a pregnant pause, then said, "I'm here to bring your attention to the latest development; unconfirmed as yet, but the rumours are flying.

Kate waited, and Barney delivered.

"As a direct result of last night's TV win, Jane Armitage has organised for the three Anzac renegades to make a personal appearance on the campus of the Wide Bay Technical College sometime in the near future."

Kate was caught off balance. "You're kidding!"

"The Wide Bay Technical College is within spitting distance of *Dad and Dave World*, which, in my opinion, is why Armitage has arranged the visit."

A frown creased Kate's brow. "What for? Specifically?"

"I can't be specific, but the Wide Bay College, like all technical colleges, has a large component of socialist students who believe that evil capitalists like Mackenzie Forbes should not be let loose on the public with extravagant theme parks that champion the decadent lifestyles of the past. Are you following me?"

With her interest captured, Kate sat forward. "Is this Tobey Groundwater's latest time bomb?"

"It is."

"What's your take?"

Barney gave out. "Tobey is rarely wrong. At this point, we can do without any kind of interference in Wide Bay, but I don't believe it can be avoided. Whatever Armitage's motives are, they're not in the best interests of the Snake Gully theme park."

"Obviously."

"Are you aware that five representatives from the United Nations in New York jetted into the country to view, in person, the results of Declan Mulqueen's handling of the *Second Guess* exposé?"

"I am. What's happened to Mulqueen? Has he gone home with a bucket of our taxpayer dollars courtesy of Lady Armitage?"

"I don't know. Neither does Tobey."

"Will he keep you in the loop?"

"He will."

Kate shook her head. "I've been hoping that Armitage would have been satisfied with the runaway success of her *Second Guess* trump card."

"Operators like Armitage are never satisfied, Kate. That's why she's who she is and why she's where she is. I'm glad I made this trip. We've got a lot to talk about and I'm free for the rest of the day.

39

TIM AND HIS GUARDIAN ANGELS

TIM WAS BURNING THE MIDNIGHT oil. He was working impossible hours and making clear decisions—at the back of his mind, his ever-present third eye kept him tuned in to Cynthia's words:

"Ride the stars—let them take you where you're destined to go."

He was on his way home from the office for a shower and a break. When he turned into his home street in Maryborough, there it was—the yellow car parked outside his house. And again—the same warm glow took him over.

He parked his car, walked up the steps and opened the door. She was waiting, cooler than a late summer day with flowers in her hair and stars in her eyes.

She watched him walk over to her and automatically opened her arms. He walked into them and felt her lips stealing his.

"I heard you when you said you needed me," said April.

"I only said that to myself."

"That's the same as saying it to me."

"You're always here when I need you."

"This time I'm not going anywhere."

"Explain."

"I'm staying until your park is open."

"No assignments?"

"You're my assignment. I'm here to look after you."

"I'm doing okay."

"You're facing a crisis."

"Cynthia told you."

"She said to be here for you."

"Is that all she said?"

"That was enough. I'm here."

His hand found hers. "You've never really told me that you love me."

"I don't have to. They're silly words."

"Lots of people don't think so."

"Lots of people don't think."

He smiled at her. "Is it okay if I say I love you?"

"I already know. Have you ever read Robert Nathan?"

"Never."

"He wrote this in the *Portrait of Jennie*: '*Is there, perhaps, one soul among all others, among all who have lived, the endless generations from world's end to world's end, who must love us or die? Who we must love in turn, and for whom we must seek all our lives long, headlong and homesick, until the end?*'"

"That's beautiful, April."

"It's how I feel when I think about you."

"I'm flying."

"Don't ever come down, baby. Not ever."

"How can I?"

"Your Aunt Charlie said hello."

"How is she?"

"She's happy. She knows I'm looking after you."

"There's nothing to eat in this house."

"I've brought lots."

"That's nice."

"Pomegranate martinis, too."

"With cherries?"

"With cherries."

"You think of everything."

"Only important things."

"When do you want to eat?"

April leaned in and kissed him on the lips. "I don't care about eating. I want to make sure you're okay."

"I am. I'm okay."

"I'm staying around anyway."

"I've never read *The Portrait of Jennie.*"

"You should—it's all about you and me."

AFTER CHECKING WITH DOTTIE AUSTIN, the Snake Gully costume heavies, and several personal fittings with Sam Winston-Smith, Diane Petersen signed off on the bushranger costumes and sent them back to the wardrobe department with a big tick.

Dottie couldn't resist a comment, "Are you sure those jeans are not too tight?"

"They fit just fine, Dottie, and they look even better when they're on."

"I didn't know they wore them that tight in the Nineteen Thirties."

"Is that important?"

"Snake Gully is supposed to be about vintage Australia, love."

Diane flashed a wide smile. "These costumes are supposed to be about creative flexibility, Dottie."

"I suppose that clears it up."

"Wait till everyone cops Dusty on his white horse, Dottie. How hot can it get?"

Diane suddenly changed pace. "I forget to tell you. We got a request from someone at the Wide Bay Technical College."

"What for?"

"One of the teachers in their Arts Department wants to know if it's possible to arrange a student inspection of the Snake Gully Railway Station before the opening day."

"What for?"

Diane picked up an official looking sheet of A4 paper and gave it her eyes.

"This letter says it's just a bunch of wacky students on some kind of assignment about old-time Queensland train travel, like refreshment rooms and the kind of food they used to serve in railway station dining rooms."

"Sounds reasonable."

"We've got all that, Dottie, the corned beef sangers and meat pasties in our station refreshment room are to die for. These kids will be having a ball."

"I'll speak to Josh."

"We've already let a few nosey groups through, haven't we?"

"We have, yes."

"This is only a small mob," Diane explained, "like about six or eight bookworms from a boring Technical College—who'd be bothered?"

"Six or eight—is that all?"

"They're saying their prayers to hear a yes."

"Then I can't see a problem," said Dottie. "I'll get an okay from Josh. You can arrange the passes and ID tags with Andy or Perry in Security. Do you have a contact at the college?"

"Professor John Sullivan is the name on the bottom of the letter."

"I'll call him and make the necessary arrangements. The students will need passes for the car park, and they'll have to arrange their own transport from Maryborough. The train is all set, but it's booked solid, and these students will also need one of the security boys on hand to check them in."

Diane's eyes rolled. "How lucky can you get?"

"Down, Di," said Dottie. "The security boys are strictly off-limits."

"You mean for now."

41

DECLAN AND THE SECOND MOVE

IN A SEASIDE APARTMENT IN Point Vernon neighbouring north of Hervey Bay, Robert McMahon delivered, in person, an urgent request for Declan Mulqueen to extend his stay in Australia instead of returning to the United Kingdom after the success of the *Second Guess* television exposé.

Declan smiled. "Tell me, laddie, what brought this urgent request on?"

"I'm surprised you have to ask."

"I never take anything for granted."

Robert explained—as if he needed to.

"The United Nations Five were off their faces about the *Second Guess* television program. Jane Armitage is Eva Peron—you're David O. Selznick and you're being given a chance to make *Gone with the Wind 2.*"

Declan's eyes lit up. "Literally?"

"Only if you approve of the script and the concept?"

"What's the concept?"

"I have it here."

"If I approve of the concept, I'll write the script."

"Understood."

Robert opened his briefcase, extracted a folder, and offered it to Declan, who gave it the once-over and said, "I'm not in a reading mood. Tell me what it says, a brief breakdown, no longer than two minutes."

"Right. Have you ever heard of Snake Gully?"

"Yes. The name plays games with my mind. Read on, please. I can feel a boredom attack saddling up."

Robert's eyes swept over the documents. He'd already studied them closely and gave out with his interpretation of the message they contained.

It went as follows:

The three re-conditioned Anzac thugs were to visit the Wide Bay College to lecture a small group of socialist students on the evils of the *Dad and Dave* theme park. With the assistance of the college's dean, Professor John Sullivan. Declan was to devise an effective protest by the Wide Bay students against the violence of the bushranger stunt to be featured on the local television coverage of the opening event.

Declan listened closely then said, "What's the object of the exercise?"

Robert's answer, "If the protest is strong enough, the UN will have reason to negate the park's ownership and install a more responsible management."

"Is that legally possible?"

'With the assistance of a corrupt judge and an outraged public, yes."

"An outraged public—is that what you said?"

"Yes."

"How outraged, Robert?"

"That's up to you."

"Then I'm expected to come up with something sensational."

'Correct."

"Something sensational enough to seal Snake Gully's fate."

"Correct."

"I'll give it some thought."

Robert frowned. "You're considering the assignment?"

"You didn't expect me to?"

"I didn't, no."

"Never pre-judge, laddie."

"Sorry."

"Have those documents been signed by Jane Armitage?

"They have."

"Is there any mention of my fee?"

"Open-ended. Whatever you want."

"Then Mrs Armitage will expect the fee to be sensational, too."

"She will."

"I want it understood that I have the last word on everything. I want no interference from your Human Rights public servants, and none from Jane Armitage. No arguments or I refuse the assignment."

Robert, still frowning, said, "Do I understand then, that you're accepting it?"

"On acceptance of my plan, whatever it is. I want my fee in advance, and I want you on a percentage."

Robert looked straight at him. "I don't want any payment."

Declan took a deep breath. "You work for the bureaucracy, laddie. Did you choose to do that?"

"Yes."

"You've told me you think the bureaucracy is corrupt. True?"

"True."

"Yet you're shocked when the bureaucracy orders you to tell me to organise something you don't approve of."

"I reserve that right, Declan."

"Let me make it clear, laddie. When you take money for something, the money buys you, it buys you and everything that makes you who you are. If you want to be a philosopher, get another job. Do you follow?"

Robert nodded and said nothing.

Declan's next question was a curly one. "Do you want to keep working with me?"

"Yes."

"Do you trust me?"

"Yes."

"Then take the money and do something with it. Buy something for someone who really needs it. Ease your conscience by being a Good Samaritan. You'll be surprised at how good you'll feel. Now, tell me you understand."

"I guess I do, Declan."

"Guessing is not the game, Robbie. Tell me you understand."

"I understand you."

"And I understand you. We've got a job to do. Now let's put everything together. I'll need you to brief Professor John Sullivan at the Wide Bay College and I'll need you to report back on everything to Jane Armitage."

"Fine."

"One thing, and it's important. We'll need to know about any changed plans for the opening day events, especially to the bushranger stunt."

Robert nodded. "That won't be a problem."

"Are you sure about that?"

"Quite sure," said Robert.

"How so?"

"Armitage has a mole in the theme park."

42

MACKENZIE: THE BIG MAN COMES HOME

AT THE REDCLIFFE HOSPITAL. DR Bruce Moore concluded his examination of Mackenzie Forbes and gave him a green light. "You're in great shape, Mack—as good as new for a man of your age. You're back in the saddle for Australia Day."

"Thanks to you."

"I only made the rules. You did the rest."

Mackenzie drove to the Noosa Homestead with Natalie on a high. There had been times during his rehab when he'd had lingering doubts about his recovery. Bruce Moore had thrown them out the window. Sitting beside him in the car, Natalie was a new woman. Her life was back on track, and the best was on the way.

At Snake Gully, the team had brought the place to its peak, and everything was raging. Mack was back; he was out of the hospital and on his way home where he belonged.

Maryborough and Wide Bay were tingling in anticipation. A miracle was waiting to rocket them into outer space. Mackenzie walked into the Homestead, took a deep breath, flexed his muscles, and said, "It feels great to be free, Nat."

She hugged him and lingered awhile. "Did you ever think you wouldn't be?"

"A man can have doubts—sometimes when he shouldn't, but it can happen. I've never been clobbered like that before."

She released him and searched his eyes. "It's all over, Mack."

"The thing is, I still can't remember what happened; it's too hazy. I try but it doesn't happen for me. Maybe it'll never come back."

"There's someone who can bring it back. I invited him around."

"Who is it?"

"Click Roberts. He was with you in the plane."

"And he remembers?"

"So far, he's kept it to himself—Bruce's suggestion—he didn't want you confused and upset when you came out of the coma, so he asked Click not to discuss anything with you until you were fully recovered."

"When's he coming?"

"He's waiting in your study."

Mackenzie entered the study through one of the shutter doors. Click stood, flashed one of his cheeky smiles, reached out and took Mackenzie's hand.

"You're lookin' one-hundred-per cent, boss. They can never keep a good man down."

"Let's talk," said Mackenzie.

Click told it as it happened from the first snap of the engine, through the shaky flight over Bribie Island, the beginning of the descent above Deception Bay, the unbelievable near tangle with the windsurfers, the final dive into the high tide at Suttons Beach, and the incredible surfboard flotilla to safety.

Mackenzie caught on. "So that's why they left the surfboard at the hospital."

"The board that floated you to the beach, Mack."

"Well, bugger me."

Natalie took over. "The whole thing was videotaped—do you want to see it?"

The tape played through twice.

Mackenzie sat like a man in a trance. When he came out of it, he said, "First things first. I want those windsurfers found. I could have died out there. As it was, all I copped was a bash on the head and a few days in a coma. Not good enough. Not good enough."

He was on a roll. "I want those boys to have shares in Snake Gully, I'll work something out. What can a man say when his life's been saved like that? What? What does he say? Thanks for stepping in and making the effort? You're in it too, Click. I saw what you did, and I can't forget."

Click was modest for once. "What else could I do, boss?"

"That's not the question. I'm permanently in your debt."

Mackenzie turned to Natalie. "I want everything squared off. I don't want to blow trumpets or make speeches. I want payback, the kind of payback an honest man gives out when his winning cards are on the table."

He turned again to Click. "Let's shake on it."

It was done. All over. All understood.

Click flashed one of his more modest smiles, turned and left the room.

Natale took Mackenzie's arm. "Tim Cameron is waiting in the sitting room."

"Wonderful."

There was a brief exchange of greetings and Tim took the floor. "I know you're busy, but this is important. *Ultimate Events* is a US telecommunications company that specialises in covering notable happenings around the world. They've contacted me and they're very keen to cover our Australia Day opening."

"What's involved, Tim?"

"They'll send a director, two cameramen, and four technicians. The rest of the crew will be recruited in Australia. They'll use state-of-the-art digital hand-held cameras for the action shots—regular digital cameras for the rest. The footage will be edited and cut here. They want Dusty to host the finished product, which will play on selected cable networks in two thirty-minute episodes. *Ultimate Events* picks up the costs."

Mackenzie's face lost ten years. "Are you telling me this stuff will play all over the world?"

"It does, Mack, entitled *The Wizards of Oz—Dad and Dave Down Under.*"

"Will it upset any of the local television coverage?"

"There's no problem."

"Have you checked?"

"Signed off, Mack. There's no problem."

Mackenzie instantly turned into the man Tim had first met. "The crews can be billeted in the Snake Gully Hotel. There are fifty rooms available for VIPs, and the catering will be first-class. How do we confirm the deal? How do we lock it away?"

"We do everything on the Internet. They don't want to waste time."

"Then set it up—immediately, Tim."

"All done, Mack. All we need is your official okay and Dan Anderson's approval of the legal arrangements."

"Can you contact him?"

"He's been briefed, he just needs an okay from you."

"Who else knows about this?"

"Josh, Dusty, Sally, Dottie, the security boys—Andy and Perry—and that's it for now. It will soon be everywhere."

"Big is beautiful, Tim."

43

SINISTER SHADOWS ON SNAKE GULLY EVE

WITH THE SNAKE GULLY OPENING closing fast, Barney Ericson, who was on Tim's VIP invitation list as Kate's partner moved into the guest suite in Kate Mallory's Maryborough residence. The town was booked solid, so too was Hervey Bay. Kate's two girls were home for the January holidays entertaining friends.

In the early evening, the day before the big day, Barney sat on Kate's wide veranda sipping chilled white wine. Outside on the streets, Maryborough was a rowdy carnival town filled with festooned lights, *Dad and Dave* banners, and Snake Gully posters.

Kate walked onto the veranda and joined Barney who sat quietly gazing at the river and the lights on the opposite riverbank.

He didn't register her entry until she spoke. "You're too quiet, Barney. Is something on your mind?"

"I've had an update from Tobey Groundwater, my trusty mole."

"Does that boy ever sleep?"

"I don't think he ever wants to."

"What's his latest problem?"

"He's worried that the underground is too quiet on the Snake Gully opening. He expected a welter of *Second Guess* talk on the Jane Armitage front, but nothing's happening."

"What's your take on that?"

"I can't call it, Kate, but it's too quiet."

"And it's not supposed to be?"

"Tobey thinks Declan Mulqueen, Armitage's secret weapon, is still in the country."

"What does that mean?"

"He's heavy money, Kate, we know he's been bought, and he doesn't stay around for fun. He was expected to take off after his win with the *Second Guess* exposé."

"And he didn't?"

"Apparently not."

"Has Tobey heard anything about him?"

"Not a thing, and that's strange. If Mulqueen is hanging around for something, it's costing Armitage a pretty penny."

"You two are incredible, Barney—Sherlock Holmes and Dr Watson."

Barney chuckled. "Traps of the trade, Kate."

"How about—*no news is good news?*"

"Or—why spoil a lovely night?"

Kate lightened up. "My seafood man delivered some Gladstone mud crabs this afternoon, cracked, cleaned, iced and ready for the table."

"How perfect is that?"

"They're in season, Barney, and they're all ours. The girls don't like them."

Barney finally smiled. "I'm being super sensitive. Does everything seem all right to you?"

"If you're talking about the opening, the organization is amazing. Josh Forbes had the final details of the train trip sent over—it reads like a movie script. There's an American events company coming down to shoot it. That means worldwide exposure, Barney."

"You've stayed with Snake Gully all the way, Kate, and you've backed the right horse. Clever girl."

Barney was smiling but at the back of his mind, he was still worried because Tobey was worried, and Tobey was too cool to be worried about nothing.

44

THE PLOT THICKENS AND TURNS NASTY

WHILE KATE AND BARNEY WERE exchanging notes on Kate's veranda, Robert McMahon was attending a private meeting with Professor John Sullivan, in his comfortable made-over Queenslander mansion two streets away. With Robert in his briefcase were explicit details of Declan Mulqueen's spectacular plans to sabotage Snake Gully's opening event.

John Sullivan was a respectable learned citizen and a lecturer in Marxist Philosophy at the Wide Bay Technical College. At the age of thirty-seven, he was married to an attractive academic wife. They had three children, and like many other upmarket Marxists, they lived a well-heeled lifestyle.

It was the last week of January. Alma Sullivan and their children were holidaying on the Gold Coast, and John was home alone.

Pictures of Karl Marx adorned the wallpapered walls of his study, and the Marx name was on most of the books that filled the study's book shelves. The trendy College professor sat with Robert McMahon in an office that smelled of furniture polish and soft leather, and he was listening intently to what Robert was saying.

"I'm following up on your written contact with Jane Armitage. I understand you've arranged with her to be involved in a demonstration to protest against the *Dad and Dave World* opening on Australia Day."

"That's correct."

"I need to confirm that you're happy to have students enrolled in your philosophy classes at Wide Bay College taking part in the demonstration."

John Sullivan looked pleased. "I am. I see this as an opportunity to make a statement against the wanton extravagance of Mackenzie Forbes, and his decadent theme park."

"Why is that, Professor?"

"Modern Australia does not belong to the past, specifically in a commercial establishment that wantonly promotes outdated habits and customs."

"So, you think it's okay to have your students indulging in a protest to uphold these views."

"Yes, I do."

"Do the students involved share your views?"

"Yes, they do."

"You understand that as a representative of the Human Rights Institute of this country, I need to make sure that neither you nor your students have been forced to do anything against your collective will."

"Far from it, Mr McMahon. I welcome the opportunity to be involved."

"You do know that the three young men who appeared in the *Second Guess* exposé of cultural racism have been approached to be involved in this protest with your students?"

"It's why I accepted the chance to join them."

"May I ask why you're so enthusiastic?"

"In my opinion, those three young men were victimised because of the colour of their skin. Australia has to change its attitude to people like that, but there'll be no changes while people like Mackenzie Forbes are encouraged to keep the country locked in the past."

"As good a reason as any, I'd say."

"I'm glad you think so."

Robert smiled, opened his briefcase, and passed a three-page document across the desk. "Now for the boring business, Professor. I need your signature on all three pages agreeing to my associate Declan Mulqueen's strategy to upset the opening day of the Forbes theme park—merely a formality for my office files; that's if you don't mind."

"I don't mind at all."

Professor Sullivan took the papers, read through them quickly, signed both with an artistic flourish of his Mont Blanc pen, and handed them back to Robert, who folded them once, and put them in the folder on the desk in front of him.

"Thank you for that," said Robert. "You understand these forms are strictly private and will not be seen by anyone outside of the Human Rights Institute offices."

John Sullivan nodded. "Yes, I do."

Robert picked up the folder and made a move to rise.

Professor Sullivan stopped him. "May I offer you a celebration drink?"

"I only drink Tullamore Dew Irish Whiskey, Professor."

John Sullivan looked disappointed. "Oh, I'm sorry. May I offer you something else?"

"Thank you, no. I have a busy evening."

Robert thanked him again, stood and walked to the door. John Sullivan walked with him, shook his hand, watched him leave, looked at his watch and closed the door.

ROBERT COVERED THE DRIVE FROM Maryborough to Hervey Bay in just under twenty-five minutes. He parked on the beachfront at Point Vernon, got out of the car and sauntered through the narrow park to look at the still water through the trees. There was no moon, but it was a bright starry night, and he thought how beautiful and fresh it all looked. Ten minutes later he was still standing there.

Declan Mulqueen had kept his promise to him. The fee for his latest escapade had been pre-paid in full, and Robert's bank account was fat enough to maintain the luxuries of an extravagant lifestyle for some time.

He tried to think of nothing, but it didn't work. His brain was racing, and he knew he wouldn't sleep. The job he'd been instructed to carry out should have been over. It wasn't, and it wouldn't be over until midnight on Australia Day; maybe not even then. As he turned to walk back to his car, a smile crossed his lips and he heard himself say, "Whatever else you are, Declan, you're never boring."

THE ARMITAGE MOLE COMES OUT OF THE DARK

SAM WINSTON-SMITH RODE THE short distance from the Brolga Guest House to Professor John Sullivan's mansion, three streets away, on a bicycle. He alighted, propped the bike against the neat paling fence, walked up the path and rang the bell.

John Sullivan opened the door immediately, admitted Sam and ushered him into the study. They sat facing each other across the polished desk.

Sam spoke first. "Has the Human Rights man met with you yet?

"He's just left."

"Is everything sorted?"

"To our financial and moral advantage."

Sam looked pleased. "We need to go over the strategy that's been worked out by the Irish hotshot that pulled off that *Second Guess* exposé. He's a friggin' genius. You've read and understood the detailed outline of the Irishman's plan I sent over."

"Three times," said Sullivan. "Is everything under control at the theme park?"

"Sweet as."

"Your *Gigs Incorporated* boys haven't twigged to anything?"

"When the shit hits the fan, they'll be as surprised as everyone else. Have you worded your students?"

"My team will be five students plus the three Anzac men in vintage thirties attire. They'll all appear to be students of the college as directed."

"Perfect," said Sam, "that adds up to security passes for eight, right?"

"They've already been sent over. My team will travel to Snake Gully on the official College bus and mingle with the crowd on the station platform."

Sam nodded and outlined the next step. "The night before the opening, I'll go to the Maryborough train station with one of the theme park security boys to set up the baggage carriage of the Snake Gully Express for the bushranger stunt. I will load the four prop gold bullion bags into the carriage—inside one of them will be three Smith & Wesson pistols and one box of one-hundred-and-fifty-rounds of 22 TCM live cartridges for the Anzac boys. That bag will be marked. Inside the three unmarked bags will be the pistols and blank cartridges for your students.

Sullivan frowned. "How will you manage to conceal the live cartridges?"

Sam's smile was a mile wide. "I'm in charge of the operation. It's my gig."

"What if the security man checks?"

"Why would he? I'm the trusted leader of *Gigs Incorporated*—I've been rehearsing my boys on site every day for three weeks. I'm part of the Snake Gully team, fella."

"Nobody's guessed that you're a Jane Armitage plant?"

"Of course not. I'm a certified professional stunt man."

Sullivan nodded. "Tell me what happens at the station on the big day."

"Okay . . . I'll walk you through it, listen carefully."

Sam explained:

"The band will start up as soon as the train enters the park to approach the station. There will be cheers and whistles from the crowd—flags will wave. The crowd on the platform; made up of actors dressed as Snake Gully towns people, will clap and cheer.

"When the train stops at the station, my masked *Gigs Incorporated* bushrangers will ride up the platform ramp shooting blanks. They will hold up the guards in the leading baggage carriage and open the doors to get at the fake gold in the bullion bags.

"Your five students, together with the Anzac shooters will break out of the crowd on the platform in an effort to foil the bushrangers. The five students will grab the pistols from the unmarked bullion bags, load them with blank cartridges and start firing at the bushrangers.

"At the same time, the Anzac boys will load the pistols in the marked bullion bag with the live cartridges I've planted there and pretend to back up the five students.

"My *Gigs Incorporated* boys and your students, still firing blanks at each other, will provide perfect cover for the Anzac boys, who will then be firing live cartridges at the VIP carriage and its guests.

Sam paused a moment. "So much will be happening that no one will know what's going on. Actors have been primed to pretend being shot—who'll know if a live cartridge hits someone in the VIP carriage? At some point, someone will discover that real cartridges are being fired and confusion will take over.

"This is when Sheriff Dusty Rivers provides further confusion by riding in on his white horse twirling his lasso at the bushrangers, who will realise the gig's up when they start dramatically dropping like wounded flies.

"In the VIP carriage will be a nest of important people— Kate Mallory, Josh Forbes, Tim Cameron, Sally Temple, Western Ridge Mining Company heavies and their wives, plus high-profile politicians and media celebrities."

Sullivan shook his head. "If any of them are hit it will be a major catastrophe."

Sam's face hardened up. "Exactly. The Irishman's brief is to make a serious statement that will be covered on live television and prove to be sensational enough to lay the blame at Mackenzie Forbes's feet, close Snake Gully and put it in the hands of the UN when the furore dies down."

"Questions will be asked," said Sullivan. "There'll be an inquiry. How will that be handled?"

"Who will know who fired the live cartridges? My boys will be firing blanks, so will your students."

"What about fingerprints?"

"The Irishman is no dummy. Everyone will be wearing leather gloves. It's in the brief. No fingerprints on any of the weapons. Nobody will know where the live cartridges came from. I pretended to stash blanks into the bullion bags under security supervision the night before. Where did the live bullets come from? That Irish mastermind knows his onions. His plan has win-win written all over it. Once Jane Armitage's cronies get involved, the coverups will take over. The shoot-up will be the work of '*unknown activists*' and Forbes will be blamed for not taking precautions. Start buying the booze, Professor."

Sullivan rose from his chair. "Why wait? How about a drink right now?"

"A short one only, pal. Then I'm off home to screw half the night away."

"Only half the night?"

"She never stays for breakfast."

"Lucky man."

46

LADIES WHO PARTY

AMONG THE FORBES AUSTRALIA DAY VIPs were the Western Mining CEO Mal Chambers and his wife, Maxine, who had taken up residence in their holiday retreat at Hervey Bay's Point Vernon in readiness for the big event. Their house guests were the prominent legal identity, Geoffrey Barkley, and his wife Jennifer, who were also on the Australia Day VIP list. On the day before the event, while Mal and Geoffrey were chasing little white balls around the greens at the Hervey Bay Golf Club just down the road, the girls were spending the afternoon sipping Louis Roederer champagne in the glassed-in conservatory of the impressive Chambers holiday house.

"I've no idea why we were invited to this thing," said Jennifer, "I thought Geoffrey was in the Forbes bad books after that legal mess-up with Tim Cameron and the Army."

Maxine waved her glass. "The Australia Day opening is hardly a 'thing,' Jen. In fact, it's the showcase of the year. Everyone who's anyone will be there."

"Apparently."

"This part of the world has been completely reinvented, and as for your invitation, Mackenzie Forbes is nobody's fool. He's aware of Geoffrey's standing in the community, and you'll both have a wonderful time. Have you studied your invitation in detail?"

"Not really. It went to Geoffrey's office."

"Maryborough will start celebrating at eight a.m. tomorrow. Throughout the day, there's a street festival, a flotilla on the river, a carnival in the showgrounds and community happenings everywhere. The Snake Gully opening will officially begin at four p.m. when the train leaves the Maryborough station, and the big night will run until one a.m. the next day. Apart from the train's ticket winners, there will be another two thousand invited guests arriving by road."

Jennifer sat up to hear more.

"Everything will be spectacle and lights. Snake Gully will be Fantasyland—food, champagne, beer, Sally Temple's stage show, *The Girls of the Golden West*, and a gourmet dinner on the main street.

"It's all glamour-plus, honey. We're on board the Snake Gully Express and we're in the VIP carriage with fifty glittery guests. A champagne buffet stretches across the centre of the carriage, and we're seated in the front section with Snake Gully executives—Josh Forbes and Tim Cameron, plus Kate Mallory, Barney Ericson and several showbusiness and celebrities . . . there's only one downer."

"Like what?" asked Jennifer

"Jane Armitage and her Human Rights cohorts will be among the guests in the second section of our carriage," said Maxine. "Harry Broadchurch and his wife will be there, too."

Jennifer frowned. "Why would Mackenzie Forbes bother with any of them? They've been nothing but critical of him and everything he's doing."

"I suppose he's simply turning the other cheek."

"It still doesn't make sense—it's only encouraging more of their criticism, isn't it?

"Who cares? We won't have to mix with them. We'll simply pretend they're not there."

THE MID-SUMMER SUN WARMED up around eight a.m. on the morning of Australia Day. Instead of the usual late January burn, the day stayed on the right side of pleasant. Not that it mattered. By mid-morning, Maryborough was in party mode. Flags fluttered in a light breeze, decorated yachts and small craft showed off on the river, kids in fancy dress zipped around on scooters and bikes, and eager folks lined the main street to ogle and yell at the sights in the festival parade.

They included marching girls in cheeky skirts, caps and boots, the resident pipe band in swinging kilts, the Army band blowing trumpets and banging drums, and a collection of colourful old-time floats with flappers in Roaring Twenties gear, guys in boaters and striped blazers, and a mock-up of the *Dad and Dave* cottage on the fictitious Snake Gully farm on the Darling Downs.

Highlight of the parade: Mackenzie and Natalie seated high on the back seat of a red and white 1950 FJ Holden convertible followed by Dusty and Sally Rivers on the back seat of a green 1950 Topless Holden. Streamers flew, flags waved, and the band played "Waltzing Matilda." How Aussie can you get!

At the Maryborough Railway Station, the spiffy made-over thirties steam engine, all black-satin shine, and the polished veneer encased carriages of the Snake Gully Express, waited in the sun. The steam engine puffed impatiently, with its three spiffy uniformed guards and two drivers eager to get going.

At Snake Gully, everything in the little town was dressed for the big night.

The streets were festooned with lights, coloured spots were ready to zap the hotel, the picture theatre, the fine diner, and the Bakery Bar. Tens of thousands of fairy lights waited to come alive around the Waterside pool, and the spotlights on the butter factory would soon shine brightly. The Snake Gully Band warmed up in a rotunda close to the railway station, and the town's Puffing Billy train with its open carriages was ready for the first of its sticky-beak tours of the town's goodies.

It was heartbeat stuff—perfect foreplay for what was about to happen.

The Security Team was set, and the costumed Snake Gully Police Force, channelling the old-time street coppers of early Sydney, twirled their batons and relaxed in the shade.

The *Ultimate Events* camera crew had been on the spot for two days, whizzing about in buggies, talking camera-crew talk, checking camera angles and adding to the Steven Spielberg buzz. A feeling of breathless anticipation hung over Snake Gully. Midday came and went, and as zero hour approached, the *Dad and Dave* giant stirred, stretched its muscles, and prepared to show its face to Wide Bay and the World.

AT THREE-FORTY-FIVE P.M. the eight-student team from Wide Bay Technical College met in the college parking lot to board the minibus. The five students, in thirties wardrobes, were chirpy and eager; the three Anzac studs in similar wardrobes looked almost normal. Professor John Sullivan boarded the bus to give his charges a final briefing. "Good luck, boys, do what you have to do and make your college proud. Do it for the future of your country." He patted the shoulder of the driver, left the bus, and watched it drive off.

ON THE ROAD FROM HERVEY BAY, Mal and Maxine Chambers with Geoffrey and Jennifer Barkley, resplendent in designer finery, were riding smoothly in Mal's Mercedes-

Benz. They drove through the festive river city to the Maryborough Train Station and boarded the VIP carriage of the Snake Gully Express. Tim Cameron and Josh Forbes welcomed them aboard, where they were joined by Sally Temple, Natalie Forbes, Bernie Ericson, Kate Mallory and her two daughters. *Posh was the word!*

Already on board were the *Second Guess* team, the press and television journalists with their camera crews, and ten costumed actors who mingled with the crowd. Click Roberts decked out as one of the infamous Kelly Gang was hopping about, ready to immortalise the virgin train ride in still-life action shots.

Maxine's eyes swept across the opposite compartment of the VIP carriage and winced when she caught a glimpse of Jane Armitage in conversation with Harold Broadchurch. The VIP carriage buffet was open, the champagne was chilled, and the company was cheery and bright. Who needed Jane Armitage?

Three-hundred-and-fifty prize-winning guests on the Maryborough Train Station platform were a colourfully wardrobed crowd, all in fancy dress. When the guard blew the boarding whistle, they moved to their seats in the passenger carriages and settled in.

At 4:00 p.m. on the dot, the whistle of the Snake Gully Express gave three sharp blasts. The train and its carriages rolled slowly away from the Maryborough platform, and the thirty-minute journey began with carriage flags and ribbons fluttering, and the prize-winning passengers hanging out of windows yelling at partying people on the street.

The road beside the train line was carrying heavy traffic. Included in the cars and buses was the Wide Bay Technical College minibus; on time and travelling well.

ON THE PLATFORM OF THE Snake Gully station, the band was setting up.

Andrew Denton and Perry Collier, together with a crowd of special guests and actors were preparing for the bushranger stunt. Close to the platform's ramp entrance, Sam Winston-

Smith and the *Gigs Incorporated* boys stood by to mount their horses. Several metres away, Dusty Rivers waited beside his white horse and checked his trick lasso.

As 4:30 p.m. approached, the distant whistle of the Snake Gully Express signalled its imminent arrival. Minutes later, Express train smoke rose above the trees in the near distance. The chuffing of its vintage engine and the sounds of its wheels on the rails grew louder. Snake Gully held its breath.

The Wide Bay Technical College minibus drove through the Security Gate near the train station, and its eight-student cargo piled out, flashed their lanyards at the security guards and raced up the ramp to join the actors and the crowd of pass holders on the platform.

On a riser at the rear of the station ramp, the band hit the opening chords of "Along the Road to Gundagai," and a flight of white doves took to the air, wheeling over the cheering crowd. At the same time, the vintage steam engine of the Snake Gully Express, belching steam and smoke, *choofed* into the park about one hundred kms away from the station, and slowly approached the platform. The crowd roared!

Onboard, the special guests in the VIP carriage watched through the carriage windows as the station's refreshment room doors and the vintage architecture of the platform glided past outside. The engine driver hit the brakes; the engine blew out a last gasp of fragrant steam and the train came to a halt.

Right on cue at the bottom of the ramp, the *Gigs Incorporated* bushrangers gave their mounts a gentle boot and took off yelping and yelling like the Kelly Gang on the warpath and rode up the ramp to the platform. They dismounted, headed for the doors of the baggage carriage, wrenched them open, attacked the two guards, grabbed the bullion bags, and tossed them onto the platform. The crowd on the platform, reacting in alarm as directed, went wild.

Brief moments later the five Wide Bay students broke out of the crowd on the platform and moved towards the bullion bags, reaching inside for the pistols, quickly loaded the blank cartridges to pump shots at the bushrangers. It was looking good, and the crowd was whooping it up. 'Wounded' actors, overdoing it like crazy, were dropping all over the place with the *Ultimate Event* cameras recording everything.

While the staged madness accelerated, the three Anzac thugs, under cover of the Wide Bay students, dived for the marked bullion bag, put the grab on the three pistols inside, loaded up, and elbowed through the crowd to move, freely firing, to the open doors of the VIP carriage.

Inside the carriage, Josh and Tim, in company with four of the actors, suddenly came to life, startling the guests with desperate shouts.

"Hit the floor! Everyone on the floor! Do it now! This is for real! Hit the floor!" Believing they were part of the stunt, everyone obeyed, taking glasses, champagne bottles and food platters with them. Outside, the fury was looking anything but fake.

The Wide Bay students, shooting blanks, covered the Anzac thugs who were closing on the VIP carriage. Everything was going exactly to Declan Mulqueen's plan.

Then, at the height of the chaos, a team of fifteen-armed security guards led by Andrew Denton and Lance Collier swarmed out of the refreshment room and charged through the crowd to hold off the Wide Bay students and the three Anzac thugs. Andrew put an arm lock on the Anzac leader, whipped the hot pistol out his hand, tossed it away, pulled him into the refreshment room, and said, "We've met before, mate. You got away with it in the courtroom, but you're all out of luck today."

In the VIP carriage, Harry Broadchurch saw Andrew's move and clutched at Jane Armitage. "This is all wrong, Jane. This is not how it was supposed to happen! What are your Anzac shooters doing here? They're not supposed to be a part of all this. It's wrong; it's all wrong, and the cameras are catching it all!"

Watching everything in a state of shock, Jane Armitage just shook her head in disbelief. Out on the platform, the crowd had swollen in numbers when the ticket holders from the passenger carriages surged into the action.

Dusty's gallant arrival on his white horse, twirling his lasso with practised dexterity, to put the bewildered *Gigs Incorporated* bushrangers on hold, sent the stunt's success worldwide via the *Ultimate Events* cameras and seeded his return to the film business. Beaming as he held Sam Winston-Smith captive while the mob cheered and yelled, Dusty's words were delivered into Sam's ear.

"I've got ya, old mate. They're gonna have you knackered for years for your part in this gig. You're done for, pal, and so are your Anzac Day thugs. It's all over buddy, sorry to spoil it all but crap happens to the best of us!"

The crowd went wild, and the band played on.

BUT APART FROM DUSTY, JOSH, *Tim, Andrew and Perry, nobody knew that the Australia Day bushranger gig had been set up to deal Mackenzie and his theme park out of the equation, and it was odds-on that nobody else would ever know.*

THE DAY WENT ON TO become Mackenzie's Everest—his greatest moment.

48

SNAKE GULLY OWNS THE TELEVISION NEWS

IT WAS SEVEN P.M. AND the National Television News Bulletins had just ended. The coverage of the official *Dad and Dave World Opening* wore the label as '*The most unforgettable Australia Day in history.*' Superlatives drenched the screen.

Mackenzie Forbes was Australia's Miracle Man. His theme park had given the country its yesterdays back in an extravagance of must-see attractions and must-do experiences for a clutch of celebrities and VIPs in big business, the media, members of the Wide Bay and Maryborough political establishments, and hundreds of lucky prize-winning voters.

Slight mention was given to a disturbing incident that occurred during the staging of the wild stunt that involved a team of bushrangers robbing the vintage Snake Gully Express when it arrived at its destination.

According to Australian movie star Dusty Rivers, who was involved in the stunt, there were indications that the special Smith and Wesson pistols used by some of the actors were loaded with live cartridges instead of blanks. This was not confirmed by Human Rights Institute executive, Jane Armitage, who was a passenger on the train.

Her official explanation on camera was that the thin timber panelling on the train's carriages was shattered by blank cartridges fired at close range, and not by live cartridges, as suggested by a few people close to the action on the platform.

"It sure smelled like live stuff," said one of the actors, but hey, nobody got hurt, did they?"

Mackenzie Forbes's comment was:

"The bushranger robbery was carefully researched and planned as a spectacular action-filled stunt, which is what it turned out to be; a phenomenally successful and safe show that fulfilled its purpose. No one was injured and it added greatly to the official opening's success."

That's what went to air.

It was a different story in the Snake Gully Administration Office, where Tim met with Mackenzie Forbes in private in the immediate wake of the stunt, to explain what had gone down.

"This morning, Declan Mulqueen sent word to me via his assistant Robert McMahon that the bushranger gig was a setup to cover a violent shoot out with live bullets to wreck the opening ceremony."

Mackenzie stared at him. "So, who planned the setup?"

"Mulqueen himself."

"Hold on here, son. If he set the bloody thing up, why did he warn you?"

"McMahon explained that Mulqueen had decided to change the brief at the last minute."

"Just like that?"

"Exactly like that."

"Who else was involved in the plot?"

Tim gave Mackenzie all the details: Sam Winston-Smith's link to John Sullivan, the Wide Bay students and the tricks with the bullion bags and live cartridges.

Tim went on: "Mulqueen purposely added the Anzac shooters as the clincher that tied the Human Rights Institute to the whole operation."

Mackenzie was honestly dumbfounded. "I don't get it!"

"Declan pulled the pin on Armitage and the Institute, Mack. That's what happened."

"Why would he have done that?"

"I don't have answers, and I didn't ask questions. I took McMahon's warning seriously and alerted Josh and Dusty.

They got Andrew and Perry to round up the security boys—
and we were ready to take care of everything."

"What about the rumoured live bullets? They could have
done real damage."

"There were no live bullets in the bullion bags. I had
them replaced with blanks at the Maryborough Station. The
Anzac thugs didn't know that, they thought they were firing
live cartridges, which was the original intention."

"Can you prove that?"

"Robert McMahon can prove it. It's all in his brief."

"Jesus Christ!" said Mack. "We'd have been finished! I'd
still be interested to know why this bloody big-time spin
doctor suddenly grew a conscience, and I'd like to talk to him
if he's still around."

"He's gone, Mack. He waited to make sure everything
was okay, then he and McMahon took off."

"That's it? They just took off?"

"Not before McMahon handed over the documented
evidence of John Sullivan's agreement to the involvement in
the bushranger stunt."

"Do you have this evidence?"

Tim handed the folder over. "It's all there, all of it, signed
and sealed."

"Okay! Let Armitage talk her way out of this. We've got
her on toast, boy. She's waiting in my office now. This is going
to be good! "

JANE ARMITAGE SAT OPPOSITE MACKENZIE at his desk. He
had the floor.

"It's all over, Mrs Armitage. Your three whitewashed
troublemakers have been caught red-handed and they deserve
everything that's coming to them."

Armitage's calm was all insolence. "I know nothing about
their part in anything, and neither does anyone in my employ
in the Institute. I agree it's been unfortunate, but you'll have
to lay the blame somewhere else."

"You had nothing to do with it?"

The response was decisive and arrogant. "I did not, and you'd be hard-pressed to connect me with anything that's happened, Mr Mackenzie."

He let that pass, waited a moment, then continued, "I'm finished with the fairy tales, I think it's time to get into the raw truth of the matter, which is anything but a fairy tale."

Armitage gave out with her best cynical smirk. "Do your best, Mr Forbes."

Mackenzie held her with a stern gaze. "Before we go any further, there's something I'd like you to see." He picked up the folder Tim had given him, unfolded the pages it contained and handed them to her.

"These papers were presented to Professor John Sullivan at the Wide Bay Technical College by Robert McMahon, a qualified representative of your Human Rights Institute. Professor Sullivan agreed to their contents and signed them."

Jane Armitage examined the papers closely and looked up. "I know nothing about these arrangements."

"Come now, Mrs Armitage, those documents were presented to Professor John Sullivan by Robert McMahon, a senior member of your team. He would never have acted without your permission. In fact, if you look more closely at this evidence, you'll notice that you authorized him to act for you. You gave him permission to brief Declan Mulqueen, the spin doctor you employed to coach the three men interviewed on the *Second Guess*, television program. You then gave Mulqueen carte blanch to do what he could to upset the opening day of my theme park, and you also directed him to brief the activists from the Wide Bay College who were involved in the stunt. It's all there, Mrs Armitage."

She was crumbling. "There's been a mistake. I told Mulqueen to use discretion."

"Carte blanch is what it says. These papers have your name all over them. Now here is something you were not meant to know. Tim Cameron, my marketing executive was alerted to the arrangements agreed to by Professor Sullivan this morning. Tim took immediate action to prevent any mishandling of the bushranger stunt as detailed on the pages you're holding. He removed live cartridges in the bullion bags that were intended to be fired at the VIP carriage by your terrorist stooges and substituted harmless blanks."

After a heavy pause, he said, "Shall I go on?"

Armitage was flustered and suddenly speechless.

Mackenzie wasn't finished. "I invited you and your cohorts to be guests on the Snake Gully Express today in good faith, but you and your Institute took untold liberties to discredit me and my theme park, and you did it in cooperation with the United Nations and its paid bureaucratic bullies in this country."

"That's ridiculous." It was a weak try.

"Dusty Rivers, my executive assistant, has also uncovered evidence that links your friends in the bureaucracy to the crash of my private plane in the water off Suttons Beach on the Redcliffe Peninsula."

She was still trying. "I know nothing about that."

"Next you'll be telling me that you didn't manipulate the court case that dismissed the charges against your supposedly reconditioned ethnic killers."

Stunned silence. Mackenzie kept coming:

"You did that by following the UN's ruling to compromise Harry Broadchurch by going public with a rumour that ties him to his alleged habit of messing with little boys if he didn't do as he was told."

Silence again from the flustered victim.

"Deny all or any of this until the cows come home," said Mackenzie. "Harry Broadchurch is in another office being grilled by Dusty and my son, and he'll be well on the way to singing like a canary about the dirty goings-on in your dodgy Human Rights Institute."

Jane Armitage was dead meat, and she knew it. She sat in her chair in emotional shreds.

Mackenzie stood and glared at her. "This is not finished, not by any stretch. I haven't decided how far I'm going to take it, but it won't be an easy ride for you, and certainly not for your bureaucratic bullies. I'm coming after you from a position of strength, and I'll act for the good of this country. That's all I have to say. I have a driver waiting to take you to the Maryborough airport. You and your accomplices will be flown to Brisbane on a charter aircraft. You can make your own way from there. Now do me a big favour, Mrs Armitage, remove yourself and your corrupt butt from my office. You'll be personally escorted to the Snake Gully minibus for the trip to the airport. It's the best I can do on short notice. Have a safe trip."

49

ROBERT MCMAHON SAT QUIETLY STARING at the sea from the balcony terrace of Declan Mulqueen's rented unit. It was seven p.m. and the National News Bulletin had just ended. Declan, seated close to Robert, had quietly taken it all in. On the table beside him sat an open bottle of Tullamore Dew Irish Whiskey.

The quiet mood was broken when Declan said, "Cat got your tongue, Robbie?"

"What does a man say to the ultimate event architect?"

"I was simply doing my job."

"Not the one you were paid to do."

"You don't approve?"

"You're trawling for compliments, Declan. I'm warm all over."

"And it's not the Tullamore Dew?"

"It isn't, and you know it isn't."

"Those three offensive louts bought their own Karma. It was my job to see that it was delivered."

"I agree that it was."

"They had a chance to prove their worth, but it wasn't in them. In spite of how I made them look, they were bad through and through. They cheated and lied and brushed aside the chances I gave them."

Robert nodded. "Too true."

"They tested me and expected to get away with it."

Robert smiled. "Big mistake."

"You don't do that to a man who lives by a code of honour."

"They sure found that out."

"You were part of it, Robbie—which is why you alerted the Cameron boy."

"Exactly what you expected me to do."

"It was your choice—the only one a worthy young man of honour could make."

"You're playing with words again."

"You don't regret what we did?"

"I'll never regret it."

"We acted as one, laddie."

"We did and they're finished," said Robert.

"They're not the only ones."

"You made sure we got them all."

"Why play favourites?"

"I'm finished, too," said Robert, "I'm quitting the Institute."

"I thought you might."

"I've applied for a job at *Dad and Dave World*."

Declan smiled. "You'll be an asset. That place deserves you."

Robert poured some of the Tullamore Dew into his glass, took a decent mouthful, and gave Declan a questioning look. "I need to ask you something."

Declan smiled. "Is that why you just refuelled."

"Yes."

"You want to know why Tim Cameron's cause was so important to me—is that it?"

"He wasn't just a boy who lost his mother and father, was he? There was something about him, something that drove you to put things right."

"You're very perceptive."

"It's impossible to work with you and not be."

Declan rose from his chair, gazed out at the fading twilight, and started speaking.

"In the early August of 1915, my father's father landed on the beach at Suvla Bay on the eastern seaboard of the Gallipoli Peninsula with the Fourteenth Irish Fusiliers. In the course of the battle, he was crippled by two bullets in his thigh but managed to pull himself up to the dry Salt Lake behind the beach. He had no water, no medication, nothing to stop the blood. He was lost, alone and hopeless—ready to meet his maker. After five hours in the hot sun, he was found by an enlisted man who gave him water, dressed, and bound his wound with leggings from his boots, and half carried him through the smoke and fire to the casualty tent at Anzac Cove, five miles away. The man signed him in and left him to be picked up by a transfer boat to be taken to a hospital ship near the Greek Islands."

Declan took a pull on the whiskey. "He recovered, came home and tried for years to find out who saved him, but he died without knowing. Not long ago, in a document that sat for years in the vintage files of the Irish Fusiliers, my grandfather's arrival at Anzac Cove was noted, and so was the name of the man who signed him in."

Declan reached into his jacket pocket and extracted a sheet of folded notepaper, opened it, and handed it to Robert.

On it was written the name *Lance Corporal Timothy E Cameron, 321 2nd Division, Australian Infantry.*

Robert looked up at him. "Tim Cameron's great-grandfather?"

"I checked."

"Are you going to tell Tim about this?"

"I'm not; neither are you."

"How long have you known?"

"All the time."

"All the time?"

"Can I trust you to keep that to yourself?"

"You have my word."

"You're a good lad, Robbie."

"You've made me a better man, Declan."

"My father and grandfather are both in the arms of heaven, and I know that the Cliffs of Mohr are smiling. I'm going home happy." With that, he clicked his heels and said, "And there's no place like home."

Robert smiled, "Like Dorothy in The Wizard of Oz?"

"Indeed. After all the fire and smoke and rowdy deception, it's good to know that the Wizard could still play one of his cleverest tricks."

Declan turned to look again at the sea, and in a sweet soft voice that didn't sound like him at all, Robert heard him say, "Home is the sailor, home from the sea, and the hunter home from the hill."

50

APRIL HADN'T ATTENDED THE AUSTRALIA Day Event on purpose. She knew Tim would need to be busy and didn't want to get in the way. When he arrived home at 10:30, she expected him to be exhausted. He wasn't. She had seen the news bulletins and she heard the full story of what had happened. She sat quietly when he called Cynthia Del Largo on her private line.

"It all came true, Cynthia—the Karma. It happened as you promised."

"Are you happy?"

"I'm free."

"It didn't just happen for you. Your theme park is free to exist because of what you gave it. You've helped give it a life to share with everyone who visits it. You've done well."

"You showed me how."

"You rode the stars, Tim."

"You made sure I did."

"All I did was open a door."

"One that will never close."

"Have a wonderful life."

Cynthia ended the call.

Tim took April in his arms, and said, "Where can I get a copy of the *Portrait of Jennie?*"

51

KATE MALLORY'S VERANDA: THE NEXT AFTERNOON

IT WAS A BRIGHT SUNNY day. Maryborough was still on holiday and would be for the remainder of the week. Kate, unable to relax, was standing on the veranda idly hosing the hydrangeas in the garden blow. Barney Ericson, mobile phone pressed to his ear, was pacing up and down listening to his well-informed mole, Tobey Groundwater. Kate's two girls were partying somewhere in town.

The big news was that *Dad and Dave World* was capacity-booked for weeks in the daytime, and for longer hours at night with the Snake Gully Express running non-stop shifts to the site and back. Maryborough was in full bloom. Hervey Bay was running hot.

Kate heard Barney's sign off on the phone, watched him return it to its holder, turned off the hose and waited to hear Tobey's latest bulletin.

Barney served it up on bright notes.

"The Wide Bay Technical College business is under control and off your agenda. It will continue to operate as a college under new administration with newly appointed staff. John Sullivan will lose everything. He's been arrested and charged with involvement in a terrorist plot. His renegade students have been expelled and they'll be similarly charged. Their weak defence was that they were recruited by the Human Rights Institute."

"Barney wasn't finished: "Jane Armitage has been relieved of her position. Her board has been sacked and the bureaucrats on her advisory panel have been told to resign. Armitage was handed an overseas appointment as a 'top level' assistant to the Australian Ambassador in Paris. The appointment was instant, a nothing move that got her out of the way. She was advised to make no statements to the media. Her connections in the UN in New York were told she'd been moved on to a more responsible international job. Her treatment is low-key, the reason being that the voting public doesn't need to be informed about what's been going on in certain sections of the bureaucracy. The government itself is extremely vulnerable at the moment."

Kate's question: "What's happening about the three Anzac shooters?"

"Arrested, in custody and charged, and there's no Harry Broadchurch to save them."

Kate nodded. "What goes around comes around. Tim Cameron can rest easy at last."

"There'll be a lot of changes in the government, and the Sutton's Beach crash is being investigated. There's not much anyone can do because the plane was sold for scrap the day after the accident, but top-level people are running for cover all over the place."

"Where's all that going to end?

"Mackenzie will let it slide. What's the point of stirring it up? He's holding a winning hand, so is Dusty Rivers. Western Mining is going ahead with the new *Outback Jackaroo* production. Sally Temple is writing it as a six-part series for one of the cable networks. The first episode features the Australia Day bushranger footage that *Ultimate Events* filmed—great publicity for Snake Gully. Josh Forbes is the Executive Producer. Snake Gully will never die while that kid's alive. It's looking good for you too, Kate. You've got Wide Bay in your pocket, exactly where it belongs."

Kate smiled an easy smile. "How about a drink?"

"A little early, isn't it? The sun's still up."

"Not for long. I've got two bottles of Moët & Chandon someone gave me for Christmas. By the time we open the second one, it'll be dark."

"You talked me into it, Kate."

"One query, Barney, when do I get to meet Tobey Groundwater?"

52

TIM STOOD ALONE AT THE entrance to Richard Russell Park in Manly. The small green triangle, shaded by trees, dressed in shrubs and pretty gardens, was fresh and calm in the early morning light. Seated in a car parked nearby in the shade, Charlie Cameron watched and waited while her nephew spent time with his memories.

Charlie didn't want to intrude, she never did, but she knew what he was thinking and feeling. Minutes passed, and Tim didn't move. She looked closely at him; at his firm young body, his manly shoulders and at the proud framework of him that held him so perfectly still.

Charlie knew the Camerons, she'd married one, she had admired Tim's father, a man who stood tall in her eyes, a family man and a loving husband. It was all gone now. Mary and Jack were at peace. Karma had evened the score.

But the seaside suburb of Manly that Tim had known and loved was not for him anymore; there was too much sadness; too many yesterdays, too many memories and too much longing for what had once been.

Tim turned away, finally, walked to the car, opened the door, and got in. Charlie waited for him to speak. When he did, he was clear and decisive.

"I'm going back to London, Charlie, I need to be free, and I can't be free here."

She nodded. "If that's how it is with you, then do what you must."

"If I stay, I'll always be the man who lost his mother and father to the bullets of that Anzac morning. It will never change. I love Snake Gully, there's so much of me in it, and I'm proud to have helped make it what is it, but now that everything has turned out right, I have to let it go. I can't let my shadow fall over it."

After a considerable pause, Charlie said, "Are you sure about this?"

"There's bound to be a backlash, there are people who will make trouble and take it out on the theme park if I'm still there. I have no choice. I have to make the move. I can't be Kit Walker anymore."

"What will you do about April?"

"She's coming with me. She's not the past. She's part of what I am now, and I can't live anywhere without her."

Charlie turned the key in the ignition and started the car. She didn't need to say anything. Sitting beside her, Tim took a last look at Richard Russell Park and said a silent goodbye to his parents and his past.

"Thanks forever, Charlie, thanks for everything you've given me—and I'll never forget you for giving April to me."

WAY UP IN THE MONTVILLE Rainforest, Enid Avery put the tray containing a pot of freshly brewed peppermint tea and a bone china cup on Cynthia Del Largo's polished desk, and said, "April Dawn called to say goodbye. You were busy but she's calling back."

"Lovely."

"Where's she going?"

"To London, Enid."

"With the Kit Walker boy?"

"His name is Tim Cameron."

"I'll always think of him as Kit Walker."

"You liked him, didn't you?"

"Yes, yes I did. So did you."

"He's an exceptional young man. He thought he'd grown a third eye, but it wasn't that at all. He learned to ride the stars, and he's discovered the secret. His future will be as bright as his newly found knowledge."

"Is that in his chart?"

Cynthia picked up the pot, poured out a cup of steaming peppermint tea, and said, "If it's not, he'll put it there, Enid."

THE AMAZING CASE OF THE ANZAC KARMA ENDS

AUTHOR BIOGRAPHY

MY EARLY LIFE WAS SPENT in live theatre: acting, direction, designing, writing. That led to a career in television: writing cop shows, panel games and soaps for Crawford Productions in Melbourne and Reg Grundy Productions in Sydney and Brisbane.

I partnered in one fine dining room and two theatre restaurants (Victorian melodrama and satirical revue . . . The Mark Twain and The Living Room Brisbane).

As a weekly columnist for the *Brisbane Courier-Mail*, *Brisbane Sun,* and *The Brisbane Sunday Mail*, I had a twenty-two-year second career writing lifestyles, food, theatre, fashion, entertainment and mainstream events (London, Paris, California, Hong Kong, Singapore, Kuala Lumpur, Hawaii, Finland, all Australian capitals). I do not write about people or places I haven't experienced. Currently freelancing.

Happily married to an amazing woman: two kids, three grandkids, one poodle.

KENN LORD

www.ingramcontent.com/pod-product-compliance
Lightning Source LLC
Chambersburg PA
CBHW031649100726
47898CB00006B/2032